ONE BIGFOOT IN THE GRAVE

ONE BIGFOOT IN THE GRAVE

A
JILL COOKSEY
MYSTERY

Lesley St. James

Madcap Mystery

Mechanicsville, Virginia

Ebook ISBN: 978-1-7361855-8-2

Paperback ISBN: 978-1-7361855-9-9

CHAPTER 1

"**Y**ou can really taste the possum in this one," said Mike McCall around a huge bite of Brunswick stew.

"Who are you?" I asked. Gone was my Upper-West-Side-dwelling, sophisticated reporter boyfriend, replaced by a cast member from Duck Dynasty. He and my father were getting along like a house afire at the annual Brunswick Stew Festival sponsored by Daddy's lodge, the Concatenated Order of the Woodbooger. The festival was a high point on the calendar for my hometown, Luthersburg, Virginia.

"Don't fill up on that one, son," said Daddy. "This next one has smoked squirrel in it. They smoke it with cherrywood before they add it to the pot. I'll make sure to bring some of that home."

"You most certainly will not, Calvin Cooksey," said my mother, Loretta. "Squirrel has never been served on my table, and it's not going to be, no matter who's company."

"Loretta, I don't know why you draw the line at squirrel when we both know your bowl is full of groundhog."

"Groundhog and squirrel are not the same thing," my

mother said with a sniff. "Groundhog is a much more refined meat for a sophisticated palate. Squirrel is just nasty."

I had been certain to get the Brunswick stew that only had chicken in it, and I clutched my bowl protectively lest someone contaminate it with rodent meat. I'm Jill Cooksey, by the way. Daughter of Calvin and Loretta Cooksey, girlfriend to Mike McCall, proud product of Luthersburg Senior High School, the First Baptist Church, and the University of Virginia. I was also a public relations account executive in New York, but I was on a much-needed vacation and had chosen to bring my boyfriend to visit my hometown during the Brunswick Stew Festival because it was the perfect opportunity for him to experience all the hometown charm…and lunacy. Where better to begin than with the Concatenated Order of the Woodbooger?

What's the woodbooger, you ask? Why, only Virginia's version of bigfoot, said to roam the Blue Ridge Mountains. By all reports, the woodbooger was a gentle giant, but then again, I didn't know anyone who'd ever seen one. Why Daddy's lodge had chosen the mythical creature for a mascot almost a hundred years ago was anyone's guess. If the higher-ups in the fraternal order knew, they weren't telling. My daddy was the number two guy in the Woodboogers, known as the Right Honorable Yeti. The top man was Daddy's best friend, Dud Scott, and his title was Supreme Squatch.

Please, do not judge us.

Why the order was called "concatenated" was another mystery. I looked up the word when I was a kid after my father was unable to define it for me. It means linked together, but the Luthersburg lodge was the only one of its kind. I suspected whoever named the order just liked the sound of it.

Today, Daddy, Dud, and all the Woodboogers were wearing their jaunty fezzes, royal red embroidered with silver thread, which set them apart from the Ruritans, the Boy Scouts, the Girl Scouts, the Frontier Girls, 4-H, Civil Air Patrol, the

Garden Club, Friends of the Library, and the Chamber of Commerce, not to mention the stew teams fielded by the Baptists, the Church of Christ, the Presbyterians, the Lutherans, and the Catholic Church. All the civic organizations came out to compete for the coveted trophy, a four-foot-tall red and gold monstrosity straight out of *The Karate Kid*, topped with a tiny golden bigfoot. Everyone wore smiles and spoke kindly, but underneath the rich aroma of stew lurked the unmistakable musk of adrenaline. Every participant, from the loftiest priest to the lowliest Daisy Scout, was in it to win it.

Luthersburg had its quirks, but it wasn't a bad place to live. I hadn't left my home for New York because there was something wrong with it. I'd left it because I wanted different opportunities than it could afford me, but I always enjoyed coming home...mostly. Nestled against the Blue Ridge Mountains, Luthersburg lay in an idyllic location. It was just far enough off the beaten path that it wasn't overrun by tourists in the summer and fall. For example, folks from Richmond had to drive an extra hour from Charlottesville to get to Luthersburg. Richmonders who were willing to drive that far were usually headed for football games in Blacksburg and passed us by, so Main Street never felt overcrowded with outsiders. We got just enough tourists coming down Interstate 81 or the Blue Ridge Parkway to keep the economy alive but not enough that there was too much traffic on any given Saturday morning.

Like many small towns, Luthersburg had one main thoroughfare, aptly called Main Street. People coming to visit for leaf peeping or apple picking mostly only ever saw the main drag with its town hall, café, tearoom, bakery, florist, antique shop, candle shop, and assorted other stores that catered to tourist tastebuds. But off the main drag, tucked into tiny side streets or up in nearby hollers, were some of the more interesting businesses and cultural experiences that Luthersburg had to offer. One of those was the Concatenated Order of the

Woodbooger, whose lodge was on a road that twisted off Main Street and up into the forest. Most people never even saw it unless they were from Luthersburg. The Woodboogers preferred it that way. Whatever rituals they liked to enact, they didn't have to worry about prying eyes, and their rites had been a secret ever since the order was founded in the 1930s.

I looked forward to showing Mike all around Luthersburg. There was a lot of fun to be had—music, food, local color. My hometown was the perfect retreat from big city life, but I had an additional reason for showing Mike around. Frankly, it was a test. Mike had been talking the m-word until I beat him at a game of cards. Because he lost, he was forbidden to bring it up again. But I knew he wanted to marry me, and I was pretty sure I wanted to marry him too. According to the rules of that particular poker game, since I won, I would have to be the one to bring it up, but I wasn't going to do that until I was certain that Mike and Luthersburg would get along. So far, he had exceeded my expectations. It was uncanny how he could blend in with the locals. Even his accent seemed to fade a bit here in Luthersburg, although he was by no means drawling. Mike's assimilation into Luthersburg was going almost too well. He had excellent manners, and he didn't put sugar on his grits. I thought the Brunswick Stew Festival, with its colorful assortment of game—everything from possum to woodchuck— would trip him up, but it hadn't. My man did not balk at vermin. But how much of it was authentically Mike, and how much was a boyfriend who wanted to please the woman he loves and her parents?

The festival was set up in the field next to the lodge, both of which were situated at the very foot of the mountain. The teams inhabited booths arranged in two rows facing each other. One row contained the safer bets, the Brunswick stews made from ham, chicken, and pork. The other row was for the connoisseurs of mountain cooking—or people who had taken a dare. Each team had a huge kettle simmering over an open fire. The teams had camped out overnight to perfect their stews under cover of darkness, so no one could steal the recipes and to give the stews enough time to simmer to perfection. The simmering concoctions were judged blind inside the lodge by the Supreme Squatch, Dud Scott, the owner of the local barbecue restaurant, Bill Cahill, and the Family and Consumer Science teacher from the high school, Mildred Oliver. Bless them. At the far end of the field was a stage where a Bluegrass band played while a troupe of cloggers wheeled and whirled. I braced myself for what I knew was coming.

"It's such a shame that you gave up clogging," sighed Momma for the thousandth time. Every time Bluegrass music played, she sang this refrain. "You were a natural."

"Clogging? Really? How interesting." Mike's smirk told me I'd be hearing about this for some time. I shifted uneasily in my wedge espadrilles, a shoe chosen specifically to prevent anyone from trying to get me to clog. The espadrilles looked super cute with my knee-length seersucker skirt and white sleeveless blouse. Sophisticated country, I liked to call it.

Daddy grinned. "Jilly was just the cutest thing in her petticoat and ruffle bloomers. I don't know why she ever stopped."

"Because I was a klutz."

"Nothing a little more practice wouldn't have helped. No, don't roll your eyes at me, young lady. Calvin, there's Jeannie Shoecraft. I need to speak with her about refreshments for the dance."

While Momma and Daddy hastened toward Mrs. Shoecraft, Mike and I tossed our empty bowls in a trashcan and meandered closer to the stage to watch the clogging. He pulled me to him, back to front, wrapped his arms around my waist, and rested his chin on my shoulder.

"I wouldn't mind seeing you in one of those short petticoats," he murmured in my ear. I tried to elbow him, but he had my arms pinned in place. "I think that would be very sexy indeed." A shiver ran down my spine, and Mike felt it. He pressed me closer. "And maybe you could show me some of your dance moves."

His lips tickled my ear as he talked, making my knees weak. Hands on my waist, he began to turn me around so he could kiss me when I spied Shirley Scott, my mother's best friend, giving us the stink-eye. That sobered me up quickly.

"Mike, honey, it's a small town. People are watching."

"So, let 'em watch," he said as he moved in for a kiss. I turned my head at the last possible second. He got my cheek instead.

"But they won't just watch. They'll also talk. In front of my parents."

"Your parents know that we kiss. They've seen it often enough."

"Duh! But it might be embarrassing to hear our kisses described by their friends and neighbors. Nobody needs the play-by-play."

"Ah, point taken…and challenge accepted."

"Huh? What challenge?"

"The challenge of finding places to kiss you breathless while we're here for the next week." He cocked an eyebrow. "Game on!"

A thrill ran through me from my head to my toes. This was going to be an interesting week.

Our momentary excitement was interrupted by a cacophony at the other end of the field. In sharp contrast to the twang of the Bluegrass band came a drum cadence executed with military precision by the high school's drumline, followed by several young men wearing royal blue fezzes. The procession stopped in the middle of the field, and when the drum line ceased, all that could be heard was the bubbling of stew pots. A young man stepped forward with a megaphone

"Hear ye! Hear ye! We have come to announce the formation of a new fraternal order that will better serve the citizens of Luthersburg. We are the Woodboogers of the World!"

I saw Daddy scurrying across the field toward the interlopers, and Mike and I hurried to join him.

"Tyler Skaggs, what in tarnation are you doing?" demanded my father. "And what have you got on your head?" He pointed to a blue velvet fez with the initials WOW embroidered in gold, I supposed for Woodboogers of the World.

"We recognize the Right Honorable Yeti of the Concatenated Order of Woodboogers. I am the Supreme Squatch of the Woodboogers of the World."

"No, you're not," said Dud Scott as he emerged from the lodge. "You're just a cub! How dare you call yourself Supreme Squatch?"

"Tyler! Enough!" boomed a voice to my right. Every head turned toward Jack Skaggs, Tyler's father. His crimson fez trembled above a face that was nearly the same shade. In contrast, his wife Betsy was white as a sheet. She clutched Jack's arm as if to hold him back.

Tyler only paused a moment before he squared his shoulders, and, ignoring his father, addressed Dud.

"I am no longer a member of your order. Like I said, we have founded our own fraternal organization."

"But why on earth would you do that?" Daddy's voice achieved a pitch I thought only my mother could produce.

"Because we have no voice," said Tyler. "Because COW is a senior-dominated, narrow-minded organization that does not possess the scope of opportunity for younger generations to thrive. You have refused to amend the rules of the organization to allow younger members to advance more rapidly, thus keeping certain privileges, such as the ability to set the order's agenda and to lead committees, to yourselves. The younger members of the organization do not feel fully involved or appreciated by the senior members. You wouldn't even let us enter our meat-free version of Brunswick stew into the festival.

"And our repeated calls for financial incentives such as life insurance products and financial advising have also gone unheeded. Therefore, we feel we have no other option but to start our own 501(C)(10) fraternal organization. We'll be offering a life insurance product and financial planning, and we'll be focusing our efforts on our environmental charities, including the fight against ocean plastics. As a tribute to the organization that showed us the ropes and that has contributed so much to yesteryear, we have incorporated the Woodbooger name into our new name, Woodboogers of the World. We mean it as a tribute to an older generation that will someday fade away, and we want to make sure there's a trace of you left behind. Anyone interested in joining WOW, please attend an informational meeting at the community center tonight at eight p.m."

The drumline erupted again, and a regiment of blue fezzes marched off the field, leaving Daddy, Dud Scott, and the rest of the original Woodboogers standing there in shock, but not for long.

"Well, it's a crying shame," said Beulah Kenilworth, President of the Ruritans, from underneath a gargantuan bouquet of helium balloons that she was selling for charity. An imposing woman with or without balloons, Beulah demanded complete loyalty from the Ruritans, and she got it one way or another. Her grasping ambition was contained in a tall, full-figured body perpetually clothed in jeans and Ruritan polo shirts. You had to admire her devotion even while you shied away from her Slytherin tendencies. "I mean, to see an organization as venerable as the Concatenated Order lose a quarter of its membership to a bunch of young upstarts. I just don't know what this world is coming to. Bless your hearts."

"Put a cork in it, Kenilworth," said Momma. "It's ugly to gloat. Everyone can see you're filled with glee that the Ruritans might finally outnumber the Woodboogers in this town." Beulah just laughed and sauntered off with her balloons to frighten the children.

"I did not see this coming," said Dud. "Everything they asked for violated our covenants, so what did they expect?"

"They expected you to rewrite the rules to suit them," said Momma. I had to agree, but as a member of the younger generation, I didn't feel I had a voice. Everyone else, however, felt fine about expressing themselves, and the whole crowd erupted.

"Society is doomed! They have no patience!"

"Don't they know they have to earn things?"

"How did this happen?"

"Oh, I don't know. Maybe because you started handing out participation trophies in Little League fifteen years ago."

"I bet the vegan Brunswick stew was the last straw."

"No, I think it was life insurance. Why people that young are so interested in life insurance I will never understand."

"It's because they're obsessed with safety!"

My father recovered before the rest of the crowd and whistled for quiet.

"I say good luck to them. Let's enjoy our Brunswick Stew Festival. Whether they choose to participate, it's still a Luthersburg tradition and a good one. Roy, let's have some music."

The fiddler picked up his instrument and began to saw. Soon the rest of the band and the dancers joined in. Merriment was restored for the most part, but I could tell people were still whispering about the incident. I looked around for Jack and Betsy Skaggs, but they had disappeared, probably in mortification. I felt for them.

In the end, it was the Church of Christ that took home the trophy that year with the Brunswick stew that was Daddy's personal favorite. I'll never know how good it was because cherrywood smoked squirrel will never pass my lips, but the judges were unanimous. Mike even waxed poetic about it.

"A dish like that takes you back in time. It's like communing with your ancestors."

I snorted.

"I don't think your ancestors in western New York were making Brunswick stew."

"My ancestors aren't from western New York."

Excuse me? Who was this man, and what had he done with my boyfriend?

"Well, where are they from?"

"Kentucky."

Momma's jaw popped open with an audible click, and Daddy's partial almost fell out of his mouth.

"You're a New Yorker," I said to Mike as if he had amnesia and I had to remind him who he was.

"I am, but my great-grandparents were from Kentucky. They moved to Buffalo during World War II to work in a war plant making fighter planes. When the war ended, they never left."

"You have Southern roots!" exclaimed my father. "My boy!" And he embraced Mike like he was the Prodigal Son.

"There was always something familiar about you," said Momma as she put her arm through his so he could escort her to the car. "I just couldn't put my finger on it."

"Was any of it the truth?" I demanded. "Is our love built on lies?"

"What?" Dazed and confused, Mike let Momma lead him away.

"Oh, don't pay any mind to her," said Momma. "She just thought she was subverting expectations, and it turns out, she isn't. She'll get over it."

CHAPTER 2

I was in heaven. Overhead, the Milky Way sparkled like glitter sprinkled on black velvet. Below that sky, on a patio overlooking a deep, dark, but friendly forest, we sat around a firepit and roasted marshmallows. We'd been out there since sunset. The lightning bugs had come and gone. The bats and martins had invaded soon after, devouring flying insects. After they settled down, Mr. Owl had announced his presence, his *who-who* the mountain equivalent of "Nine o'clock and all's well."

Daddy played his guitar softly while Momma roasted marshmallows and popped them in his mouth. Adorable. I felt a burning in my chest, right where my heart was. I had lost my father for a few years, and to see him reunited with my mother like this was perhaps the greatest blessing of my life. Not that I wasn't still a little miffed that my mother and half of Luthersburg had known he was alive all along. In fact, I was compiling a list of people who had kept that information from me. I was up to two hundred and three.

Catty-corner from my parents, Mike and I were seeing how many marshmallows we could put on one many-branched stick, like Snoopy in the old Peanuts camping cartoon. At the same time, I was peppering him with questions. What else didn't I know about Mike McCall?

"Religion?"

"Presbyterian."

"Alma mater?"

"SUNY Oswego. Go Lakers."

"Number of siblings?"

"Three. You know all of this."

"Beach or mountains?"

"Both."

"Myers-Briggs type?"

"INTJ."

"Have you ever killed another human being?"

"What? No!"

"Have you ever been arrested?"

"Jill, I was a cop. How can you ask that?"

"They say cops and criminals are two sides of the same coin."

"Loretta, how do I make her stop?"

"Shove a marshmallow in her mouth. Make it three."

So, he did or attempted to. Only one and a half made it into my mouth. The rest ended up smeared on my face. I shrieked and launched myself at him while scraping burnt marshmallow off my face so I could smear it back onto him.

And that's how the Woodboogers found us, with Mike on the ground and me straddling his torso and trying to rub my face against his because I'd had no luck getting the marsh-mallow off with my fingers.

"We hate to interrupt, Cal," said Dud Scott. He was with two other men I recognized as Lester Tidwell and Hi Graham.

"Think nothing of it, Dud. The young'uns are just wrasslin'. What can I do you for?"

"Jill!" hissed Momma. "Get off that man!"

The members of the COW took seats around the fire, which were just chunks of logs that had been sanded and varnished. I had known these men all my life. They were trusted uncles and my father's closest friends. Dud, Daddy's best friend, was the tallest of the three. An attorney practicing family law, he was always neatly dressed, tonight in khakis and a button down shirt. Lester was shorter than the others and, while not pudgy, softer in his features, probably because his wife Gladdy, who ran the tearoom, was a legendary baker. His best friend was Hi, short for Hiram, the most dapper of the three. As mayor of Luthersburg, he had an image to maintain, and he rarely left the house without a sport coat and shined shoes.

"We need to talk about the Woodboogers of the World," said Dud. "We just came from their meeting, and it was alarming, to say the least."

Daddy glanced at Momma, Mike, and me. "Do we need to go somewhere to talk?" He sounded nervous.

"No need," said Lester. "The point is, Tyler Skaggs has poached a passel of our members. A passel!"

"And Beulah Kenilworth is just eatin' it up!" muttered Hi. No surprise. Beulah had been a harpy for as long as I could remember.

"The position of the COW in this town will be weakened by the WOW. That's just facts. We need a plan." Lester slapped his knee to punctuate his assertion.

"How will the Order be weakened?" Mike asked. "You're all service organizations. What does it matter if some of your members make another one?"

"It matters," said Hi. Then he stared into the fire gloomily.

"What you don't realize," said my mother patiently, "is that Hi is the mayor of Luthersburg, and he was elected to that position in part because of the Woodbooger voting bloc."

"I see," said Mike. "The fraternal organizations represent political power in Luthersburg."

Daddy added another log to the fire. "That they do. They also represent manpower for raising money for our charitable endeavors." He looked significantly at the other men. Their faces were grim. "Our primary focus is the nature preserve that starts right behind our lodge and covers all of Woody's Mountain. We get something of a tax break because it's a preserve with no hunting, but it's not much. A lot of our fundraising goes to paying the real estate taxes."

"We have other charitable endeavors," Dud quickly added. "We support the local hospital and the bookmobile as well."

"How many did you lose tonight?" Mike asked. Was it my imagination, or had he slipped into reporter mode?

"Forty-two," grunted Lester.

"Forty-two!?" shrieked Daddy. "Forty-two of our brothers betrayed us? Forty-two followed that whiny infant and his life insurance product? Please tell me none of them were Loyal Knights!"

The Loyal Knights were the highest level of the order, followed by Squires and then Pages. I whispered as much to Mike so he could follow the conversation.

"I am proud to say none of our Loyal Knights have betrayed us," pronounced Dud solemnly. "We lost mostly Pages, but a few Squires also went over to the dark side."

"This bodes poorly for the future," intoned Lester like a doomsayer.

"Indeed, it does," agreed Daddy. "What are we going to do?"

"You could always let women join," I suggested and got a swift kick in the shin from my mother in return. She shook her head *no* and implored me with her eyes to keep silent. That wasn't like Momma. I thought she'd be all for the integration of women into the Order. The Woodboogers did have a Ladies Auxiliary, but it wasn't the same thing.

"Let's not be hasty," soothed Momma. "This might be a flash in the pan. What does Tyler Skaggs know about starting, let alone running, a lodge? Nothing. When his members see that, don't be surprised when they show back up, fezzes in hand."

"I'm sure you're right, Loretta," said Daddy more cheerfully. "You usually are. I just hope we don't lack manpower at the dance tomorrow night and the ice cream social on Sunday."

"We'll help," volunteered Mike, bless the man. I could almost forgive him for all his lying. Kentucky, indeed.

"That's mighty kind of you, son." Daddy beamed with pride. "You know," he said, turning to the other Woodboogers, "Mike's people hail from Kentucky."

"Is that a fact?"

"Well, I'll Swannee."

"You a bourbon drinker?"

"Oh, for the love of Pete. Momma, give me the marshmallows before I say something I shouldn't." I grabbed the bag and shoved two in my mouth.

The Woodboogers left soon after. Then my parents drifted off to bed, leaving me to finish Mike's inquisition by the glowing coals of our dying fire.

"Where are your ancestors really from?"

"Kentucky. They were coal miners who wanted out of the mines."

"Really?"

"Really. Why do you find that so hard to believe?"

Why did I? Maybe because I had an image in my mind of my life in New York, and it included my thoroughly New York boyfriend. He had an apartment in the Upper West Side. He wore loafers and chinos. He brunched. Rural southern roots, no matter how distant, didn't figure in.

"I don't know. I guess it was just so unexpected. The next thing you'll tell me is you're not Irish."

"I'm not. I'm Scottish. Well, my McCall ancestors were."

"But you hang out in an Irish pub!"

"Do you have to be Irish to hang out in an Irish pub?"

"*Gaah!*"

"What is the deal? Do these facts about my life count against me? Do you have something against people from Kentucky, or Scots for that matter?"

"Of course not! I just wonder if we know each other well enough to..."

"To what?" His sharp gaze told me he knew exactly what I was thinking.

"I just think we need to get to know each other better. That's all."

Mike put his arm around me.

"Jill, we know everything we need to know." He gently tapped my chest with his index finger, just above my left breast. "We know what's in here."

Was that enough?

CHAPTER 3

The next morning found Daddy, Mike, and me hiking the trail up Woody's Mountain. Daddy had wanted to take Mike hunting, which would have meant a trip to the National Forest, but I put my foot down. I wanted to show him Woody's Mountain and my favorite spots. I'd been hiking it since I was a small child and knew the trails like the back of my hand. I also knew the special spots like Fern Forest, a wooded hollow so filled with ferns that it resembled the Pacific Northwest. And Bridal Veil Falls, my favorite place to go wading as a child. And, of course, Baldy's Pate, a smooth granite outcrop that provided incredible views of the valley below.

I hadn't hiked Woody's Mountain in a long time—too long —and as we ascended the trail through the hardwood forest of oak, tulip poplar, and sweet gum, I felt all of my cares and worries recede. As much as I loved living in the city, nature was my happiest place. Mike seemed to relax, too, although I could tell something was brewing in his mind. Nothing stressful, but something exciting. A story perhaps?

Our first stop was Fern Forest. Under the canopy of maple and birch trees, lacy wood ferns and maidenhair ferns grew in abundance. The overall impression was of infinite shades of cool green.

"When I was little," I told Mike, "I used to imagine Ewoks lived here."

"I half expect a Stormtrooper on a speeder bike to come zooming out of the trees."

"Exactly!"

We kept moving up the trail, and soon we could hear the distinct tinkling of running water, one of my favorite sounds in the mountains.

"That's the stream that leads from the bottom of Bridal Veil Falls," I said. "We've probably got another thirty minutes before we reach it. I can't wait to go wading."

"You wade all you like," said Daddy. "I'm going to keep my toes nice and dry and out of that frigid water. No, thank you!"

We hiked mostly in silence, which is how I liked it. Conversation on the trail ruined the experience, and Mike seemed to know that instinctively, which made me glad. But the sight that met us when we rounded the next curve provoked exclamations from all of us.

Two maple saplings on either side of the trail had been bent, forming a gothic arch. Below this arch, sprawled face down across the trail lay Tyler Skaggs. His head was a rusty red mess, his arms scraped and bruised, and I assumed the rest of his body underneath his clothing was in the same state. His hair was crusted with blood that had flowed and then dried. A rock as big as my fist lay nearby, stained with a brown substance that could only be dried blood.

Mike raced to the body and checked for signs of life.

"He's alive! Call 911."

I didn't have my cell phone on me, but I knew that Daddy did.

"Daddy?"

He stood transfixed at the scene.

"Daddy!" I shook him slightly. "Call 911!"

He snapped out of it and rummaged in his pocket for his phone. Soon he was speaking with the local dispatcher.

"They're sending a rescue team," he said minutes later. "But I'm going to stay on the phone with them. If he stops breathing, we'll have to do CPR."

Mike was already rolling up his sleeves, preparing to do that should the need arise.

"Jilly," said Daddy. "Why don't you pull those saplings apart and get them out of the way for the EMS."

"No," said Mike. "This is a crime scene. We can't touch anything. This man has been attacked. We need to preserve the evidence."

"Do you think the saplings are evidence?" Daddy countered.

"Well, they've probably been positioned here on purpose. Some sort of ritual or sign? Is this a killer's signature?"

"Okay," said Daddy. "If you insist."

While Mike monitored Tyler and Daddy stayed on the phone with EMS, I looked at the scene more closely. The rock had surely been used as a weapon, but I couldn't see any other signs of a struggle. Not wanting to destroy any evidence, I stayed put and scanned the scene with my eyes. A flash of blue and gold pinpointed Tyler's fez as it lay in a bush.

Soon I heard the *whoomp-whoomp-whoomp* of a helicopter. There was no place to land except in the field by the Wood-booger Lodge where we had just attended the Brunswick stew festival. The trailhead was right behind the building, so if they could get him down the mountain, they could get him in the chopper and to a hospital. The problem was getting him off the mountain in a way that wouldn't injure him, but the EMTs were professionals trained to do just that. They'd hauled people off nearby mountains countless times. Woody's Mountain hadn't seen an incident like this in living memory, but that was because the use of the mountain was restricted to members of the lodge and their families.

Half an hour later, I heard the scuff of boots, and an EMS team of six with a stretcher appeared, followed by Luthersburg Police. I recognized one of the paramedics, Tater Shoecraft, Jeannie's husband and a loyal knight of the COW.

While the EMTs descended on Tyler to provide aid, Sheriff Bagby and his deputies gave orders for how to render aid without disturbing the crime scene. They moved the three of us away and began processing. Photos were taken of Tyler in situ and from every angle. The whole crime scene was photographed from every angle. It was fascinating to watch them work. I'd never seen a crime scene processed, even though I had been near more than one murder. I pointed the deputies toward the fez in the bush.

As soon as the EMTs thought Tyler was stable, they moved him to the stretcher, strapped him in, and set off down the mountain. By using six different people, they lightened the load for everyone and were able to move quickly down the trail.

"It's lucky for Tyler this happened so close to the trailhead," I said.

"No luck about it," said Mike. "He was attacked here on purpose. This spot was chosen. The attacker wanted him found. Otherwise, why would he stage the body so elaborately?"

"Who could have done this? One of the Woodboogers?" I asked.

My father started.

"No! No Woodbooger did this."

"The guys were pretty mad about Tyler poaching members, but would that be enough to make someone attempt murder?" I looked at Mike, but he just shrugged.

"I suppose it's possible," muttered Daddy. "It's just hard to believe."

We emerged from the trail to find Dud Scott, Hi Graham, Lester Tidwell, and Beulah Kenilworth waiting for us.

"I heard about it on the police scanner," explained Hi.

"And you invited Beulah?" asked Daddy.

The Ruritan president smirked. "I have contacts in law enforcement who keep me informed."

"Who cares?" cried Dud. "What happened to Tyler?"

Daddy quickly explained the scene on the mountain. When he finished, the faces of everyone except Beulah wore grim expressions.

"How many do you have left in the Concatenated Order?" she asked Dud innocently.

"Why do you want to know?"

"I just want to tell Sheriff Bagby how many suspects he has for this attempted murder." Beulah grinned wickedly. "Later, Woodboogers!"

"Yeah, get on your broom, you hag!" Dud nearly threw his fez at her swiftly retreating form, but Lester stayed his hand.

"Dud, your blood pressure."

Once Tyler was on his way to the hospital, the police turned their attention to us. We said goodbye to Dud, Hi, and Lester, who went forth to spread the word among all the Woodboogers, and submitted to police questioning. Afterward, we didn't feel like continuing our hike, so we headed for the car.

"I think we should go to the hospital," said Daddy. "Let's get your Momma."

Momma had stayed behind to prepare for the dance that night. I wondered if it would still go on in the wake of this vicious attack.

We found her at the community center, where she and the other women of the auxiliary were busy hanging decorations and arranging chairs and tables under the direction of Jeannie Shoecraft.

"Loretta," called my father. She glanced over her shoulder,

took one look at his face, and said, "I've got to go." She picked up her purse and hurried over. "What's happened, Cal?"

We filled her in on the way to Mountain Regional Hospital.

We found Tyler's parents, Jack and Betsy Skaggs, in the waiting room. The pair sat with their heads bowed, praying for their son. Daddy gently placed a hand on Jack's shoulder. When he saw my father, he sprang up, and the two men embraced. Momma sat down next to Betsy and put her arms around her.

When the hug ended, Jack, looking stricken, gripped my dad's arms.

"Cal, I had no idea he was planning a defection. He kept it from me. I would have warned the order if I'd known."

"Jack, it's all right. Tyler is a grown man. If he wants to start his own club, he's allowed. The important thing right now is that he gets better."

"They're saying…they're saying a woodbooger did it."

"I know, but you and I both know that's just not possible." Daddy gently patted Jack on the arm.

"Excuse me," said Mike. "I don't mean to butt in, but how can you be certain that none of the Woodboogers did this? It seems that many, if not all, of the order had a motive."

A moment passed as Daddy and Mr. Skaggs stared at each other in silent conversation.

"Well, that's true," said my father eventually. "It could have been a member of the order. But there's no way this was a woodbooger."

"I don't follow," said Mike.

But I did. I held my breath, waiting for someone to say it.

"What he means," said Momma, "is that while a member of the order could have done this, a real, live woodbooger couldn't."

And there it was.

CHAPTER 4

"Have any of them actually seen a bigfoot?" asked Mike as he added hot sauce to his collards.

We were seated in a corner booth at Cahill's, our family's favorite barbecue spot, on the road between the hospital and Luthersburg. Over plates of pulled pork, fried okra, collards, pinto beans, and cornbread, we discussed the latest revelation that some people in Luthersburg believed in bigfoot.

"Of course not," said Daddy. "Because they don't exist."

"We're educated, rational people," sniffed Momma.

"But the Skaggs family believes in them?" pressed Mike.

Momma dabbed at her mouth with a napkin before she spoke again. "Not just the Skaggs family. Other folks around here do too."

"Fascinating," said Mike.

"Well, Luthersburg isn't any different from the rest of the world." Daddy slathered his cornbread with butter under my mother's watchful eye. He had put on some weight since leaving his employment on the cruise ship. "Some people believe in bigfoot and some people don't, just like some people believe in aliens and the Loch Ness monster."

"I believe in the Loch Ness monster," I piped up. "At least I want to believe."

"Of course, you do." Momma moved the butter dish out of Daddy's reach. "We'd all like to believe the world still holds some mysteries, despite satellites and CCTV cameras."

"But why would people immediately assume a bigfoot attacked Tyler?" Mike put the cap on the hot sauce bottle. "Even if they believe in the hairy guy, isn't it more likely that a person attacked Tyler, especially after his display at the stew festival?"

"Of course it's more plausible he was attacked by a human." Momma put a liberal helping of chow-chow on her collards and handed the dish to me because I, too, adore chow-chow. "But the clues point to a woodbooger."

"What clues?" Mike asked.

"The arch," pronounced Daddy around a big bite of corn-bread and pulled pork. He then swallowed and explained. "Many people believe the woodbooger leaves signs of its presence in the woods. One of those signs is a sapling arch."

Mike nodded slowly. "Like the one over Tyler."

"It's so silly." My mother rolled her eyes as only she could. "Even if the woodbooger were real, which it isn't, why on earth would it go around bending saplings into arches? To what purpose? The creatures of the forest are more interested in survival than gothic architecture." Everyone laughed except Mike.

"So that means someone was trying to frame bigfoot for Tyler's attack." Mike shook his head in wonder. "Ingenious!"

"Simmer down, son." Daddy patted Mike on the back soothingly. "No one in law enforcement is going to believe Tyler was attacked by the woodbooger. Can you imagine putting that on a report? Or saying it in court?" Daddy laughed. "They'll find the son-of-a-biscuit who did this. Don't you worry."

"You can't say woodbooger, can you?"

It was after lunch, and Mike and I were hanging decorations in the community center in preparation for the Brunswick Ball. As promised, we had rolled up our sleeves to help. Mike was perched on a ladder, and I was handing him swathes of craft paper covered in amorphous blobs of color.

"What do you mean? I can say it."

"Then why do you keep calling the woodbooger bigfoot?"

"Well, aren't they synonyms?"

"They are, but everyone around you is saying woodbooger. Normally, you have no trouble relating to people. That's why you're a good reporter. Heck, you've practically been assimilated into Luthersburg like it's the Borg…but you can't say woodbooger."

"Fine!" Mike threw his hands up in the air. "It's just the silliest word I ever heard. Okay? Are you happy?"

And there he was—my New Yorker boyfriend. I smiled broadly at his rant because this was the Mike I knew and loved.

"And it sounds like someone blew their nose in the forest. Woodbooger. Gross!" He made a retching sound just to make sure I got the point.

"Booger doesn't refer to mucus." I laughed, and Mike retched again. "It's just a country form of boogeyman. So, a woodbooger is a boogey man who lives in the woods."

"Really, Jill, I had no idea. If only I were as smart as you." I stuck out my tongue at him. "I know what booger refers to, but it still sounds gross."

I hoisted up the last of the large sheets of craft paper, and Mike secured it in place with removable adhesive strips. Then I stood back in awe and wonder.

The theme of the dance was "Starry Night." As a result, I was now looking at a reproduction of Van Gogh's masterpiece covering an entire wall of the converted barn that was our community center.

"It's not half bad," said Mike as he descended the ladder.

"Understatement of the year." It was incredible. No, it wasn't perfect, but it was the result of untold hours of labor by so many hands. All the groups who participated in the festival, from the Daisy Scouts to the Ruritans, had created panels. Jeannie Shoecraft divided up the Van Gogh painting into the required number of sections, assigned one to each group, along with specific dimensions and a materials list, and visited each group as they were making their panels to ensure consistency. I was looking at a beautiful facsimile of a masterpiece, and I was also looking at what my hometown could achieve when everyone worked together.

"The Daisies need to work on their scissor skills." Momma eyed the wall skeptically. "They're spending too much time on physics in kindergarten and not enough time on fine motor skills."

"It's breathtaking," I countered. "Jeannie sure knows what she's about."

Momma chuckled and patted my shoulder. "Thank you for your help." She squeezed Mike's arm. "And yours too. I don't know what we would have done. Tyler Skaggs' attack has everyone discombobulated."

"I suppose it's natural for the town to be in an uproar after a native son is almost murdered." Mike was beginning to speak in headlines. So cute!

"*Weeeeelll*, Tyler has never been anyone's favorite, except his parents. He's a bit of a know-it-all, if you know what I mean. Of course, folks feel bad for him, but what's got them jumping like water on the griddle is that there might be a rabid wood-booger on the loose."

Mike laughed loudly, but his laugh trailed off when he saw my mother's face.

"You can't be serious."

"There has been talk of canceling the dance, but the ladies of the Auxiliary wouldn't stand for it."

"That's right!" chimed in Jeannie Shoecraft as she entered the hall from the adjacent kitchen. "We have to set the example and show the people of this community that superstition is just that."

"Hi, Mrs. Shoecraft." She wore her daily uniform of pencil skirt, twin set, ballet flats, and pearls. We swiftly kissed each other on both cheeks, the way the French do and the way she had taught me when I went to her for elocution and deportment lessons as a preteen. Her home was the Luthersburg equivalent of a finishing school, and almost every pubescent child endured cotillion under Jeannie's tutelage.

"Hello, my dear. And who might this be?"

I introduced her to Mike using my best manners. No matter how old I got, I would always use my best manners with Mrs. Shoecraft. Luckily, Mike could read a room and responded in kind.

"So, I hear you encountered Virgil out on the mountain in the aftermath of Tyler's unfortunate mishap."

"Virgil?" Mike was puzzled.

"She means Tater, her husband."

"Oh, the EMT. Yes, he was there."

"Virgil said you all kept your heads and responded well to the crisis."

"That's kind of him," I said. "Mike used to be a policeman."

"Is that a fact? What do you do these days, Mr. McCall?"

"I'm a journalist. I write for the New York Gazette."

"How thrilling! You must tell me all about it. Maybe you'll have a moment at the dance tonight."

"It would be my pleasure."

"Wonderful. Now I must scoot. I have an appointment. Loretta, Jill, Mr. McCall."

And then she was gone in a whiff of Chanel No. Five.

I looked at Momma and we both grinned. Mike looked puzzled.

"That woman is married to a man called Tater?"

I burst out laughing.

"To her everlasting chagrin," chuckled my mother.

"What am I missing?"

Mom explained.

Jean Custis Lee had become engaged to Virgil Shoecraft while he was at Virginia Military Institute and she was at Hollins College. She was an art history major, and he was studying military science intending to make a career in the army. Jeannie had been looking forward to her life as an officer's wife, helping her husband climb the ranks and being the perfect partner and helpmeet. Upon graduation, Virgil entered the army and Jeannie began planning a wedding. Then Operation Desert Storm happened. Virgil spent his time liberating Kuwait in a tank, and when it was over, he unexpectedly resigned his commission and came home to Luthersburg. He never said much about what happened in Kuwait, but it changed him forever. Jeannie, her head spinning from his abrupt decision and all the wedding plans in motion, went ahead and married him.

"She had no idea what life would hold for them at that point," said Momma. "I think everyone was surprised when he became a firefighter and then an EMT, but no one was more surprised than Jeannie. She has George Washington and Robert E. Lee in her family tree, so a military life with all its moving from station to station was just fine with her. But Virgil put on a fireman's uniform, and they never left Luthersburg. Jeannie has traveled a bit. She went to Paris, Rome, and Florence—all the places she could see the art she spent years studying—but she never got to live abroad as she hoped."

"How sad," said Mike.

"Well," said Momma, "I suppose you could look at it that way. Or you could call it beautiful. You see, you have to love your spouse unconditionally because you never know what life will throw at you. Jeannie Shoecraft is resilient. She held on to all that breeding and education despite the change in her circumstances. It may look like she's putting on airs, but what you're seeing is the real Jeannie Shoecraft."

~

"So, what kind of story are you planning?" I asked. Mike and I were at home, with the house to ourselves for a brief blissful time while Momma finished dance preparations with the Ladies Auxiliary and Daddy had another emergency meeting of the COW.

"I'm not planning a story," replied Mike smoothly. "Not yet anyway. It will depend on what the sheriff has to say. If he thinks a bigfoot attacked Tyler Skaggs, that's a story worth reporting."

I could see his point, but I had concerns.

"You know if that happens and you write a story, it could be bad for the town."

"I wouldn't write it with a slant, but the fact is grown adults trying to lay blame for a criminal act at the feet of Sasquatch does seem ridiculous, and there's nothing I can do about that."

"Beyond that, it could bring a bad element to the town."

"What do you mean?"

"Bigfoot hunters."

Mike laughed. He'd been laughing a lot in Luthersburg, which was nice, but I didn't like it when he laughed at me.

"Bigfoot hunters? Jill, you've been watching *Harry and the Hendersons*."

"I mean it! There are plenty of crazy people out there on the trail of bigfoot. If we give them a real live woodbooger attack here in Luthersburg, who knows what's going to crawl out of the woodwork with weapons and crackpot ideas and tin foil helmets? They could start shooting up the place. Wreaking havoc. No one wants that."

"Well, I doubt the sheriff's going to say Tyler's attacker was a woo—bigfoot. In fact, I'd bet money on it. It would be too humiliating." He pulled out his laptop and earbuds. "I'm going to do some research."

That was fine with me. I had a good book to read, the latest installment of my favorite time travel romance series. Mike sat at one end of the sofa, the laptop perched on his knees, while I snuggled at the other end.

I don't know how much time passed, but one of the characters in my book had just been tortured due to a case of mistaken identity (poor man) when I heard Mike chuckle.

"You gotta see this!"

I scooched down the sofa to see what was so funny on the computer. He pulled the earbuds out of the jack and pressed play on a video.

"Who are these guys?" I asked.

"Bigfoot hunters."

"Where is this?"

"New Jersey," Mike snorted. "One of the smallest and most populous states in America. If bigfoot lived there, I think someone would have found him by now. But these guys insist bigfoot lives in the hills of western Jersey."

As I watched, three guys in camo tramped through the forest carrying all manner of equipment.

"Those are parabolic microphones," said Mike. "They're trying to capture vocalizations."

"Bigfoot talk?"

"That's right."

I listened carefully, but all I could hear was crackling, like an animal moving through fallen leaves.

"He's watching us," whispered one of the guys. "He knows we're here. He may be hunting us."

Then one of them yelled, and they all took off running.

"Oh, for heaven's sake. It's The Three Stooges Hunt Bigfoot!"

"That's an insult to Larry, Moe, and Curly."

"Fine. The Three Doofuses then."

The three doofuses (Doofi? What's the plural of doofus?) entered a clearing and stopped short.

"Would you look at that?" breathed Doofus Number Two.

The camera zoomed in on two young trees at the edge of the clearing that were bent together to form an arch.

"That's proof right there that he's playing with us," seethed Doofus Number Three.

"I wish I was seeing this at night," said Doofus Number One, "so I could tell if it's following the correlation of Orion."

"The what?" I blinked at Mike. He paused the video.

"These guys think bigfoot is an astronomer who can spot constellations and creates these tree arches in such a way that they point to Orion."

"This is insane."

"Yes. Yes, it is."

"Somebody needs to tell these guys that saplings bent in the forest are a natural phenomenon. Do you think Tyler's attacker knew about this?"

"Check this out." Mike pointed to the number of views of the video—over a million.

"So, a lot of people know about this."

"Yep. I have to admit," sighed Mike, "I thought I had seen everything as a cop and a reporter, but this…this is brand new territory."

CHAPTER 5

My childhood home was called Cooksey's Corner. It was a two-story white clapboard house with black shutters and doors and a wide wraparound porch. It was a large home that had been built by my great-great-grandfather on the site of an earlier, smaller home that was part log cabin. Great-great-granddaddy had saved the cabin part and turned it into a family museum of sorts. The succeeding generations had kept the tradition alive, and now my dad tended the cabin museum lovingly and stored all his uniforms and equipment for Civil War reenactments there. The Cookseys had family on both sides of the conflict, so Daddy alternated weekends between reenacting the Union and the Confederacy.

The house sat on half a cleared acre with forest on three sides. It had been a wonderful place to grow up. The property extended into the forest for several acres, so we had plenty of woods to explore. Daddy tried his best to teach us how to be safe, to avoid snakes, and to come home in one piece.

The house itself boasted a large living room that had once been divided into a parlor and a sitting room, but my parents had taken down a wall to create a larger living space with a big stone fireplace and lots of windows looking out on the porch. On the other side of the entry hall was the door to the kitchen and breakfast nook. Two sets of stairs led to the second story, one from the foyer and one from the kitchen, a configuration that was a source of never-ending amusement for us as children and made playing hide and seek exciting because you had two ways out of the second floor. It was very difficult to get cornered in that house.

Upstairs were four bedrooms, two baths, and another set of stairs that led up to the attic. As homes went, it was practically perfect. During this visit, I was in my old bedroom, as usual, and Mike had been put in the guest room. Between those rooms lay my parents' bedroom, and that was no accident.

My room was exactly as I had left it when I moved to New York several years before. The antique maple furniture shone from my mother's conscientious polishing. The rainbow quilt and pillow shams on the bed had been made by Granny Zaricor. Daddy had constructed the window seat flanked by bookshelves that held all my favorites: *The Boxcar Children, The Chronicles of Narnia, Little House on the Prairie, Anne of Green Gables,* and *Nancy Drew.* The books went on and on. What a precious place—not just the room but also the house and the town. How fortunate I was to always have this retreat, a place of refuge from the outside world.

That evening, as I prepared for the Brunswick Ball, I felt like a teenager again, getting ready to go to a school dance. Making sure I picked the right outfit. Curling my hair. Touching up my makeup. But instead of the excitement of wondering if a boy would ask me to dance, the excitement I was feeling stemmed from knowing that I would be in the arms of the man I loved. I also wondered what the night would bring. The Brunswick Ball was always a good time full of colorful characters and fabulous music.

I had chosen a cotton sundress in coral with a double white stripe around the hem of the skirt and a sweetheart neckline. A darker coral ribbon cinched the waist. I paired the dress with white ballet flats that wouldn't get hung up on the dance floor. My hair was pulled back from my face with barrettes but otherwise fell to my shoulders in loose waves, difficult to achieve with heat styling, but I had worked hard. Silver hoops glinted at my ears, and a silver heart locket echoed the neckline of the dress. Pretty but practical was my motto for the dance, to prevent sweating and injury. A girl's got to think ahead.

I grabbed my clutch purse and stepped out of my bedroom just as Mike was coming out of his.

"You look beautiful," he said and pulled me in for one of those breathless kisses he promised.

So did he in his gray pants and French blue button-down shirt, open at the neck.

"You approve," he said with a cocky grin. "I can see it in your face." I rolled my eyes but took his offered hand, and we descended the stairs and met my parents by the front door. They were adorable in their matching square dance outfits. Daddy wore a green gingham shirt with blue jeans, and Momma wore a green gingham dress with puffed sleeves.

"Are you ready to do a little buck and wing, Loretta?" asked Daddy.

"Just don't step on my feet, Cal."

"I've never stepped on your feet."

"You stomped all over them at the last practice, while I was wearing my new shoes, I might add."

"I hope you broke those puppies in. Otherwise, it's gonna be a bloodbath on that dance floor."

I smiled sheepishly at Mike, but my parents' bickering didn't seem to faze him. This man was too good to be true.

We decided to drive separately so my parents could, as Momma put it, "after-party" with their square-dancing group without having to bring us back home. Mike had rented a pick-up truck for our trip to Virginia because he wanted to blend in, so we climbed into the Chevy and followed my parents for two miles to the community center. The place was packed because everyone wanted the latest gossip on Tyler Skaggs and the Woodboogers of the World. As soon as we arrived, Momma and Daddy bustled off to join the square dance troupe.

You could always tell the tourists from the townies at the annual Brunswick Ball. The locals were busy flitting from group to group saying "hidey" and catching up with neighbors like they hadn't seen them already that day at the Piggly-Wiggly. The tourists, on the other hand, grabbed a table and hugged it all night long for security, never moving from their chairs except to get food or drink, but always remembering to leave something at the table to mark their territory. The tourist's greatest fear was being ambushed by a group of locals and being forced to interact.

Mike and I began by making the rounds. I introduced him to several of my elementary school teachers and classmates, my Girl Scout troop leader, and my former clogging teacher, who laughed out loud when I told her Momma and Daddy said I never should have quit clogging.

"It was only a matter of time before you did yourself or someone else irreparable damage," she said.

I saw more than one admiring glance cast Mike's way from gals I knew from high school and some of the older widow ladies in the garden club. I slid my arm around Mike's waist in a blatant attempt to signal "Hands off! He's mine!"

Every group we visited meant a new interrogation for Mike. Southerners love to find a connection.

"I know some McCalls down in Pulaski County. Are they any kin to you?"

"My McCalls are from Kentucky."

"My aunt married a man from Kentucky, and they settled

down near Bowling Green. Do you have any family down there?"

"No, ma'am. My folks were from coal country."

"Like Loretta Lynn! I just loved her!"

I heard a variation of this conversation four, maybe five, times. Mike handled it like a trooper. He was sweet and polite to everybody. Frankly, I don't know how he did it, but I chalked it up to his deep and abiding love for me.

Eventually, I took pity on the man and dragged him over to the punch bowl. I poured a glass, sniffed it, and tasted it.

"This one's going to be pineapple juice, orange juice, Seven-Up, and grenadine. Pretty sure, anyway."

"What's the stuff floating in it?" He eyed the cup I offered him warily.

"That was an ice ring, but it has broken up into a bunch of little icebergs. You want to get a chunk of that in your punch cup to keep it cold. If you want something stronger, just ask Daddy. He probably has a flask unless Momma has pickpocketed him."

"This is fine." He took a sip, evaluated, and took another. "I need to keep my wits about me. The good people of Luthersburg are keeping me on my toes."

"You're handling it fine. You're practically a native already." I stood on my tiptoes and kissed him on the cheek. Then someone grabbed me and yanked me off my feet.

I was pressed into the chest of a huge bear, but Mike made no move to rescue me. Then my face felt shirt buttons hard at work leaving imprints on my cheeks, so I knew it wasn't a bear. Then I recognized the voice.

"Jill Cooksey! How's my favorite PR executive and private detective?"

Hoss Buckworth lowered me gently to the ground and beamed down at me. The huge Texan was my client two times over. I headed up the PR for his cosmetics company and the cruise line he had recently bought. Both businesses had been plagued by murder, and I just happened to solve those cases, saving the businesses in the process. In the case of the cruise line, an adventure that had occurred just three months before, my work had landed me a much-needed and, dare I say, well-deserved promotion. I was now Account Supervisor Jill Cooksey. I should have been VP Jill Cooksey, but my boss, Pamela, had acquired the company I worked for, Waverly Communications, in her very recent divorce from the company owner. She had never been inclined to do me any favors, or, for that matter, reward me for my hard work. Hoss had offered to take his business elsewhere, anywhere that would make me a VP, but I didn't want to get my promotion that way. After all, I reasoned, it shouldn't be too long before Pamela needed rescuing, and when I saved her ridiculously small butt, I would ask for what was coming to me.

Before I could respond to Hoss, a much smaller creature hug-bombed me too. It was Juliet, Hoss's new wife and my old friend. Juliet was a famous actress and the daughter of my parents' best friends, Dud and Shirley Scott. We had grown up together, making her considerably younger than her husband, but the pair adored each other and had endured some trials and tribulations on the way to their happily ever after.

"It's so good to see you, Jill! When I heard you were spending your vacation in Luthersburg, I knew we had to come. After all, Hoss has never been to the Brunswick Ball. It's going to be so much fun!"

"It's just too bad you missed the stew festival," said Mike as he shook Hoss's hand. "It was a feast!"

"Let me guess," Juliet whispered to me. "The winning stew was possum."

"On the contrary, cherry wood smoked squirrel."

"Gross!"

"So gross!"

I glanced over Juliet's shoulder, intent on seeking out my parents, who would want to greet Juliet and Hoss, but my eyes never made it past the face of my old clogging teacher—her eyes wide like saucers, her jaw slack. Slowly, she raised an arm and pointed to someplace behind me. I turned and saw the wide wall of windows, and on the other side of the glass, I saw the woodbooger.

Finally, my old teacher managed the scream she'd been cultivating, and it was worth the wait. Horror movie-style, it got everyone's attention, and all eyes turned to the hairy creature right outside the window. In response, the creature raised its arms in menace and shook its head in fury. Had the windows been open, I believe we would have heard a bellow or a growl from the woodbooger, as well. Some detached part of my brain wondered if it was as scared of us as we were of it. A moment later, it was gone. As we recovered ourselves, someone (inevitably) yelled, "It tried to kill Tyler. Let's get him!" and a group of young men ran out of the community center to enact vigilante justice.

"What did I just see?" asked Hoss.

"Bigfoot," said Mike at the exact moment I said, "The woodbooger."

"Well, alrighty then," replied Hoss. "I think I'll go find me a drink." He walked off in a daze followed by his concerned spouse.

Mike turned to me with purpose.

"What did you see? What exactly did you see?"

"I saw…" I racked my brain to remember exactly what my eyes had perceived. "I saw a hulking figure, dark in color, with an undefined silhouette, like it was covered in fur."

"Did you see its face?"

Had I? No.

"I didn't. It was lit from behind by the landscaping lights. I only saw a silhouette."

"Same here," said Mike. "It could have been anything. A bear. A large man."

"What are you saying?"

"Look around." I did. Everyone had recovered enough to be talking about only one thing—the woodbooger. I could hear speculation coming from every direction. Was this the same woodbooger that had attacked Tyler? That's all anyone wanted to know. That and whether anyone was safe in the community with a rabid woodbooger on the loose. People were talking about the precautions they would take and what type of firearm would be strong enough to take down a woodbooger.

"Everyone has bought into what we just saw," continued Mike. "Everyone believes, and that's just what Tyler's attacker wants. I know it's inconvenient, but, Jill, someone has to investigate this logically. We can't even be sure the police will because, news flash, the chief of police is in your father's lodge. He may be buying into this crap, too. Someone has to think clearly."

"And that someone is?" I already knew the answer.

"You and me."

There went our vacation.

We began our investigation in the flower beds on the other side of the windows. Giant footprints were easily discernible in the mulch thanks to the landscape lighting. We took photos with our phones and put a quarter in the frame for reference. Mike wanted to take an imprint like he had seen on a bigfoot video, which led to my mother raiding the community center art supply closet for plaster of paris while Mike and I stood guard over the prints. My mother, a veteran Sunday school teacher of thirty years who had imprinted the palms of countless toddlers in plaster for Christmas presents, then took over and made the casts. Thirty minutes later, they were set, and we gently removed them with a snow shovel and placed them in cardboard boxes for the ride home.

By then, the dance had broken up. The people were rattled and just wanted to lock themselves in their homes. We found out that, while we were making the casts, the police had come and gone. They had dismissed the incident as a prank or a bear and didn't even look outside. Oddly, this made Mike feel better because it showed that the police weren't seriously entertaining the bigfoot rumors regarding Tyler's attack.

"But we're still looking into this," he said. I just smiled and nodded. I knew the set of his jaw. My reporter boyfriend had sniffed out a story.

CHAPTER 6

At church the next morning, the town was still buzzing about the "woodbooger" at the dance, but at least my boyfriend wasn't the main topic of conversation, which made for a nice change. Many people who had been at the dance and had seen us making casts of the footprints asked what we had discovered. Sadly, we didn't have much to tell them. The footprints were very large and maybe had five toes. The mulch was too bulky for a clearly defined print, so the number of toes had been a hotly debated topic at Cooksey's Corner the previous evening.

As we were settling into the pew at First Baptist, I heard a commotion at the back of the church. I turned to see a handsome, youngish man with bright blue eyes, oodles of wavy blond hair, and a custom-made suit making his way down the aisle, shaking hands with all and sundry.

"Who's that?" asked Mike.

"Jeremy. My brother."

"Lord, love a duck," I heard my mother whisper.

Eventually, after making every blue-haired lady swoon and accepting a packet of Smarties from Elder Bledsoe for old times' sake, Jeremy made his way to our pew. The organist had been forced to play the prelude a second time while my brother made his entrance, but she didn't mind. His former piano teacher beamed at him from behind the enormous Wurlitzer. When he reached our pew, he solemnly shook hands with Daddy.

"Father."

Then he kissed Momma on the cheek.

"Mother."

I stood for the obligatory hug. "Jelly belly," he whispered in my ear. I sighed. Same old Jeremy. Then he released me and offered his hand to Mike.

"You must be Mike. Pleased to meet you." The two men shook hands, Jeremy squeezed between me and Momma, and we all sat down.

Mike leaned toward me. "He seems like a nice guy," he whispered.

"*Seems* being the operative word," I whispered back, and then I stopped whispering because Mrs. Taylor in the pew in front was glaring at me. Her glare turned into a beatific smile as she gazed upon the Second Coming that was Jeremy Cooksey. Some things never changed.

You need to know a few things about Jeremy Cooksey. First and foremost, he was a snake in the grass. My brother made Eddie Haskell look like Mr. Rogers. There was an entire file of unsolved larcenies and vandalism in the Sheriff's filing cabinet that were all my brother's handiwork. He cheated his way through school, rigged school elections so he would win class president, spiked the punch at every dance, and took a baseball bat to most of the town mailboxes. Jeremy was a menace to society.

But he had never been caught.

Meanwhile, I had been a Girl Scout and high school valedictorian, had babysat every kid in town with a spotless safety record, helped my momma teach Sunday school, volunteered at every COW charitable event, and read to senior citizens at the nursing home in my spare time. But all I ever heard growing up was how wonderful Jeremy was.

After high school, my brother had gone to Virginia Tech where he promptly found the smartest and loneliest girl in his class. He made her his girlfriend, and she did his homework for four years while he fed her promises of marriage, all the while stepping out on her. He broke up with her right before graduation, got a job with a prestigious company, and moved to Atlanta.

Meanwhile, I graduated from UVA after doing all my own homework and now had a successful career in public relations in New York. I had even saved the life and career of America's sweetheart, Juliet Scott.

But when I came back to Luthersburg, I still only ever heard about Jeremy.

He called me Jelly Belly, and I called him Jerkemy. Now don't get me wrong. I loved my brother...but I didn't necessarily like him.

Thankfully, my parents were wise to his shenanigans. They were wise because Jeremy had made the mistake of documenting his crimes, along with his disdain for everyone in Luthersburg, in a journal that Momma found when she was putting away his clean laundry. (I might have retrieved it from under the false bottom Jeremy had installed in the drawer and laid it atop his tighty-whities.) The revelations led to a summer of hard labor on the Cooksey property for Jeremy. My parents hoped they could work the mischief out of him, and, boy, did they try. But my brother was just biding his time. After his punishments, I know for a fact his reign of terror continued, but he was never dumb enough to incriminate himself again.

And now, here he was at church. Whatever Jeremy was doing in Luthersburg, I knew it wasn't the Lord's work.

~

"So, you just drove up here on a whim?" asked my mother as we stood in line to get food at the church picnic and ice cream social. The church was situated on a few acres of land, partially a cemetery, so there was plenty of room for a picnic, especially if you didn't mind breaking bread with the deceased.

"Can't a man come see his family and meet the man who's courting his sister?" Jeremy flashed a one-hundred-megawatt smile. I was pretty sure he'd gotten veneers. Like the rest of him, his teeth were too perfect.

"You must have left early to get here from Atlanta in time for church," remarked Momma pointedly.

"I left yesterday. I stayed the night in North Carolina."

"Well, it's good to see you, son," said Daddy. He slapped Jeremy on the back affectionately. Daddy would never admit it, but I think he was a little in awe of Jeremy's ability to get away with murder, so to speak. Momma always said the mischievous streak came from the Cooksey side. Evidently, I was pure Zaricor, Momma's family, a rule follower to the letter.

We made our way down the long line of tables, gathering paper plates, napkins, and cutlery first, and then all the best food in the world: fried chicken, macaroni salad, deviled eggs, cornflake chicken casserole, Catalina taco salad, green bean casserole, strawberry pretzel salad, and the staple of all Virginia gatherings from weddings to funerals, ham biscuits. My mouth was watering long before I sat down on our family blanket, near the graves of Granny and Granddaddy Cooksey, with my heaping plate and a red Solo cup full of sweet tea.

"I think I've put on ten pounds since I got here," said Mike around a mouthful of deviled egg, "but I'm not going to stop. This food is amazing."

"That's because the special ingredient is love," said Jeremy nauseatingly. Was he really trying to Eddie Haskell my boyfriend?

"More like Duke's mayonnaise," said my mother. "There wasn't a jar left on the shelf at the Piggly Wiggly yesterday. Luckily, I found some at the Dollar General."

"Now save some room for dessert, son," said Daddy to Mike. Jeremy flinched when Daddy used the word *son* to refer to someone other than him. "If you think the main course is good, just wait until you taste the cakes, pies, and homemade ice cream, courtesy of the Concatenated Order of the Woodbooger."

"You mean courtesy of the Ladies Auxiliary," Momma corrected.

Hoss, Juliet, and her parents joined us for dessert.

"Well, I'm just pleased as punch to meet another member of Jill's family." Hoss pumped Jeremy's arm violently, but my brother held his own. There was no way Jeremy was going to lose face in front of Hoss Buckworth, billionaire business mogul. "Your sister is like family to me, so any brother of Jill's is a brother of mine."

Oh, boy. I needed to have a quiet word with Hoss.

"The pleasure is all mine, Mr. Buckworth."

"Call me Hoss."

"Okay then, Hoss."

The giant Texan and my brother settled down on the blanket where the rest of us were shoveling dessert into our mouths as fast as we could. I opted for coconut cake and home-made Tutti Frutti ice cream. Mike, a Baptist church supper neophyte, had fallen into Satan's trap and created a sampler platter from at least five different pies. He would spend the afternoon moaning on the sofa. I'd bet good money on it.

"Loretta and Cal tell us you live in Hotlanta," continued Hoss. "Where do you work? What other company has the honor of having a Cooksey on the payroll?" Hoss's bombastic, hyperbolic style was fertilizer for my brother's ego. I swear I saw his head grow right before my eyes.

"I'm with the Malevia Group."

Hoss's smile fell, and a deep crease appeared between his eyebrows.

"Is that so? How are things over there? I mean, in light of the government investigation."

An awkward pause ensued during which I saw my parents look at each other. I knew what they were thinking. If there was an investigation, there was a good chance Jeremy was the cause.

"A tempest in a teapot." Jeremy was all smiles. He was so good at faking, he should have been in PR. "It will soon blow over."

Luckily for everyone, our third-grade teacher, Mrs. Huffines, chose that moment to drag Jeremy away to meet her single, twenty-something granddaughter. I felt the group breathe a sigh of relief when he left. I looked at Mike, and I could see the wheels turning in his mind as he studied the now-silent group. Everyone seemed to be paying close attention to their desserts, but no one was eating. Jeremy often had this effect on my family.

Finally—thankfully—Shirley Scott spoke up.

"I don't see the Skaggs here today. I don't suppose they were up for a picnic, what with Tyler still in the hospital."

"Jack and Betsy don't deserve to suffer like this," said Dud, "even if karma is coming for Tyler."

"David Scott! That's awful!" Shirley grabbed her husband's arm. "How can you say such a thing?"

Dud wrenched his arm from her grasp and got shakily to his feet. "You're right, Shirl. I'm so sorry, folks. I don't know what got into me. Please excuse me." Then he stumbled off farther into the cemetery. Shirley made to follow, but Momma intervened.

"Let him go, Shirley. He's under a lot of stress with this Woodbooger splinter group. We know he didn't mean it. He'll pull himself together."

"Dud's a good man," agreed Daddy. "We don't always mean words spoken in anger."

I had never in my life heard Dud Scott speak that way, so his anger must have been great.

"We should go to the hospital today, Cal," said Momma. "We'll carry your regards, Shirley, yours and Duds."

"Yes, we should," replied Daddy.

Shirley smiled her thanks as her eyes filled with tears.

"We'll go too," added Mike. I squeezed his arm. "And we'll learn a little more about the victim," he whispered.

After church, we bid goodbye to Hoss, Juliet, and the Scotts, and headed home to change clothes before going to the hospital. Jeremy made the excuse of needing a nap after the long drive from Atlanta and stayed behind. Momma and I had made plates of food and dessert for Jack and Betsy and stored them in a cooler for transport.

When we saw Tyler's parents at the hospital, they didn't look like they'd be interested in eating. Jack sat in a chair next to Tyler's bed with his head bowed while Betsy read to her comatose son from the Bible. But when Daddy touched Jack's shoulder, the man looked up and managed a weak smile. So did Betsy. If I had to guess, I think they were relieved to learn they hadn't been forgotten.

We pulled in more chairs from the hallway and sat down. Momma doled out the food, and Jack and Betsy narrated their meal for Tyler's benefit.

"Why, lookee here. There's strawberry pretzel salad, Tyler, your favorite. You just open your eyes now, and I'll give you a bite," said his mother brightly.

"I see coconut cream pie in that cooler, Tyler," added Jack. "You listen to your momma and wake up so we can share it."

It about broke my heart.

"Does the sheriff have any leads," Mike asked quietly.

"None that he's sharing," replied Jack.

"But that's okay." Betsy's smile was steely. "Because Tyler's going to wake up and tell us who did it, and then there will be somebody else in the hospital."

I felt my eyes grow wide in disbelief. Betsy Skaggs was one of the gentlest people I knew. My surprise at Betsy's implied violence turned to curiosity, though, when I caught sight of Jack's expression. Tortured was the only way to describe it.

"Did you see Jack Skaggs' face when Betsy said she was going kick the as—butt of whoever hurt Tyler?" asked Mike later while we were driving home.

"How could you miss it? It was pure agony."

"Jack and Betsy are going through hell right now," pronounced Momma, as if that explained it all.

"Would you say," continued Mike, "that Jack was embarrassed, angry even, when his son announced he was starting his own lodge?"

"Of course, he was angry and embarrassed by Tyler," said Daddy, "but not enough to hurt his son. I know where you're going with this, Mike, but remember, whoever attacked Tyler clubbed him with a rock. Jack Skaggs could never do that to his son."

"He was probably anguished over his gentle and loving wife transforming into a vigilante right before his eyes," Momma added.

"I'm sure you're right," lied Mike. I knew him, and I knew that Jack Skaggs was on his list of suspects.

"We didn't get much information from the Skaggs family," whispered Mike in my ear.

"I know, but the timing wasn't right."

Mike nodded in assent. "We'll have to get the skinny on Tyler someplace else. This is your turf. Any ideas?"

"Oh, I know exactly where to start."

When we got home, Mike found a comfy chair in the living room and promptly fell asleep. (Behold the power of pie!) Daddy announced he had to meet his lodge brothers, and Momma announced she had to meet the Ladies Auxiliary. I supposed they were all in a kerfuffle about the supposed woodbooger on the loose. I headed for the porch swing with my e-reader and found my brother.

"Jelly Belly"

"Jerkemy."

I sat on the swing next to him and hugged him. This might seem odd given what I've revealed about my brother, but, as I said, I loved him even though I didn't like him. It was complicated. Jerkemy hugged me back.

"So, how bad are things at your company?"

He laughed archly.

"Not bad for me but definitely bad for some other folks. Don't worry, little sis. They can't pin a thing on me." In Jeremy speak, that meant he had a fall guy all set up. I felt bad for whoever that was.

"Please tell me you haven't set up someone innocent to take the blame." I couldn't help myself. I had to believe there was some good in him. After all, I was a huge fan of *Return of the Jedi*.

"I'm not a monster, Jelly Belly. Don't lose any sleep. Any indictments will be well-deserved. Now let's talk about your boyfriend. He's a do-gooder like you, isn't he?"

"Of course. He used to be a cop."

"I could smell the righteousness from several feet away. So, what does he think of all this woodbooger hysteria?"

I groaned. "I'm pretty sure he's looking for his next story, but that's not why I brought him to Luthersburg."

"Why did you? You have the island of Manhattan and all its delights. Let me guess. A test of his devotion?"

"Not exactly."

Jeremy arched an eyebrow.

"I mean, it's a little bit of a test. Even though you despise Luthersburg, which is rich considering the entire town worships you, I love it. It's part of me. I need to know if Mike and Luthersburg are compatible."

"Oh, heavens! You're thinking of marrying the guy." Jeremy shuddered in horror.

I threw up my hands. "Why is that a crazy idea? I'm getting close to thirty. You're past thirty. Have you never thought of marriage?"

"I think of it...like I think of death, war, pestilence, and famine." He shuddered again, and I had to laugh.

"I think you've just never been in love," I said smugly.

"You would be correct because love doesn't exist."

"Ha!" My outburst startled some crows who squawked back and flew away in disgust. "You've seen love all your life in the form of our parents. Don't you dare tell me love doesn't exist."

"Mutual dependence exists, and if humanity needs to romanticize it, so be it. But I don't need anybody else. I'm perfectly happy flying solo."

"Whatever, Jerkemy. I look forward to watching you eat those words. I'll even buy you a drink so you won't choke."

"That'll be the day."

On Monday morning, Mike and Daddy headed to the barber shop "to have their ears lowered," as Daddy liked to say. Momma and I were going to meet Shirley and Juliet at Tidwell's Tearoom for lunch. Jeremy had to work remotely and was holed up in his bedroom having virtual meetings.

By the time I got out of bed, Momma had already been up and running for two hours. She'd baked banana nut muffins, so I grabbed one and a cup of coffee and headed to the backyard, where I found her weeding a flower bed.

"Let me caffeinate, and I'll help you."

"I won't say no. I hate weeding. It doesn't matter how much newspaper I put under the mulch. The weeds just come back."

The coffee was strong and the muffin moist and delicious. I soon finished my breakfast and knelt beside my mother in the flower bed. She handed me an extra pair of gardening gloves.

"So, how much trouble is Jeremy in?" she asked as we yanked on crabgrass, nut grass, and spotted spurge.

"He says he's in the clear. I think he's telling the truth."

"It's only a matter of time before Jeremy discovers he's not as smart as he thinks he is."

I laughed. "It hasn't happened yet. Face it. Your son is an evil genius."

Momma didn't laugh with me. "I know exactly who my son is. I've always been a step ahead of my daughter but two steps behind my son." I wasn't sure how to take that, but I wasn't going to think about it because my super-capable mother had just admitted a failure…for the first time EVER.

"Momma, Jeremy is as capable as he is because of you. He gets it from you."

Momma sighed. "Zaricor ingenuity coupled with Cooksey mischief." She shook her head. "Is it any wonder we produced a Professor Moriarty?"

"Well, you also produced a Sherlock Holmes."

My mother gave me a pitying smile and patted my hand condescendingly. "Of a sort."

Et tu, Momma?

When the morning heated up, we quit weeding and got ready for the tearoom.

Shirley and Juliet were already there, sitting at the best table—the perks of being a movie star. As soon as we sat, Gladdy Tidwell, wife of Lester, bustled over to take our order: afternoon tea for four with pots of Earl Grey and green tea. Gladdy hurried off to make afternoon tea magic. I had a feeling we were going to get great service since Juliet was there, and I was going to take full advantage of it.

Ten minutes later, a tea trolley arrived. Two étagères were placed between the mother-daughter duos, with an assortment of tea sandwiches on the bottom tier, scones on the second tier, and desserts on the top tier. Steaming pots of fragrant tea followed, and Gladdy herself poured our first cups.

"Enjoy, ladies."

I started with pimiento cheese and red pepper jelly on homemade white bread. I could eat my weight in those sandwiches. Mike and I would be hitting the gym when we got back to New York, make no mistake. Next, I tried the cucumber and cream cheese with dill, then country ham on a mini-cheddar biscuit, and curried chicken salad with golden raisins on Irish soda bread. The last one was so good, it almost brought me to tears.

The scone course consisted of fresh strawberry scones with clotted cream and cinnamon raisin scones with whipped butter. The dessert tier included mini lemon meringue tarts, milk chocolate dipped shortbread, melt-in-your-mouth walnut baklava, and coconut macarons filled with dark chocolate ganache.

Over tea, we discussed Juliet's career. Her hit show, *Singletons*, had been renewed for another season, and she was making a rom-com for Netpix. I asked about her stepson, Dustin, whom I knew from when he worked for Hoss's cosmetics company.

"He's devoted to his surfboard company," she told us. "And I think he's much happier for it."

"And how is married life?" asked my mother.

Juliet blushed. "It's wonderful. Hoss is simply amazing." Juliet patted her stomach, and I thought she was about to announce that she was expecting when Beulah Kenilworth dropped by our table.

"Well, if it isn't the queen consorts and princesses of the Concatenated Order of the Woodbooger. My condolences ladies." Beulah's smile, thin lips stretched grotesquely in a grin under a hawkish nose and beady black eyes, told otherwise. The tall, broad-shouldered woman had actually dressed up for tea. She loomed over our table in an orange linen pantsuit that should have been left on the rack.

"Condolences for what?" Momma's tone was sharp, but Beulah didn't seem to notice.

"Why, because of the fall of the Woodbooger empire, of course. Splinter groups. Attacks, either by a real live woodbooger or one of the members of your husbands' order. Anarchy. Chaos. Perhaps a new mayor. Things will never be the same in Luthersburg. We're looking at the dawn of a new day, and while it will be bittersweet for some, it will be triumphant for others. Like I said, you have my deepest condolences. Don't forget, there's always room for you in the Ruritans." With that, she strolled off.

"It'll be a cold day in Key West before we darken the doorstep of the Ruritans, Beulah! Do you hear me? A cold day!" Shirley was on her feet shouting, and the entire tearoom was riveted.

"Get a hold of yourself!" hissed Momma. Shirley collapsed in her chair and went rummaging under the table for her handbag. To my surprise, she extracted a flask. "I just need a little brandy in my tea. A restorative. You understand."

Her teacup was almost empty, but she filled it nearly to the rim. Then Momma gently took the flask away and stashed it in her own handbag. Juliet smiled apologetically, but Momma patted her hand and said loud enough for the whole tearoom to hear, "Never you mind, Juliet. This is a stressful time for everyone, and most of all for the Supreme Squatch and his fair lady. No one is judging your sweet mother."

Chastened, the other patrons went back to their teas, and so did we.

Gladdy came back as we were draining the last drops of our teapots.

"More tea, ladies?"

We all groaned in chorus to show just how full we were, and Shirley hiccuped, which made Gladdy smile. No one enjoyed feeding people more than she did. As she reached over to take the teapot nearest me, I saw my opportunity.

"Gladdy," I said quietly, "you hear everything. What have you heard about the Tyler Skaggs attack?"

Gladdy froze. "Now, Jilly, you know the tearoom is like a confessional. It wouldn't be ethical for me to reveal what I hear every day. What I know," she looked right and left in case anyone was listening, "could destroy the world."

"Please, Gladdy," pleaded international superstar Juliet Scott. "Just this once? It could really help the investigation."

I watched Gladdy melt under Juliet's gentle pressure. "Well," she said as she knelt by the table, "everyone is so quick to blame the woodbooger, but I know a human or two who had better reasons to go after Tyler Skaggs. Since he moved back in with his parents last year, he's been running around with Lacey Shoecraft, but I heard he broke up with her last week and that she was devastated with a capital D. Lacey has always been the apple of her daddy's eye, so if I were the sheriff, I'd be looking at Tater Shoecraft before I'd go looking for a beast no one has ever proven exists. But that's just me. I'm practical like that. Now, you didn't hear that from me, got it?"

We all pantomimed buttoning our lips. Shirley did it several times.

"Now, will that be cash or charge?"

As we exited the tearoom, the Buckworth limo eased to a stop at the curb, and we said our goodbyes to Juliet and Shirley with promises to see them later. Juliet got her tipsy mother into the car and they left.

"I wouldn't start with Virgil," said Momma as soon as they were gone.

"I wasn't going to. Where might I find Lacey on a Monday afternoon?"

Momma smiled approvingly.

"Exactly. Never underestimate a woman scorned, I always

say. You will find Lacey up to her eyes in Mildred Oliver's monthly perm and blue rinse at the Beauty Box Beauty Salon."

I flipped my hair and said archly, "I do believe my hair could use a trim."

"Those split ends are a fright." Momma grasped my hair and tugged it to her face until her eyes were crossed. "Have you been deep conditioning like I told you?"

"I was joking, Momma."

"It's all that heat styling. You should sleep on rollers instead."

And look like a Miss America contestant circa 1987? No, thank you!

When we got to the Beauty Box, Lacey was indeed rolling Mrs. Oliver's hair tightly onto rods, but that was the least interesting thing happening at the beauty parlor. The place was buzzing like a beehive, and I guessed it had something to do with the woodbooger.

The Beauty Box had been in business since my mother was a child, and it had changed hands several times through the decades. The latest owner had enlarged the place since my last visit several years before.

"Who owns the beauty box now?" I asked Momma.

"Lacey does. Her daddy bought it for her."

This didn't bode well. Lacey and I had a complicated history. We had been great friends in elementary and middle school, maybe even best friends, but it all changed in high school when we had what could be politely referred to as a falling out. In reality, our friendship had exploded in a mushroom cloud. What kind of missile could cause that much damage? A scud named Jeremy Cooksey.

Lacey had had a crush on my brother since elementary school. She came over to my house to play with me, but she was always on the lookout for Jeremy. For years, he didn't know she existed, but once we were freshmen in high school, he no longer saw us as a lesser species and would occasionally speak to Lacey. I never understood why she cared. I knew who my brother was, and I most certainly didn't want a friend of mine dating the town criminal, even if my friend, and the rest of the town, didn't know his true nature.

It all came to a head at the end of freshman year when Lacey decided she would ask Jeremy to the Sadie Hawkins Dance. I put my foot down. I told her she could either be my friend or Jeremy's girlfriend but not both. She demanded that I give her one good reason why not. I had about a hundred good reasons in Jeremy's journal of larceny and vandalism, but I couldn't tell someone outside the family. I couldn't rat out my brother to the community. The worst I could do was make sure my parents found out what he'd done, which I did, but I couldn't tell Lacey. She thought I was just being a selfish cow. In the end, Jeremy refused to go to the dance with a freshman, and it was all for nothing. But Lacey never forgot my ultimatum.

She joined the cheerleading squad and found other friends, popular ones who dated all the football players. We didn't have many classes together, so we just coexisted in high school. I knew that sometimes those girls had whispered behind my back because, let's face it, as high school valedictorian, I was a little bit of a nerd. And maybe Lacey fueled those whispers. But high school was a long time ago, and I hoped that it was all just water under the bridge and that Lacey would be amenable to my questions. The Beauty Box complicated things. I wasn't just walking into Lacey's place of employment. I was walking onto her territory, and that meant she had the advantage automatically.

Lacey saw me coming.

"Jill Cooksey, as I live and breathe!"

The entire room became silent.

"Let me just put Mrs. Oliver under the dryer, and I'll take care of you personally."

My heart sank. Lacey hadn't been that friendly to me since I was fourteen. I wasn't sure if it was the product of nostalgia or curiosity or something more sinister.

There you go again, looking for the worst in people. A lot of time has passed.

I was soon ushered to a sink where Lacey herself washed and conditioned my hair. She was very gentle, and the water was the perfect temperature. I relaxed as she prattled on about what the last ten years had been like for her.

"As you can see, I've expanded this business. I have a lot more chairs and a lot more stylists in my employ, and I offer more services. We do waxing, threading, hot stone massage—all manner of beauty services. You should book some when you have more time."

"I'll be sure to do that. Hot stone massage is one of my favorites."

Was it my imagination, or had the pressure of Lacey's fingers increased infinitesimally when I expressed my preference for hot stone massage? The pressure eased, and I was pretty sure it was my imagination.

Soon, I was in the chair with a cape around my shoulders.

"So, what are we doing today?" asked my former best friend.

"Just a trim. I want to get rid of the split ends."

"And maybe a few layers," piped up Momma from behind an issue of *Southern Lady Magazine* in the waiting area. "Let's give it a little bit of body, a little bit of movement."

"Just a *few* layers," I cautioned. "And nothing shorter than my chin." I wanted to be able to put my hair in a ponytail for working out, and I didn't want anything resembling bangs.

"Piece of cake," said Lacey. "You just relax, and I'll have the split ends off in no time."

As Lacey got to work parting, combing, and trimming, I ventured my first question.

"So, what do you think about all this woodbooger stuff? Do you think it's real?"

"People say it is."

"Have you ever seen one?"

"I haven't," she said, "but I know people who say they have."

"Do you think they're telling the truth?"

Lacey paused for a moment. "I think they think they're telling the truth, but as to whether they've really seen a woodbooger, I reckon there's no way of knowing."

"Were you at the dance the other night?" I asked. I didn't remember seeing her there, but that didn't mean she wasn't.

"I skipped it. If you've been to one Brunswick Ball, you've been to them all."

I distinctly heard the pages of a magazine rip.

Lacey went back to cutting my hair and said no more. I'd hoped the mention of the woodbooger would prompt her to talk about Tyler and his attack, but it hadn't worked. Did I dare be more direct?

Before I could formulate a new question, Momma interjected.

"I see someone I need to talk to." She gestured to the window behind her. "Be right back." She was out the door in a flash.

I screwed up my courage and let 'er rip.

"I heard you were dating Tyler. I'm so sorry about what happened to him."

I jerked as Lacey swung my chair around so I was no longer facing the mirror. I must have made a sound because she said, "Sorry! The light is better this way, and I'm about to put your layers in." She didn't say anything more, nothing about Tyler.

"I've been to the hospital," I ventured. "Tyler is stable but in a coma. Jack and Betsy are taking it hard, as you would expect."

"Is that a fact?" she murmured and continued to snip away.

"I just keep praying he'll come out of the coma and be able to tell us all who attacked him."

"Hmm," was Lacey's only response.

After that, I gave up. Lacey clearly didn't want to talk about Tyler for whatever reason, so I turned my attention to the rest of the salon. I glanced over at the pedicure station and saw Nancy Jo Clark getting her toes done. She was a member of Lacey's clique in school. I waved to her, and she smiled and waved back. I continued my inspection and saw Mrs. Oliver under one of the dryers, and next to her was Amanda Mitchell, another cheerleader from days gone by. I waved to her, but she only smirked at me and went back to her magazine. I cut my eyes to the chair next to the one I was sitting in and found Destiny Woods having red streaks added to her do. Destiny had been the captain of the cheer squad. I was about to say something to Lacey about how nice it was that she and her friends were still so close, but she started up the hair dryer and cut me off.

Usually, I love having my hair dried. The warm air and constant brushing of my very straight hair would soothe and relax me. Not so today. I was on edge. My eyes darted around the room to find all of Lacey's pals now actively watching me. They were smiling. Why? Was my hair looking particularly good? Or did they sense my discomfort? Did they find it amusing?

You're looking for the worst in people. Stop it!

We were all grownups now. We had a shared history and culture. There was no reason to feel as if I'd landed in a nest of smiling crocodiles. I was overreacting.

Be an adult.

I took a deep breath and forced my shoulders to relax. Then I smiled back at everyone.

That's when the laughing started.

Lacey switched off the hair dryer.

"So, what do you think, everyone? It's a masterpiece, isn't it?"

In the blink of an eye, cell phones appeared and photos were taken.

"What's going on?" I started to bolt from the chair, but Lacey swung it around towards the mirror, and I froze.

I had a mullet! An honest-to-goodness mullet. And the whole room was laughing at me, except for Mrs. Oliver who had fallen asleep under the dryer.

The front was short and feathered. The back came to my shoulders and flipped up at the ends. I was an Eighties nightmare.

Horrified, I could summon no words, but that was fine because Lacey had plenty.

"Did you honestly think I wouldn't see through you? That you just wanted to pump me for information about Tyler Skaggs? Miss high and mighty big city detective! Did you think we didn't know about the murders you solved? Your mother made sure everybody knew what a superhero her daughter was. And then you come back to show off your boyfriend. *I'm Jill Cooksey. I'm Little Miss Perfect. I live in New York City where I have a glamorous job and solve murders and date a super-hot guy. Why don't you just stay in New York?* On second thought, they'll probably revoke your New Yorker card when they see this hairdo."

The room erupted in raucous laughter that woke Mrs. Oliver. Coming to under the dryer, she caught sight of me and yelled, "Are mullets in again? Finally!"

I bolted from the chair, threw off the smock, and grabbed my purse.

"It's on the house," said Lacey. Like I was going to pay her! I burst through the door and ran smack into Momma.

"It's on Insta," she cried. "Everyone has seen it!"

She pulled an umbrella from her purse and thrust it into my hands.

"Cover up!"

"But it's not raining," I protested even as I opened it. I kept the umbrella low and hid under it as best I could while Momma guided me to the car. Occasionally, I heard her shout, "No paparazzi! No paparazzi!"

Luthersburg, how could you?

CHAPTER 8

"Business in the front. Party in the back!" Jeremy cackled as only an older brother can when faced with a younger sister's abject humiliation.

We were home. Momma had drawn all the curtains, and we were sitting in the living room trying to figure out what to do about my hair. Momma had pulled some wigs out of the attic, but they were past their prime in both style and quality.

"You'll just have to wear a hat until we can get you to a proper salon in Charlottesville. Or maybe Richmond." Momma tossed the wigs back in their box. "But those feathered wings are so short, I'm not sure what a stylist is going to do about them. I'll start calling salons." Momma left the room.

"Lacey did it on purpose!" I seethed and grabbed the hand mirror I'd been using to try on the wigs. I looked like a meth addict except I had all my teeth.

"You could shave your head," giggled Jeremy. "Then you could paint your noggin to be any number of sci-fi characters. You'd be a hit at Comic-Con."

"Not helping, Jerkemy."

"You could become a Hare Krishna. A Sinead O'Connor

impersonator. You could pretend to be a cancer patient and commit fraud—"

"Shut up, Jerkemy!"

"And to think, you work in beauty public relations! They're going to ride you out of town on a rail when you get back to New York!" Jeremy collapsed on the sofa in laughter, hugging his sides. I contemplated smothering him with a throw pillow.

I heard the kitchen door open and close, and before I could hide my head under a sofa cushion, Mike and my father walked through the door. Upon seeing me, the two froze in their tracks. Daddy attempted to speak but only managed a few choking sounds, and Mike was rendered completely speechless by the abomination that was my hair. Jerkemy, true to form, collapsed in another fit of laughter.

Momma burst into the room.

"The salon can take you in half an hour, so we have to hustle our buns! Get a move on, girl!"

She threw me a baseball hat—correction, a trucker cap— which I pulled down as low as I could. It didn't have the desired effect. Jerkemy wheezed and gasped and managed to say, "Put...the...pedal...to the...metal!" Then he pumped his arm. "Honk! Honk!"

I ran to the car.

Two and a half hours later, I returned, but most of my hair didn't. It was on the floor of a salon in Charlottesville. The wings inflicted on me by Lacey (who was going to pay for what she did) were so short that there was little the stylist could do. In the end, my only option was a pixie cut, a style I never would have chosen for myself.

"Not a word!" I hissed to the menfolk as I entered the house and headed straight upstairs to my room, where I planned to remain for the next year until my hair grew out. I threw myself on the bed and covered my head with a pillow, which is why I heard rather than saw the door open and close softly.

"Jill." It was Mike. "Let me take a look."

"No!" I clasped the pillow tighter to my head.

"Jill, you can't spend the rest of your life under that pillow."

"I'm only going to spend the next year under here waiting for my hair to grow."

Mike chuckled.

"Jill, let me see."

I sighed in resignation, slowly slid out from under the pillow, and sat up, keeping my eyes closed the whole time because I didn't want to see his reaction.

"It's cute," he said as he arranged some of my short locks with his fingers. "I never imagined you with this hairstyle, but it suits you."

"You must love me," I said as I dissolved into tears, "because you're lying through your teeth." I threw myself into his arms, buried my head in his shoulder, and cried while he patted my back, kissed my temples, and tried to say the right things.

Just then, my mother yelled up the stairs. "Y'all get ready. We have to leave for dinner at the Scotts' in half an hour!"

I burst into a fresh round of tears while Mike burst out laughing. I pushed him away.

"Okay, give me a break. This is pretty funny."

I pointed imperiously at the door.

"Okay, okay, I'm going." When the door shut behind him, I threw my pillow at it for good measure.

I emerged half an hour later, having given my best effort to compensate for the hair from hell. I had donned a peridot green sundress and had accessorized with sparkly rhinestone drop earrings and a matching pendant on a silver chain around my neck. A small rhinestone barrette accentuated my hair, which I had made a tad spikier with some mousse. I had to admit, the cut brought out the different shades of blonde in a way my long hair never had, and the shorter length, I thought, might direct more attention to my eyes. After fussing with it, I wasn't hating it as much, although I was still planning to grow it out as soon as possible and had already ordered some hair growth vitamins online. Overall, as I took one last look in the mirror, I felt pretty good about myself.

"Well, if it isn't Peter Pan!" crowed Jerkemy as I came down the stairs. "Ms. Martin, may I have your autograph?"

"More like sexy Tinker Bell!" countered Mike. "She was always my favorite."

I flounced over to my boyfriend, raised my hand above his head, and pretended to sprinkle something over him. I cut my eyes to my brother.

"No pixie dust for you, Jerkemy!"

"That's right," said Mike as he wrapped his arms around my waist. "I get all your pixie dust."

"You guys are so gross!" Jeremy high-tailed it out of the house while we laughed, but the sound of an impatient car horn soon had us running out of the house, as well.

We were headed to the Scotts' for dinner because it was Hoss and Juliet's last night in town. They were flying to L.A. the next morning because Juliet had to report to the set of her new rom-com.

Shock and awe is the only way to describe everyone's reaction to my new do, even though everyone had seen the mullet (shudder) on Insta.

"We made a pact not to mention it," admitted Juliet. "We were going to act like nothing was wrong. Thank goodness you dealt with that crime against hairmanity!"

"This short hair is right cute," said Hoss. "Unexpected, but cute. It brings to mind someone, but I can't quite place her."

"Mary Martin?" prompted my brother.

"Sandy Duncan?" urged Dud Scott.

"Rosemary's Baby!" cried an elated Hoss.

"Lord, help us," murmured my mother.

"You mean Mia Farrow?" asked Mike as he took my hand and squeezed it.

"Pretty little thing," confirmed Hoss. "It's too bad her baby was the devil."

My brother was in tears from trying not to laugh at Hoss Buckworth. Mike's face had gone strategically blank. I was torn between hysterical laughter and sobs, so I stayed quiet.

"Let's have dinner!" declared Shirley, and she ushered us all toward the dining room.

Over Shirley Scott's famous lasagna, a church supper staple, Juliet did indeed reveal that she was pregnant, and dinner turned into a celebration.

At one point, Jeremy whispered in my ear, "Well, I'm certainly glad I let that one get away in high school. Breeders! Ugh!"

"Whatever, Jerkemy. Like you ever had a shot." Then I rolled my eyes so hard I gave myself a headache.

After dinner, we took our dessert, Shirley's first and wildly successful attempt at tiramisu, to the family room and settled in for a chat. Eventually, the conversation turned to Tyler Skaggs and the woodbooger, and we shared what we had learned at the tearoom.

"Lacey Shoecraft is a very likely suspect, in my opinion." I stirred my coffee so violently that I felt Momma start, concerned for Shirley's grandmother's Haviland china. I tried to relax. "She's vindictive enough to want to hurt an ex. I think we've all seen the proof."

"But she'll never talk to you," said Momma. "You need to come at her from another angle."

I blew out a frustrated breath. Getting to Lacey was going to be very difficult.

"Such as?" Hoss put more tiramisu on his wife's plate. So cute!

"Maybe through her mother," suggested Mike. "What Lacey

did to you was the epitome of bad manners. When Jeannie Shoecraft finds out, she might feel badly enough about her daughter's behavior to sing like a canary."

Everyone agreed it was an excellent idea, so Mike and I started to make plans to approach Mrs. Shoecraft when my father interrupted.

"Don't make any plans for tomorrow. You have to visit Aunt Minty."

"It doesn't have to be tomorrow, does it? We have all week."

"It has to be tomorrow because I told her it would be tomorrow, and you know how she gets."

It had to be tomorrow.

Aunt Minty was my Great Aunt Araminta Cooksey, Daddy's daddy's sister. She considered herself the matriarch of the Cooksey family, and as such, commanded a certain level of respect and attention. She was also my favorite aunt.

"Fine," I conceded.

"That won't take the whole day, surely," Mike put in hopefully. I laughed weakly and shoved more tiramisu in my mouth.

At nine-thirty, the mother-to-be started yawning, and Momma and Daddy started making noises about leaving. Mike started to stand, but I tugged on his belt until he sat back down.

At ten, we stood up and headed to the foyer, chatting all the while. Mike went to open the front door, but I inserted myself between him and the portal and shook my head no, tempering it with a smile. The poor man looked so confused.

At ten thirty, the front door was finally opened and we moved out onto the porch. Mike headed for the car, but I took his hand and arrested his progress. I noticed he was now frowning. It was so cute.

At ten forty-five we moved off the porch and into the driveway. I managed to get between Mike and the car because it just wouldn't do to leave in a rush. (Yes, I was laughing at Mike on the inside. Does that make me a bad person?)

At eleven, we finally piled into the car, but we rolled down the windows so we could keep talking. Mike looked shell-shocked and so very, very confused.

At eleven fifteen, Daddy put the car in gear and backed down the driveway while everyone shouted goodbye a hundred times. And then we were gone.

"What the heck just happened?" asked my adorable, confused boyfriend. Finally! Something about Luthersburg he wasn't taking in stride. Hallelujah!

"Was that his first?" Jeremy's voice was full of excitement.

"It was indeed"

"My first what?" asked Mike bewilderedly. He was about to crack, and the awful Cooksey family just burst out laughing.

"Your very first Southern goodbye," said my mother as she wiped tears from the corners of her eyes. "Welcome to the family."

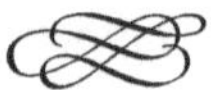

CHAPTER 9

Mike let out a low whistle when we pulled up to Aunt Minty's house the next morning. No surprise there. The property was impressive. Aunt Minty's was one of my favorite haunts as a child. Her two-story brick colonial with a sleeping porch sat in the middle of three cleared acres dotted with ancient specimen trees of linden, oak, and tulip poplar. The clearing sat at the base of a small mountain that was heavily forested. Aunt Minty's total property was something like twenty acres, and it had been a wonderful place to roam as a child. Easter egg hunts were particularly exciting at her house.

We were there by nine-thirty in the morning, and I had already warned Mike that we would be served breakfast. We would also be expected to stay for lunch.

"Why?" he asked.

"Because she's an older lady who lives alone and only gets to see me a couple of times a year."

"Fair enough."

"I think you're going to like her."

What I didn't tell Mike was that Aunt Minty was about

three quarters short of a dollar. I figured it would become apparent soon enough. Why add to the stress?

I didn't bother knocking. I had never knocked on Aunt Minty's door in my life. I let us in, called out a hello, and was met with silence. The front door opened into an entry hall with a staircase—classic center hall colonial. The foyer even had the requisite chair rail, wallpaper, and grandfather clock. I peeked into the parlor on the right. The same furniture that appeared in sixty-year-old black and white family photos still graced this room, in pristine condition, I might add, with all wooden surfaces polished to a high gloss. To the left was a small library with dark floor-to-ceiling shelves filled with books from the last one hundred and fifty years. Two wingback chairs flanked a small fireplace, and a glossy desk with a green-shaded banker's lamp was tucked into a corner. Under the window was a thickly cushioned window seat, the coziest place to sleep during overnight trips to Aunt Minty's house when I was a child. Mike took it all in, and I could tell he was impressed. His eyes were huge.

There was no sign of Aunt Minty, so we continued down the center hall to the back of the house. To the left was the family room. It had originally been a formal dining room, and, indeed, the dining room furniture was still there. The buffet now sported an immense flatscreen television that faced a huge modern sectional sofa. The gateleg dining table was collapsed and placed up against the wall near the hutch, which show-cased Minty's china and crystal. Four dining room chairs were dotted along the walls here and there, but I knew the other six were in the attic. A substantial ottoman in front of the sofa was littered with books, newspapers, throws, and several television remotes. While the parlor and library were for company, this was where Aunt Minty truly relaxed.

But there was still no sign of her.

We crossed the hall to the kitchen and found the beating

heart of the home. The kitchen was a fascinating mix of the ancient and the modern. The colonial revival builder had gone all out with a huge colonial-style cooking fireplace with a crane for hanging pots and kettles and a built-in bread oven, but directly opposite was a sleek, modern kitchen with polished concrete countertops, subway tile, and high-end European appliances. On a central island were several dishes containing slices of bread in varying states of decay. Nearby was a chemistry set partially put together to accomplish some sort of science experiment. Next to that, bent over a microscope, was dear Aunt Minty. She was dressed in a lab coat, and her snow-white hair had been braided and coiled into a bun at the nape of her neck.

"This is unexpected," said Mike, but she couldn't hear because her ears were covered with huge headphones. I waved my arms about, hoping to catch her eye, and it worked.

Rising to her full height of about five feet, she pulled off the headphones

"Sorry, young'uns. I was just listening to my podcast. You must be Michael. Nice to meet you!"

"It's a pleasure," said Mike as they shook hands. He gestured to the headphones. "True crime?"

"Prepper. Jilly knows my motto," she smiled as I leaned down to kiss her cheek.

"Always prepared." Her cheek was soft as down. I studied my aunt and determined she hadn't changed a bit since I'd last seen her. *Please, Lord, let me have her genes.*

Mike gestured to the moldy bread bits on the counter.

"Is this another part of being prepared?"

Minty laughed.

"I'm trying to make penicillin. I read about how to do it in a book. I figure if a time-traveling doctor in 1700s North Carolina can do it, so can a modern woman of the twenty-first century. It will come in handy when society collapses. I'm sure, since you're dating my infinitely capable niece, that you are aware that society is on the verge of collapse. She wouldn't date a numbskull. Let me show you my preparations."

Minty led the way to a door on the far side of the kitchen that led to the cellar stairs.

Here we go. It's make-or-break time.

What appeared to be a typical door turned out to be a self-sealing, lead-lined, sci-fi portal that would keep out radiation and chemical and biological agents, or so Aunt Minty told us as she gave us the grand tour. The cellar itself was a mixture of cutting-edge technology and all the comforts of home.

"I've got solar power and a wind turbine. For heating and cooling, I have geothermal. My well water is treated with reverse osmosis." She opened a door that led to a pantry lined with freeze-dried food. "I could survive down here for decades. I'd even thrive if I had a handsome beau like you down here with me." She winked at Mike. *Minty, you cougar!*

"This is an impressive setup." Mike wasn't patronizing my elderly relation. It truly was impressive. I only hoped that if the world went to pot, Aunt Minty would open the door to her ark and let me in. If Mike came along, she probably would.

"I've been working on this since Kennedy was assassinated. LBJ was the writing on the wall for me. Some people can't look ahead and see what's coming. They can't see all the possibilities. But I'm not one of them. What about you?"

Mike was nonplussed. "I like to believe I can add two and two together and make four," said Mike cautiously.

"That's not what I meant. How are your preparations? Do you have a planned escape route from that rat trap known as New York City? You need an on-foot route as well as a driving route. When the day comes, they'll close all the bridges and tunnels. Do you have a raft? And have you cached food, money, and weapons somewhere outside the city? What is your ultimate destination? We can plan a route together!"

Mike turned to me with eyes pleading for me to get him out of this conversation.

"Do I smell something burning?" I smelled nothing but the pleasant aroma of baking biscuits.

"My biscuits!" Aunt Minty sprinted up the stairs to the kitchen, and Mike exhaled.

Over a breakfast of country ham, red-eye gravy, biscuits, and assorted homemade preserves, I endeavored to steer the conversation away from prepping and toward current events.

"Have you been following this woodbooger case, Aunt Minty?" I asked as I soaked another biscuit with gravy.

My aunt made a derisive noise.

"No woodbooger attacked Tyler Skaggs. Woodboogers are peaceful. They just want to be left alone to raise their families, just like all normal people. Salt of the earth are the woodboogers. Give you the shirt off their backs, if they wore clothes."

Mike choked a little, and I pounded his back.

"Don't bolt your food, young Michael. Chew it. You'll live longer."

After Mike took a gulp of coffee and cleared both his esophagus and trachea, he asked, "How do you know what big —woodboogers are like?"

She fixed him with a stare that made him sit up straight.

"Because I've met them."

"Come again."

"It was in the summer of 1940," began my aunt as she laid down her knife and fork and briefly touched her napkin to her lips. "I was just a slip of a girl, but I ran wild in these mountains. I wasn't afraid of anything. Up with the dawn and out until the moon rose. I roamed every hill and holler. Daddy was proud of me because I wasn't a sissy girl. I could hunt and fish better than most boys, so nobody worried much about me until I didn't come home one night.

"You see, I got stuck in a tree. I wanted to know what it was like to be a squirrel. They could scamper up and down the trees with ease, and I got to wondering what the view was like from way up in the treetops. So, I found me an ancient tulip poplar perched on the side of a hill, with lots of big branches close to the ground, and I started climbing. It was plum easy to scamper up that tree. I just didn't look down until I reached the top.

"The view was out of this world. I didn't feel like a squirrel. I felt like an eagle. There were even wispy clouds below me, and I imagined launching myself from my branch at the tippy top of that tree and circling down to the valley floor below. But I wasn't an eagle or a squirrel, and when the sun started to set, I knew it was time to descend. But when I started to climb down, I had no idea how I'd ever climbed up. All the branches seemed too far apart. Worse, I realized just how high I'd climbed and that if I lost my footing, I was dead meat. On the top of that tulip tree, I froze.

"I'm not ashamed to say I cried my eyes out. But it was a good thing because the woodbooger must have heard my crying. The moon was up and it was way past my bedtime when I heard a noise below me. Soon after, a head popped up from below. I screeched and nearly fell out of the tree, but the woodbooger steadied me. He patted my head and my cheek to let me know he was friendly. He had kind, soft eyes. Then he gestured for me to climb onto his back. I didn't have a better option, so I did, and he took me down to safety.

"But he didn't stop there. When he hit the ground, he kept going until he reached the edge of the woods right behind this house. Then he crouched down so I could slide off his back. He patted my head again, and I hugged his leg because he was so tall. Then we waved at each other. He went back into the forest, and I went home.

"You see, he knew who I was. I'd been wandering all over

the mountains, and he must have seen me, but I never saw him until that day. He knew who I was and he brought me home."

We were quiet for a while. I applied myself to my ham biscuits and avoided looking at Mike directly. Aunt Minty carefully buttered a biscuit and layered on some damson plum jelly. Then she looked up again.

"I can tell by your silence that you're torn. You want to believe me, but some part of you just won't allow it. Probably that New York City part." She leaned over and patted Mike's hand. "But I don't hold it against you. I like you, Michael." Then she grinned. "You can hang out in my survival shelter any time."

Much, much later, we took our leave of Aunt Araminta. It had been a full day of disaster prepping, woodboogers, a short hike, a game of croquet, and, finally, a lunch of fried green tomato sandwiches with pimiento cheese. I enjoyed myself immensely, and I thought Mike had too.

"Well, she's crazy," he said when we were buckled into the truck. "But she's the best kind of crazy."

"I quite agree," I laughed. Aunt Minty was the best.

"So according to her, I need a cache of money, food, and weapons in upstate New York, preferably buried in a state park somewhere along Interstate 87. You know, for the zombie apocalypse." Mike cracked himself up.

I didn't tell him my cache was in New Jersey. The Watchung Reservation, to be exact.

CHAPTER 10

*L*uthersburg had yet to be invaded by the craft brew/craft cocktail community, and it didn't possess a proper bar per se, but outside of town was a honky-tonk that was popular with…well, I didn't know exactly because I'd never been there, and I didn't know anyone who had. So, it seemed like a good place to stop for a drink where no one would see my haircut. Mike was surprised when I suggested stopping at the dive bar, but we needed to have a conversation away from prying ears.

The interior of the bar was exactly what I expected. A pool table. A dart board. Neon beer signs. Some posters of scantily clad women. A random assortment of tables and chairs. The tang of cigarette smoke laced the air. We chose a table against the wall not too far from the door and sat down. Mike went to the bar for drinks and returned with bottles of beer.

"When in Rome," he said. I wasn't a beer drinker, but I could pretend if it would help us blend in. Okay, who was I kidding? We stuck out like a tourist from Iowa in Times Square. We were getting some annoyed looks from the other patrons, but I couldn't blame them. If I were a badass biker, I wouldn't want my honky-tonk invaded by yuppies either.

I took a sip of beer and looked everywhere except at Mike, delaying the conversation for as long as I could. Silently, I cursed my decision to stop. I could have kept silent. Did Mike need to know what I was thinking? Would it change anything?

"Jill. Talk to me."

I took a deep breath and looked into Mike's beautiful blue eyes.

"I believe Aunt Minty."

Mike looked at me for a long time before taking a slow gulp of his beer. When he looked at me again, I could see the incredulity in his face, clear as day.

"What? You believe society is on the verge of collapse?"

"I believe she met the woodbooger. I...I believe the wood-booger is real."

"Jill—"

"Hear me out. Aunt Minty is as eccentric as they come, but she has never told me a lie, not once. She hates people who lie. She despises conspiracy and values transparency."

"And she probably sees conspiracy at every turn."

"Perhaps she does. But Aunt Minty would never be part of one. She would never manufacture a lie or cover up the truth. She just wouldn't."

Mike closed his eyes and sighed.

"Is this a deal-breaker, Mike?" I whispered. "Does this put us too far apart in our beliefs for us to be together?"

Mike's eyes popped open.

"What?! Of course not! Jeez, Jill, you're allowed to believe in the tooth fairy if you want. That's not going to change how I feel. What's gotten into you?"

What had gotten into me? I couldn't say, but I was beginning to realize that something was indeed different, off even, about me.

"I don't know. Maybe it's the combination of finding Tyler nearly dead on the mountain, spying the woodbooger outside the community center, and having my hair chopped off by a harpy. Maybe it's because my dreams of a pleasant vacation with you in my quiet hometown have been thoroughly dashed by small-town craziness. Maybe I'm just waiting for the straw that breaks Mike McCall's back."

"Are you calling me a camel?" he deadpanned, and it had the desired effect. I chuckled in spite of myself.

"Jill…love of my life…"

Tears began to prick behind my eyes.

"Life has been crazy since the day I met you. I'm still here. Clearly, I like crazy."

And then he kissed me, softly, warmly, and my worries melted away. Then he abruptly broke off the kiss, the tease.

"But I am going to enjoy proving to you that bigfoot isn't real." He grinned at me.

"And I'm going to enjoy proving that the woodbooger is."

He raised his beer to me. "Game on."

"Game on!" We clinked bottles. This was going to be fun.

Our moment, however, was interrupted when the steel door opened and bright sunshine flooded the room. Several people tramped in, and it wasn't until the door shut and our eyes adjusted that recognition dawned. Then I nearly dropped my beer.

"Look!"

The Bigfoot Brigade had arrived in Luthersburg.

Three men had walked into the bar, and I recognized them as the three doofuses (doofuses is the plural; I looked it up) in the online videos. In army-style jackets festooned with bigfoot patches of all sorts, they blended in a lot better than we did. They all had patches on their breasts with their names, and I learned that Doofus Number One was named Larry, Doofus Number Two was named Darryl, and Doofus Number Three was named (sorry, classic TV fans) Mario. The men approached the bar with Larry in the lead, and I was amazed to see the bartender, a huge bald man with a handlebar mustache and a leather vest, simper like a middle school girl at a K-Pop concert.

"You're the Bigfoot Brigade! I watch your videos. I can't believe you're here."

"We go where the evidence takes us," said Larry as he removed his aviator sunglasses.

Was this guy for real?

"Do you think bigfoot attacked that kid over in Luthersburg?" The barkeep's eyes were as wide as saucers. I mused that it doesn't matter how big and tough we are, when it comes to things like bigfoot and the Loch Ness monster, we're all kids inside.

"That's what we're here to find out."

"Are you gonna trap him?"

"That, my friend, is easier said than done, but if the bigfoot hurt a human, we'll bring him to justice, one way or the other."

"Oh, my stars," I whispered. The expression on Mike's face showed he shared my worries. Vigilantes could stir up a lot of trouble in my hometown, even vigilantes after something that might or might not exist. Somebody real might get hurt in the process. We needed to find Tyler's attacker ASAP.

Mike started to rise from his chair—"I'm going to talk to them"—but then my phone chirped.

"Hold on. It's Momma." I scanned the text message. "Tyler is starting to respond to stimuli. We should go to the hospital. He's coming out of the coma!"

Tyler would soon be able to tell us who attacked him before any more crazies descended and Luthersburg was plunged into chaos. Well, more chaos than usual. I felt myself relax as I gathered my purse and prepared to leave. Soon, we would have the truth.

CHAPTER 11

*O*ur journey to the hospital was cut short when Momma called and said not to come. Tyler was only wiggling fingers.

"Disappointing," said Mike, echoing my feelings. I was ready for the whole woodbooger thing to be over. I just wanted to enjoy being in Luthersburg with my boyfriend.

And I'm sure Tyler's parents are also ready for their son to no longer be at death's door, said my conscience, which sounded a lot like my mother. Chastened, I resolved not to be a selfish cow and to do whatever was required to help the Skaggs family.

Back at home, Mike went off to do more research while I went in search of Jeremy. I called out for my brother, but there was no answer. I looked in his room, but all I found was an unmade bed and clothes on the floor. (Some things never changed.) Was he home? His car was parked in the most secluded part of our driveway, a little dog leg that ran under the trees where Daddy used to park a camper when we were kids, and I couldn't remember if I'd seen it when we arrived home. So, I went outside to check.

Jeremy drove a very nice, very new BMW, and there it was parked under the trees. *Maybe he's chilling out in his car*, I considered as I approached the bright red coupe. But then my attention was snagged by something hanging out of the trunk. On closer inspection, it appeared to be black fur. I popped the trunk and nearly cursed at what I saw inside. The empty eyes of a gorilla mask stared up at me from atop a matching furry suit that had been hastily thrown in the trunk. Next to the suit were the gorilla feet, constructed of fur and latex and made to wear over shoes. They were covered in mulch.

"What are you doing in my car?" yelled Jeremy from behind me.

I whirled, nearly crying out from fright, but pulled myself together. Jeremy was vibrating with anger, or was it fear? I knew how much he hated getting caught.

"What are you doing impersonating the woodbooger?" I countered. "I assume that was you we saw at the dance." I crossed my arms, jutted a hip, and stared him down.

"So? What if I did?" Jeremy pushed past me and slammed the trunk shut. "You gonna tell Mom and Dad? I know you'll tell your boyfriend. You always loved getting me in trouble."

Rather than backing down, I took a step closer and got right in his face.

"Dude, you get yourself in trouble! Shouldn't your prefrontal cortex be mature by now?"

"It was just a joke."

"What exactly was a joke, Jeremy? Scaring us at the dance? Or did you have something to do with what happened to Tyler?"

"Jill!" Jeremy looked horrified, and he stepped back as if I'd pushed him. "How can you think…? Of course, you think the worst of me. You always have. For the record, I didn't get into town until the night of the dance. I heard about the wood-booger hysteria going on, and I thought it would be funny to get the town more riled up. And it was! But I didn't attack Tyler Skaggs. Do you believe me?"

Jeremy's expression was earnest, and he was looking me straight in the eye. While he was a mischief maker when we were kids, he had never sought to physically hurt anyone. Mayhem, yes. Murder, no.

"I believe you."

"Well, that's something."

"But you can't impersonate the woodbooger anymore." I told him about the Bigfoot Brigade. "The hysteria is bringing weirdos to town, and someone might get hurt. Especially someone dressed up as bigfoot."

"Okay, okay." Jeremy was smiling again, mollified by my concern for his safety. "No more woodbooger impersonations." Then he laughed a deep rumble that started in his belly before it exited his mouth in the form of guffaws. "But you should have seen everyone's faces at the dance. It was priceless! I have no regrets!"

"Whatever." I turned to walk away, but Jeremy jumped into his car and started the engine.

"Where are you going?"

"To pick up my date!" He waggled his eyebrows. "You're not the only one who can bring someone home to meet the parents. Don't worry. You'll thank me later." He barked a laugh and threw the car in reverse. I was barely able to jump out of his way.

Jeremy returned home with his guest just as darkness descended, and Daddy was quick to throw open the door in welcome. He loved company.

"Come on in…" The welcome died on his lips as Jeremy ushered Lacey Shoecraft into the foyer.

You could have knocked us over with a feather. All four of us stood rooted to the hardwood as Jeremy took Lacey's jacket and formally introduced her to the family. Both he and Lacey seemed thoroughly entertained by our reaction, if their gloating grins were any indication. Thank heaven for Momma's ingrained good manners. She was the first to recover.

"Welcome to our home," she managed.

"Wait just a second—" Mike began, but I cut him off and dragged him into the kitchen before he could say anything else.

"Jeremy winked at me," I hissed in his ear.

"What does that have to do with anything? You're about to break bread with the woman who sheared you like a sheep! Don't you have a problem with that? I certainly do!"

"Don't you get it? Jeremy brought her here on purpose."

"I'm sure he did, the little weasel."

"No, he told me I would thank him later. I think he brought her here so we could have another go at getting information out of her."

Mike thought it over for a moment.

"She's probably wily enough to figure out what he's doing."

"Unless she thinks he hates me too and wants to rub my nose in it."

Mike sighed.

"It's possible."

"So, we have to play it cool. Can you do that, Detective McCall? Can you be nice to the bad guy?"

"If I must."

The next surprise of the evening greeted us when we rejoined the others. They were in the living room enjoying a drink before dinner, something we never did, but Daddy had procured a bottle of moonshine from somewhere. He was pouring it into Momma's sherry glasses, and he slid one into my hand as I entered the room. I looked to my mother, who made sure alcohol was rarely consumed in our house, and she winked at me. Either she and Daddy had figured out what

Jeremy was up to or they just thought we would need fortification to get through the evening.

"Cheers!" said Daddy, and we all raised our glasses.

I took a sip, and the fire of Mount Doom flowed across my tongue and down my throat. To my credit, I didn't choke, but when I tried to politely say "It's smooth," no sounds came out.

Lacey crowed with laughter. Her glass was already empty, and she held it out for a refill. There went that plan. No one would be outdrinking Lacey Shoecraft that evening, so I set my glass down as we headed for the dining room.

Daddy had spatchcocked and smoked chicken until it was falling off the bone. He paired it with his homemade, secret-recipe barbecue sauce. Mike and I took care of the sides: parsley-buttered potatoes, grilled corn on the cob, and green beans flavored with onions and ham. We also put out sliced tomatoes, onions, and cucumbers because, hello, the South. For dessert, Momma made her famous-in-three-counties yellow cake with chocolate icing.

Jeremy held a chair for Lacey, and as she sank onto the needlepoint cushion created by my grandmother, she shot me a look of triumph. Holy cow! No water had flowed under Lacey's bridge. She was still holding a grudge against me over Jeremy, but now, in her eyes, she was finally getting her chance. Desperate pixie cut notwithstanding, I felt kind of sorry for her. Jeremy was only using her to get information on Tyler. She wasn't winning at all.

Once grace was said and the food was passed, Jeremy tried to get the conversation started.

"So, what do you think of Jill's new haircut?"

Daddy choked on his corn cob, and Mike laid down his knife and didn't touch it for the rest of the meal. Momma and I just looked at each other and kept on eating as if everything were normal.

Lacey tossed her long, perfectly waved, chestnut locks over her shoulder before she answered.

"I think it suits her perfectly."

"You know, I think so too." Jeremy winked at Lacey, and she tittered.

"I think only the most beautiful women can pull off short hair," said Mike as he cut his chicken with the side of his fork. Thank heaven it was tender. "I think of Audrey Hepburn and Elizabeth Taylor. Jill is fortunate she's so beautiful."

Heavens to Betsy! I was never going to make it through dinner. Five minutes in, and I was already sick to death of all the passive-aggressive bullpucky. I decided to take that bull by the horns.

"I believe the woodbooger is real!"

Momma and Daddy both froze with forks somewhere between plate and mouth. Mike paused almost imperceptibly before resuming eating. And Jeremy and Lacey—well, they burst out laughing.

"Of course, you do!" hooted Lacey.

"She's always been nutty as a fruitcake," chortled Jeremy, earning a glare from Mike. I tried to mentally remind him that Jeremy was playing a part, and maybe he got my telepathic message because he picked up his corn cob and took a big bite. Or maybe he just remembered on his own.

"I really do believe in the woodbooger," I persisted. There was no way we were going to talk about my hair anymore, and we needed to discuss something somewhat related to Tyler Skaggs. "After Aunt Minty told me her story, I'm a believer."

"The nut doesn't fall far from the fruitcake, does it?" quipped Lacey, and she and Jeremy exploded in laughter again.

"Aunt Minty is as sane as anyone at this table," I said sternly. "She told us how a woodbooger saved her when she got stuck in a tree. Aunt Minty doesn't lie. I believe her."

"Jilly Bean," said Daddy soothingly, "I'm sure Aunt Minty believes she's telling the truth, but there's no such thing."

"Jill," said Momma, again with the infuriating patience that made me feel mentally incompetent, "in an age of satellite surveillance and advanced technology that our government hasn't even shared with the world, if the woodbooger were real, we'd know it."

"Now who sounds like Aunt Minty?" I countered. Before Momma could protest, I went on. "Aunt Minty is certain no woodbooger could have attacked Tyler. She says they're too gentle and just want to live in peace with their families. But I wonder if Tyler could have done something to aggravate the woodbooger. Maybe he threatened the creature somehow."

"What was Tyler doing in the nature preserve anyway?" spat Lacey. "He wasn't even a real COW anymore. He didn't care about that preserve. He always droned on about ocean plastics. No, if Tyler was on Woody's Mountain, then he was meeting someone there, and that person almost killed him."

"But who'd want to meet there?" asked Jeremy. "It's isolated."

"Isolated places can be fun," cooed Lacey as she batted her eyelashes at Jeremy.

"Someone who was up to no good," Momma said drily. "They wanted to meet in private in case things got messy, which they did."

"So, it was someone who had beef with Tyler," put in Mike.

"Yeah, like maybe one of the members of the lodge," offered Lacey. "The Loyal Knights and the Squires were none too pleased. Neither were their wives. I heard it all in my salon."

"Maybe it was a woman," I offered. "A romantic, early morning hike gone wrong?"

"Tyler wasn't a hiker," scoffed Lacey. "He liked a treadmill in a gym, not the great outdoors. If he was meeting a woman, it wasn't to hike."

"Maybe it was to break up with her," said Momma.

"Or maybe it was someone he'd already broken up with. Maybe he wanted to get back together…or she did." I held my breath. Had I gone too far?

Lacey glared at me from under her false eyelashes. She took a breath, and I thought she was going to let me have it until Jeremy got there first.

"I highly doubt it." My brother chuckled. "Tyler Skaggs is a wet blanket. I think any woman who dodged that bullet would only feel relief." Jeremy casually draped his arm around Lacey's shoulder. "Momma, I'm ready for dessert. Is there cake?"

When the cake was half eaten, we rolled ourselves out the backdoor to the firepit.

"I'll make coffee and bring it out," I offered.

"I can help you," said Lacey.

Crap.

"Don't be gone too long now," said Jeremy, winning a brilliant smile from Lacey.

You don't have to lay it on so thick, Jeremy.

Back in the kitchen, I started making the coffee and putting a tray together while Lacey leaned against the counter and watched.

"I guess it was all for nothing," she finally said.

"What was all for nothing?" Dang it! I fell into the trap.

"All your protesting, trying to keep me away from your brother. You know he doesn't like you very much. That makes two of us."

I suddenly felt a keen sense of *déjà vu*. Once again, Lacey was pining for my brother, and once again I knew a secret I couldn't tell her. This time it was that Jeremy didn't care one iota about her. I felt just as bad this time as I had fifteen years ago.

"I think he was impressed by what I did to your hair."

Well, almost as bad.

She chuckled. "Jeremy likes a woman with guts, and I have plenty. So now he's choosing me, and there isn't a thing you can do about it, even if you do think I'm not good enough for him."

I whirled around to face her.

"I never thought that! Never!"

"Oh, sure." The sarcasm was thick as chocolate frosting. "Then why were you so against us?"

"You two weren't an 'us.' Remember? He said no to the Sadie Hawkins dance."

"Because you talked him out of it, I'm sure. Who knows what you said about me?"

"I didn't! I would never!"

"Then why didn't you want me to date him?"

"Because Jeremy is a complicated guy!"

"What does that even mean?"

"It means he's not the perfect person everyone in this town thinks he is."

Lacey barked out a bitter laugh.

"Who is? You? Of course, you think you're perfect. Miss valedictorian. Miss UVA. Miss friends with Juliet Buckworth. Well, some of us aren't perfect and don't want to be with perfect people."

With that, she nudged me aside and picked up the coffee tray.

"I'll take the coffee out." She whirled on her heel and was through the door in a flash. I heard Jeremy call out to her as she approached the firepit.

I took a moment to regroup. Lacey was speaking in ignorance, I reminded myself. She didn't know what my brother really had been or who he was now. I wondered if there was any way I might be able to straighten it all out. Would Lacey even believe the truth if I told her all of it? Was it my truth to tell? I took a deep breath and let it out slowly. Then I rejoined the group only to find that Jeremy and Lacey were gone.

"Lacey said she had the beginnings of a headache and asked Jeremy to run her home," explained Momma. "I know that headache was sent by the Almighty to spare us any more time in that woman's company and to keep me from laying hands on her."

Sweet relief. I sat close to Mike who put his arms around me as if he knew what I had just been through in the kitchen. How thankful I was for that man.

Momma's cell phone rang as Daddy poured me a cup of coffee. The conversation was over before I could finish adding cream and sugar.

"That was Betsy Skaggs. Tyler squeezed her hand when she asked him a question. The doctor says it's only a matter of time before he opens his eyes. Isn't that wonderful? Jack and Betsy are on their way home to get some rest. I bet this will be the first time in a week that Betsy has slept."

Daddy rubbed his hands together with glee. "Soon he'll be able to tell us who attacked him, and all the woodbooger nonsense will go away."

"And Betsy and Jack will get their son back," added Momma firmly.

"That too!" agreed Daddy, and he leaned over to kiss her cheek.

I was glad about the improvement in Tyler's condition, but something worried me.

"Momma, who all has Betsy told about Tyler coming out of the coma? Is she just keeping you and Daddy in the loop, or is she telling lots of people?"

Momma laughed. "Well, she calls me because she knows I don't go on the socials much, but she's been posting regular updates on Facebook, Insta, and Snapchat ever since Tyler was brought down from the mountain."

"Oh, dear."

"What's wrong with that?" asked Daddy.

Mike jumped in before I could respond. "What's wrong is that Tyler's attacker, most likely a member of this community, probably knows that Tyler is waking up and will soon be able to reveal his or her identity. Tyler is still in danger."

"Land o' Goshen!" Had Momma been wearing pearls, she would have clutched them.

She quickly called Betsy to warn her, while I gathered the coffee things and Daddy and Mike pulled the car around. I tried to call Jeremy, but there was no answer. I texted him instead. I had a bad feeling about what we would find at the hospital, and I wanted all Cookseys present and accounted for.

CHAPTER 12

We pulled up to the hospital just in time to see the woodbooger come barreling out the front door. Daddy screeched to a halt, and Mike jumped out of the car to give chase. I was mesmerized by the sight of the legendary creature booking it across the parking lot. The yellow light of the street lamps in the parking lot made it hard to tell if the creature was brown or black. He was, however, big and hairy. The woodbooger had great form and was leaving Mike in the dust. My boyfriend had been shot in the line of duty back when he was a cop and had only shed the resulting limp pretty recently due to intense physical therapy. He was moving well, but he was outmatched by the forest dweller. Soon the wood-booger disappeared into the forest, but Mike followed.

"He's going to break his neck running in the dark," I muttered. I wished I had gone with him to hold a flashlight, but it was a foolish thought. I would have been far behind both of them.

"What should we do?" Daddy breathed.

"I don't know." I was torn between waiting for Mike to return so I could see he was okay or running into the hospital to check on Tyler. "You and Momma see to Tyler while I wait for Mike."

They took off towards the building, while I headed towards the edge of the woods. I don't know why I thought Mike would emerge from the same spot he had entered the forest. In my fright and concern, I may not have been thinking clearly. So, he surprised me when he came jogging out of the trees from a different direction and caught my arm.

"I lost him." He was gasping for breath and didn't notice me practically jump out of my skin. Mike bent over double and took some deep breaths. When he stood upright again, I was ready with the questions.

"Did you get close to it? Did it make any sounds? Do you think it was a woodbooger?"

Mike looked at me like I was raving.

"Yes, Jill. It was certainly a woo—bigfoot. He checked his Facebook feed and saw that Tyler was improving, so he came down here to finish the job he started on the mountain."

"Point taken," I sniffed. I felt the need to justify my questions. "It's just that he looked so real running across the parking lot."

"Well, it was a real hominid running across the parking lot, just a homo sapiens instead of a…whatever the bigfoot is called in Latin. Homo fabularis? I don't know. I'm pretty sure it was wearing shoes. It didn't sound like skin slapping the pavement."

My phone rang. It was Momma.

"Tyler's been attacked again. Get up here!"

We took off running.

When we got to Tyler's room, Momma and Daddy were outside watching through a window as a team of doctors and nurses worked on Tyler.

"He'd been suffocated," said Daddy. "A nurse surprised the woodbooger holding a pillow over his face. She scared him off, and they went to work on him. We called the police."

Sheriff Bagby arrived a few minutes later and took statements from all of us and then from the doctors and nurses as they became available.

Jack and Betsy arrived next, looking like death warmed over, and a doctor came out to update them.

"Someone, something, attempted to suffocate your son. A nurse interrupted the assailant, but we aren't sure how long Tyler might have been without oxygen. He's breathing on his own again, but he's unresponsive."

Betsy fell to her knees with a cry of anguish.

"How did the woodbooger get in here without anybody seeing?" yelled Jack. "Is no one protecting my son?" He knelt to comfort his sobbing wife.

Sheriff Bagby stepped forward. "We're looking at the security video now. We'll have answers soon."

"Not soon enough for my son." Jack's voice broke as he held his wife. "The damage is done."

"We don't know that," said the doctor. "There's every reason to hope that this is a minor setback. Tyler hadn't been alone for long when the nurse returned and surprised the...er... woodbooger."

"Can we all just stop calling the assailant a woo—bigfoot?" Mike had reached his limit. "It couldn't possibly be bigfoot! How does bigfoot know how to smother someone?"

"Their ways are mysterious!" boomed a familiar voice. We turned as one to see the Bigfoot Brigade marching down the hall with Larry in the lead. "We're only beginning to understand the limits of their intelligence. We know they build things. They probably use tools. Wouldn't the pillow be a tool? In this case, a tool for attempted murder."

Betsy, who had calmed down slightly, began to cry again.

"How would bigfoot even know Tyler was in the hospital?" demanded Mike, his face reddening to the color of a ripe apple. A Winesap to be precise. "You know what? I'm not going to discuss this with you. This is ridiculous." He turned to the sheriff. "The bigger question is, how are you going to keep Tyler safe from now on? He needs round-the-clock security and should have had it already."

"Now, wait just a minute, son." Sheriff Bagby ambled forward until he was squarely in Mike's personal space. "Don't you be telling the Sheriff's department how to do things. Just because you USED to be law enforcement in the big city doesn't mean we need you Yankee-splaining things to us ignorant Southern folk. We have it under control."

"Do you have men and dogs tracking the perp through the woods?" demanded Mike, unperturbed. "Have you put out an APB? When that guy sheds the costume, he will come out of the forest, and you need men on the perimeter ready to nab him! Have you asked for aid from the surrounding counties?"

The Sheriff's face was taking on a dangerous hue, something akin to eggplant. Either a volcanic explosion or a stroke was in the offing. Thank goodness for the three doofuses.

"He's not coming out of the woods," said Mario confidently. "Big has gone to ground, probably to one of his nests. He'll sit tight and wait for things to calm down."

"Yeah," added Darryl. "He's not stupid."

"You know what?" asked Mike of no one in particular as he threw his hands in the air. "I'm out!" He marched off, shaking his head and fists and talking exasperatedly to himself and possibly to his maker.

"It's not his fault." Larry smiled patronizingly at me. "He's just not ready to have his mind expanded. We must be patient with those who lag behind. Every man runs his own race."

I snorted in disgust and ran to catch up with Mike. I found him in the parking lot, leaning against the car with his arms crossed so tightly that I worried for his breathing. His eyes were closed, but he trembled with rage.

"You ready to go back to New York?" I asked, fully

expecting him to say yes. Instead, his shoulders sagged, and he exhaled heavily. I could practically feel the anger exiting his body. He opened his eyes and his arms to me, and I went to him gladly.

"No," he said after a long hug. "I'm ready to prove everyone here wrong. Tyler's attacker is human, and we're going to catch him."

CHAPTER 13

**Woodbooger Strikes Again:
Local man again targeted by forest beast as
Bigfoot hunters assemble to deal with menace**

The headline in the next day's newspaper had my blood pressure up before I'd even had coffee. Worse, the Bigfoot Brigade was no longer the only fringe bigfoot-hunting group in Luthersburg. Teams from Searching for Sasquatch and Cryptid Corps had set up shop as well. Who knew how many more were on the way?

"I called it! All the crazies have come out of the woodwork, and they're going to wreak havoc on Luthersburg." I stabbed the butter a bit too hard and rattled the butter dish. "Just you wait! By the end, this town will be the butt of jokes. Jackie Jordan Show, here we come! Florida Man has nothing on Luthersburg!"

"Calm down, drama queen!" Momma snapped. "There are more important things at stake than the town's reputation. There's a killer on the loose."

"And it ain't no woodbooger!" Daddy swilled down his

coffee and grabbed a biscuit for the road. He had an emergency meeting of the Concatenated Order to attend. He jammed his fez on his head and high-tailed it out the door.

"He's in a mood," I remarked.

"Everyone's on edge with these bigfoot hunters around. Your Daddy's afraid they're going to storm the nature preserve so they can see where Tyler was attacked."

"Should someone go with him?" Mike helped himself to a piece of sausage and popped it in his mouth.

"He's got a couple hundred Woodbooger brothers. If he needs more help, he'll let us know." Momma said all this while giving me the stink-eye. I had my phone at the table looking at the news online, which irked her to no end. "Jilly-Beth, you know how I feel about phones at the table."

"Sorry Momma." I put the phone away. Suddenly, something occurred to me.

"You know who we haven't heard a thing from?"

"Your cousin Margot. Not even a Christmas card in four years."

"Momma!"

"I'm just messing with you. Who?"

"The Woodboogers of the World?" said Mike before I could.

"Exactly!" I snapped my fingers. "What happened to all those young men and their quest for a new Luthersburg order? Have any of them even visited Tyler at the hospital? Are they having meetings without him? Have they disbanded?"

"These are excellent questions for which you and Mike will find the answers, I'm sure," said Momma as she put her dishes in the sink and gathered her purse. "Now, I'm late for the Ladies Auxiliary. Let me know what you find out. And wake your brother before you leave." Then she was gone.

"Have you noticed," began Mike, "that whenever your father has a lodge meeting, your mother almost always has a Ladies Auxiliary meeting at the same time?"

I thought about his question.

"Well, I guess I have noticed, but I haven't thought it strange, although I'm not sure why."

"It's probably nothing."

"Probably."

While Mike loaded the dishwasher, I went to wake Jeremy. I needed a debrief with him to find out what else Lacey had said. I also wanted to caution him to let her down easy. She didn't deserve to have her feelings hurt any more by the Cooksey family, even if it had been unintentional…unless, of course, she was Tyler's attacker. Then she deserved a jail sentence plus anything else we could think of.

"Jerkemy, get up!" I barked as I pounded on the door. I was in full little sister mode, I have to admit. In our younger years, he would have yelled something profane at me, which would have prompted me to threaten to tell Momma, and a sibling squabble would have ensued. Today, however, my barking and pounding was met with silence. After my third attempt to wake him, I tried the door. It was unlocked, and a quick perusal of the room showed me that Jeremy had not slept there last night.

Is it so wrong that my mind immediately focused on the worst-case scenario? Did that make me a bad sister? He had promised he wouldn't impersonate the woodbooger again, but if he had, that also meant he had tried to kill Tyler. Was my brother capable of such a thing? And what motive could he possibly have? What a terrible sister I was even entertaining the possibility that my brother could be so violent and ruthless.

No. He couldn't be. He had beaten plenty of mailboxes to death as a teenager, but he couldn't beat another human being. He just couldn't! And if he was Tyler's attacker, why would he bring Lacey home to dinner so we could try to question her? Any information about Tyler could lead us to Jeremy. No. My brother was too smart for that. I was sure that whoever or whatever I had seen at the hospital was not him.

I had another awful thought.

"Oh, Jeremy. Tell me you didn't."

While I was certain Jeremy couldn't attempt murder, I was less certain that he wouldn't take advantage of Lacey Shoe-craft's adoration. If he had lured her to our home under false pretenses AND taken advantage of her afterward, I was going to rip him a new one. Lacey was no innocent angel—my hair could attest to that—but our conversation in the kitchen showed me just how hurt she had been back in high school and just how much she adored my brother. The hurt and the hero-worship ran deep.

Jeremy, please don't be a jerk.

I didn't share any of my thoughts about Jeremy with Mike. I couldn't risk damaging the relationship further by merely speculating about my brother's activities. Instead, I focused on the task at hand.

We began our search for the Woodboogers of the World online. Since they claimed to be a forward-thinking group, we expected them to have a web presence, and they did, sort of.

"Site under construction," I read on the screen. "Do you think it's really under construction, or do you think they took it down?"

"Fifty-fifty."

So, we went to the community center, where the WOW had held their informational meeting. We were able to find a flyer still tacked to a bulletin board, so we took it. The phone number on the flyer went to Tyler's voicemail, and the email address was tskaggs207@gomail.com, clearly Tyler's account. There was no other contact information.

"I guess we could ask Dud Scott for a list of COWs who defected to the WOWs," suggested Mike. "Then we can start knocking on doors."

I flipped the flyer over and laughed out loud.

"Or we could pay Beulah Kenilworth a call and demand some answers."

I held up the flyer to show Mike the Ruritan letterhead on the back of it.

While the Concatenated Order of the Woodbooger had its headquarters tucked away out of sight, the Ruritan headquarters sat proudly on Main Street. A two-story brick building painted cream, with burgundy shutters at the windows, it looked a lot like a real estate office. A shingle hanging over the sidewalk proclaimed "Ruritans of Luthersburg Headquarters." A bell jingled as Mike and I walked through the door, but Beulah Kenilworth could already see us through the glass door of her office and was rising from her chair.

"Welcome to the Ruritans. I'm the president of the organization, Beulah Kenilworth." Beulah offered me her hand to shake. "Are you interested in joining our esteemed service organization?"

"What are you up to, Beulah?" Instead of taking her hand, I planted mine firmly on my hip and gave her my best stink-eye.

"Why, Jill Cooksey! Heavens! I didn't recognize you with that new coiffeur. It's quite a sudden change. Now, to what do I owe the pleasure?"

"You can explain this," said Mike as he thrust the flyer at her. Personally, I wanted to thrust something else—like my fist into her face.

Beulah eyed the flyer. "Ah. Well, that was careless, wasn't it?"

"So, you don't deny you had a hand in this?" I demanded.

"I don't deny that a young man came to me for advice on how to start a civic organization, and I gave it to him. I also let him use our color laser printer to print some flyers. There must have been some letterhead in the tray. What of it?" She thrust the flyer back at Mike.

"Cut the crap, Beulah. You don't do anything without a

plan, and you planned to use Tyler Skaggs to bring down the Concatenated Order."

Beulah yawned dramatically.

"Was there something else? I have an important nap to take."

I heard a crunching sound; then I realized it was me grinding my teeth. Beulah grinned.

"What kind of deal did you have with Tyler Skaggs?" Mike asked before I could say something angry and incoherent.

"Deal? I'm not sure what you mean?" Beulah's eyes were wide with feigned innocence.

"Did he promise you mayoral votes if you helped him?"

Beulah laughed. "Nope. He didn't promise me anything. Now, about that nap."

I took a step closer to Beulah, but Mike took my arm gently and backed me towards the door.

"This isn't over," I seethed.

"Isn't it? Toodles!"

Back on the sidewalk, I vented my frustration by pacing and ranting, two things I'm very good at.

"That snake! That worm! What's lower than a snake or a worm? I'll tell you! Beulah Kenilworth! And I'll tell you something else. She doesn't do anything for free. She always expects something in return. She's like the devil that way."

"Well," began Mike in an irritatingly rational tone, "maybe this time she didn't get anything in return, and maybe, just maybe, Tyler paid the price a different way."

I stopped pacing.

Was Beulah Kenilworth the woodbooger? She was certainly tall enough. Wouldn't it be great, I mused, if we proved she was Tyler's attacker and she went to prison for a long, long time?

It was lunchtime when we left the Ruritan offices, so we headed to the local meat and three. I held my breath as we walked into the full dining room, but, by and large, the patrons were more interested in fried chicken than they were in my haircut. I caught a couple of women I knew stealing glances at me, but I ignored them. It couldn't be helped if I wanted to be out in the world solving this mystery, which I did. I was also feeling more confident in the new do, not that I wanted to keep it forever.

We found a table, and soon we were tucking into the day's special—hamburger steak smothered in onions, butter beans, and creamed corn, washed down with iced tea and a coconut cream pie chaser. All together, we paid less than the price of lunch for one back in New York, a fact Mike would repeat several times throughout the day.

By tacit agreement, Beulah Kenilworth was not discussed over lunch. We both valued our digestion too much, and she didn't come up until we were once again strolling down Main Street.

"Would you say Beulah Kenilworth is as tall as the wood-booger you chased through the woods, Mr. McCall?"

Mike smiled. "Why yes, Ms. Cooksey. I believe it's possible."

"And do you, Mr. McCall, believe she might have an adequate motive for the attempted murder of Tyler Skaggs."

Mike paused in front of a florist's shop. "Of that I'm less certain." He sighed. "The only motive I can think of is mayoral votes, but are votes in a small-town mayoral race worth killing for?"

"I should say not, young man!" cried the florist, who had been arranging bouquets in a display in front of her shop.

"Pay no mind to us, Mrs. Thompson." I smiled at the woman I'd known my whole life. "We were just…that is…"

"I know what you're doing."

Just then, Jeannie Shoecraft passed the shop, marketing basket in hand full to overflowing with fruits and vegetables, and saved us from further scrutiny.

"Jeannie!" called out Mrs. Tompkins. Mrs. Shoecraft paused and nodded to us politely.

"Eleanor, dear, I must dash. Please forgive me for not stopping."

"Not at all, Jeannie. I just wanted to tell you that a new selection of wedding invitations came in yesterday, in case you want to look at them sometime."

Jeannie Shoecraft blushed. "Well, I don't think that's appropriate now."

"Aw, honey," said Mrs. Tompkins sympathetically. "We must keep hope alive."

"Uh…yes…well, as I said…must dash." Mrs. Shoecraft hurried off as fast as her ballet flats could take her.

"Wedding invitations? Whose wedding?" I asked.

"Lacey and Tyler, although I guess it's all up in the air now," sighed Mrs. Tompkins. Then she perked up. "But, as I said, we must hope that Tyler wakes up soon and the woodbooger leaves him alone once and for all."

CHAPTER 14

The attic stairs at Cooksey's Corner may have been steep, but they were immaculately kept by my mother. There was no fear of dirt, bugs, or spider webs, thank goodness, which couldn't be said for my apartment in Queens. I paused at the top of the stairs, boyfriend in tow, and opened the door. As always, a sense of peace descended on me. I was entering my happy place.

The Cooksey attic had been my playroom growing up. It was large and fully finished. There was plenty of room for the detritus of yesteryear and my toys. Jeremy always preferred being out in the world wreaking havoc, so the attic was my domain. Entering it again after a long absence, I saw that very little had changed. Momma and Daddy had put the Christmas decorations in new containers, and some furniture and art pieces had been updated and stowed in the last couple of years, but my toys, including my chalkboard, were right where I'd left them.

"Why, exactly, are we in the attic?" Mike looked around, taking it all in.

"Because we need a base of operations, a war room."

"And the attic is the best war room because…"

"It has a chalkboard."

"Of course."

"It also has chairs." I pointed to the two rows of metal folding chairs lined up in front of the board.

"This looks like a miniature classroom."

"Does it?"

"You used to play school here, didn't you?"

"You will get nothing from me except name, rank, and serial number."

"Who did you get to be the students?"

"Jillian Elizabeth Cooksey."

"Let me guess. None of the neighborhood kids wanted to play school, so you used your dolls."

"Account supervisor."

"And maybe some pets?"

"730-64-1859."

"Didn't you have a cat?"

"Squiggles was an excellent student! I taught that cat to count, thank you very much. I most certainly did!"

Suddenly, I was being hugged, and Mike was chortling in my ear.

"Cooksey, you are just the cutest!"

"I know."

"Are we interrupting?" It was my father.

"I'm just learning more delightful things about your daughter," said Mike over my head. "Like she used to play school."

"She taught Squiggles to count," Daddy cried. "I saw it with my own eyes."

"That cat was too smart. There was something wrong about that cat." Even with my head buried in Mike's shoulder, I could imagine Momma shaking her head ominously.

When my beloved finally let go of me, I made my pitch to the family.

"I propose we use this as our war room. We can track our suspects on the chalkboard, and no visitors will be able to see what we're up to since no one but us is coming up to the attic."

"Makes sense," said Daddy. "But do we have any suspects?"

"We certainly do," said Mike, and he wrote Beulah Kenilworth's name on the board.

"I'm liking this plan more and more," said Momma.

"We also have another." I added Lacey's name; then Mike and I filled my parents in on what we had learned that morning.

"Beulah Kenilworth doesn't surprise me at all," said Momma, "but I am shocked that things had gotten so serious between Lacey and Tyler. Jeannie never said a word."

"Lacey may be hiding some very strong feelings about Tyler Skaggs, which would be natural," offered Daddy. "She's a proud woman."

"That's putting it mildly," I murmured.

"But she might be hiding those feelings for another reason," added Mike. "Attempted murder."

"She's mean, no doubt about it," sighed Daddy. "Jilly's hair is a testament to that truth, but there's no way she could have been the woodbooger we saw at the hospital."

Momma put two and two together. "But Beulah Kenilworth could be. She's an Amazon!"

"What would bring Lacey and Beulah together?" I just couldn't see it. "How would such an unholy alliance come about?"

"A lot of secrets can be revealed at the beauty parlor," Momma pronounced mystically. "When you trust someone with scissors around your eyes and ears, you let your guard down completely."

"Truth."

Out of the corner of my eye, I caught Daddy and Mike eyeing each other skeptically.

"Maybe," said Mike. "But there may not even be an alliance. Beulah could be acting alone, or Lacey could have a different accomplice."

Don't think of Jeremy. Don't think of Jeremy.

I thought of Jeremy.

"What are you thinking, Jilly?" asked my mother in a very suspicious tone of voice.

Play it cool, Jill. Play it cool.

"Not a thing."

"You're a terrible liar."

"Nothing I wish to share with the group at this time," I amended.

"Well, just so long as you don't say that you knew it all along when we finally do unmask Tyler's attacker," said Daddy as he headed for the stairs. "That's just not sporting. Now come with me, young Michael. We're smoking ribs for dinner!"

The three of them headed for the stairs, but I stayed behind. When I heard them tromping down the steps, I eased myself behind the chalkboard. It was double-sided. I picked up the chalk.

In the center of the board, I wrote my brother's name.

WHEN JEREMY SNUCK in at one o'clock in the morning, I was lying in wait at the kitchen table. My pot of tea had grown cold an hour earlier, but my legal pad was covered with questions for Jeremy that I had worked and reworked, trying to get the tone right so I wouldn't put him on the defensive. I knew the effort was potentially fruitless, but my PR training demanded I try.

He saw me through the window before he came in, and I'm pretty sure he rolled his eyes. When he came through the door, however, he was all smiles.

I held up a plate of peanut butter cookies, his favorites, that I had spent the evening baking with this moment in mind.

"Cookie?"

His eyes narrowed. *Sigh.* He knew exactly what I was doing. Why did I think I could lure my brother into a sense of security and get him to talk? Desperate times.

Jeremy took a cookie.

"Thank you."

"Join me?"

Another eye roll, but he pulled out a chair and sat down.

"There have been some developments," I began, but he cut me off.

"Tyler was attacked by the woodbooger again. Yes, I know."

"How did you find out?"

He gave me his classic "Is my sister a complete idiot?" look.

"Everyone knows. I heard about it from K.B."

Kenny Beveridge was Jeremy's best friend from high school and persona non grata at the Cooksey house—and most houses in Luthersburg—due to the fact he had a police record a mile long and had no intention of reforming in the foreseeable future. Jeremy hanging with Kenny was potentially very bad news.

"Is that where you were last night? At Kenny's?"

Jeremy cocked his head and regarded me shrewdly.

"What are you worried about, little sister? That Kenny might rope me into one of his schemes?" He cocked his head to the other side as another thought occurred. "Or are you worried that I might have taken up with Lacey in earnest? Or worse, not in earnest? Is that what this is about?"

I glanced at my legal pad. My line of questioning was already shot to Hades, but I desperately searched the page for the right words anyway.

Quick as lightning, Jeremy grabbed the pad. I tried to

snatch it back, but he rose from the table and moved across the kitchen.

"Let's see. 'I was concerned when you didn't come home last night. Is everything okay?' Next, we have 'I love you very much, Jeremy. If you need someone to talk to, I'm here for you.' Seriously, Jill? The next one is better. 'The woodbooger hysteria is heating up. Have you considered getting rid of the costume, just to be cautious?'" He slammed the pad on the kitchen counter. "I told you I wasn't going to impersonate the wood-booger again! Do you actually think it was me at the hospital last night? Do you think I tried to smother Tyler?"

I couldn't speak. What could I say? That I had doubts? It would destroy the fragile détente we had established. But I couldn't lie either. Jeremy was perfectly capable of going back on his word. He would just call it changing his mind.

But is he capable of murder?

I threw up my hands in frustration, which took Jeremy by surprise.

"Of course not! I'm grasping at leads, trying to make sense of everything that's going on, and you're in and out of the house, operating on your own agenda, which you aren't sharing. I don't even know how long you'll be in town. Don't you have a job? You bring Lacey to dinner, leave with her, and don't come home for over twenty-four hours. She's still hung up on you, by the way. She made that clear last night, and she's looking to right what she believes is a wrong I perpetrated against her back in high school. If she hasn't thrown herself at you yet, she will. Your moral code is flexible, to put it mildly, and I don't want to see her hurt again by any member of this family, even if she is a vindictive cow. I especially don't want to add to the hurt Tyler caused when he broke off their engagement—"

"They weren't engaged."

"Um, yes they were."

"No, they weren't."

"I know for a fact that Jeannie Shoecraft was planning a wedding. It's why Lacey is on the list of suspects in Tyler's attack, although she must have had an accomplice."

"I know they weren't engaged because Tyler told me so."

Jeremy's expression went from ticked off to wary the instant he realized he said something he shouldn't.

"You've been in contact with Tyler?"

Jeremy walked to the table, grabbed a handful of cookies, and surprised me by planting a kiss on the top of my head.

"You need to stop worrying so much. You'll get wrinkles."

Then he was gone.

I sat at the table for a long time, consuming cookies mindlessly while my brain desperately tried to make order out of chaos, before I finally dragged myself to bed.

CHAPTER 15

At breakfast the next morning, Mike proposed a council of war, so, after oatmeal, we all tromped up to the attic, including Jeremy.

"I believe that owing to the bizarre nature of this case," began Mike, "we've ignored police procedure. We don't have some basic facts. What did the crime scene reveal? What time was Tyler attacked? We don't know what the police know. At the very least, if we find out the time of the attack, as indicated by Tyler's wounds—we can start looking into the whereabouts of our suspects at that time."

"Shouldn't the police have already done that?" asked Jeremy.

"It's possible," Momma put in, "that our suspects and the Sheriff's suspects are not the same." She gestured to the chalkboard where Beulah Kenilworth and Lacey Shoecraft had pride of place.

"Beulah Kenilworth, huh? How do you figure that?" asked Jeremy.

"She helped Tyler start the Woodboogers of the World," replied Daddy crisply. "All part of her master plan."

Jeremy's expression remained neutral. Beulah wasn't the

only person who had been in contact with Tyler before the attack. Why had Jeremy been talking to someone he once referred to as "a wet blanket"? He didn't suffer fools lightly.

"So how do we get the information from the sheriff?" I asked Mike. "You and he didn't exactly part on the best of terms at the hospital."

Mike turned to my father. "Isn't Sheriff Bagby a member of the Order?"

"He's a Squire," said Daddy. "He declined to become a Loyal Knight. Said it might look like a conflict of interest to the citizens of Luthersburg."

"But he might be amenable to a request for information coming from you as the Right Honorable Yeti," encouraged Momma.

Jeremy put a hand over his mouth to hide a smile.

Daddy opened his hands in supplication. "I can but try."

And try he did, to no avail.

"Stymied!" cried Daddy as he climbed into the truck where Momma, Mike, and I were waiting. Jeremy had stayed home to do work (I hoped). "He said that because the crime happened on COW property, he couldn't reveal details of the ongoing investigation to me as a member of COW leadership!"

"I should have seen that coming," muttered Mike. "Now what?"

"Now we go where we should have gone in the first place," sniffed Momma. "To the victim's family. Surely the sheriff has shared some details with Jack and Betsy."

After a short drive to the hospital, we found them at Tyler's bedside looking very much worse for wear. Momma immediately went to organize a meal for them, leaving the rest of us to talk to Tyler's agonized parents. Daddy took the lead.

"We're doing everything we can to bring Tyler's attacker to justice," he began. "But we're a little fuzzy on some of the details, and we're hoping you can fill in the gaps. What have the police told you about the original attack? Have they pinpointed a time?"

Betsy Skaggs stiffened and turned away. She straightened Tyler's blankets unnecessarily. I also noticed that Jack was having a hard time looking my father in the eye.

"We don't know anything," he mumbled.

"You mean the police haven't shared any details of the case with you, the victim's family?" said an astonished Mike. "That's outrageous!"

Betsy whirled around.

"What he means is the police won't tell us anything because one of us is a suspect!" Betsy trembled with anger. She pointed to Tyler. "You see that bruise on his cheek? That didn't happen when he was attacked. It happened before. Tell them, Jack!"

"I did that." Jack's quiet confession said as much about his feelings as Betsy's shouting said about hers. "I hit my son. After the stew festival, we fought over, well, you know what we fought about. We came to blows. I knocked him down."

Betsy turned her back again, and her shoulders shook as she sobbed quietly.

"It wasn't me on Woody's Mountain," said Jack, "but it might have been me that drove him there."

No words of comfort came to mind, no matter how hard I tried to conjure them. Daddy couldn't think of anything to say, either, so he did the only thing he could. He wrapped his arms around his lodge brother and hugged him for a long time. I followed his lead and did the same for Betsy. What else could we do?

After Momma returned with the meal, we left the Skaggs family. I felt a little lost as we emerged from the hospital. Trying to investigate in an orderly, professional way wasn't getting us very far. Nothing about this case was straightfor-ward. Information was hard to come by, and the clues we had turned up were plain confusing. Were we stuck in a criminal

Twilight Zone? A dimension outside of space and time where in was out and up was down? The one constant was the attacks on Tyler. The woodbooger's appearance at the dance didn't count because that was my brother. All we had were two "woodbooger" attacks.

Then a van jacked up on monster truck wheels and emblazoned with The Bigfoot Brigade logo sped past with lights flashing and sirens wailing.

Had two become three?

By the time we got in the truck and pulled out, the van was long gone. We resorted to rolling down the windows and following the sirens in the distance. The wail led us into town where the good people of Luthersburg were out on the sidewalks in force. Hiram Graham waved us down, and Daddy screeched to a stop.

"Hi, what happened?" demanded my father.

"The woodbooger, that's what! He was spotted at the corner of Main and Poplar. Then he ran up Poplar in the direction of the lodge."

"Quick! Get in!"

Hi made to climb into the bed of the pickup, but Mike hopped out and offered his seat before the sexagenarian could hurt himself. Mike sprang into the bed and tapped the back window, and Daddy was off.

As we hurtled towards the lodge, I couldn't help but wonder where my brother was. He had stayed at home, claiming he had to work, a legitimate sounding excuse as it was a Thursday. I resisted the urge to call him. What would I say?

Hey, there's a woodbooger impersonator on the loose. Just wanted to make sure it wasn't you.

Nope. I just had to take Jeremy at his word.

When we arrived at the COW lodge, chaos reigned. The parking lot was filled with paramilitary vehicles decked out with logos for The Bigfoot Brigade, Search for Sasquatch, and

Cryptid Corps, at least two news vans, and the assorted vehicles of the members of the Concatenated Order. More members were arriving, and the parking lot was just a big jumble. Lester Tidwell and Dud Scott were blocking the gate to the nature preserve, the Supreme Squatch nose to nose with Larry from The Bigfoot Brigade.

"You can't keep us out!" shouted the bigfoot hunter.

"This is private property!" shouted Dud. "You can't set one foot on this nature preserve without being arrested."

"The world has a right to know! The signs are there, right where Tyler Skaggs was attacked. The world has a right to see the proof of bigfoot's existence." He brandished a pair of wire cutters in Dud's face, and I thought Dud might deck him. "You can't patrol the entire perimeter of the fence, old man."

I heard the cocking of a firearm, and I turned to see Sheriff Bagby with a shotgun aimed at Larry. "Like the man said, this is private property. If you don't clear out, I'll have no choice but to arrest you."

Larry laughed, tossed the wire cutters, and caught them neatly with one hand. "I'm sure there are other ways onto this property. Let's go, everybody." He waved at all the bigfoot hunters to follow. "Mount up!" With a spray of gravel and a cloud of dust, the wackos departed, leaving behind an anxious group.

"What exactly happened?" demanded Daddy.

"I saw the whole thing!" Lester stepped forward. "I was on Main Street when the woodbooger just appeared in broad daylight, right at the corner of Main and Poplar. Then he took off running, and I ran after him. He was faster than me, but I saw him run right through this gate and up the trail."

Dud and Daddy just looked at each other for a long minute. Then Daddy spoke.

"Lester, do you think it was really a woodbooger or someone dressed up like one."

Lester got real still, and I could see the wheels turning in his mind as he accessed his memory of the event.

"Well now, I'm sure it was someone in a costume because, I mean, there's no such thing as a woodbooger." Then he laughed the fakest laugh I ever heard. I looked at Mike, and he shook his head faintly. He wasn't believing it either. Lester Tidwell was lying. If he believed he had seen the woodbooger, why wouldn't he just say so?

"We need to give chase," said Sheriff Bagby. "Dud, I assume I have your permission to pursue the suspect into the nature preserve." He reached for his radio, presumably to call for backup.

"You do not," pronounced the Supreme Squatch. "Not without a warrant."

"Dagnabbit, Dud! We have a chance to apprehend the son-of-a-biscuit who tried to do in Tyler Skaggs twice! Tyler Skaggs, the son of Loyal Knight Jack Skaggs! Doesn't that matter to you?"

"Sheriff," interjected Mike, "why would Tyler's assailant show himself in a woo—bigfoot costume in the middle of the day? What would he have to gain by making himself a target? Most likely this was just a prank to play on the woo—bigfoot hysteria going on in this town."

"Well, if it isn't the little ol' Yankee-splainer!"

"Actually, his people come from Kentucky," piped up a voice from the crowd.

"I don't care if his people come from Hahira, Georgia, Nashville, Tennessee, or Mobile, Alabama. This Yankee-splainer needs to keep out of police business! The assailant is trying to frame the woodbooger, a mythological beast. Mythological as in it doesn't exist! Of course, he's going to pop up now and again to make people believe in the woodbooger."

Now, I had to admit, that was possible. But I also had to admit that I believed in the woodbooger and that he was a peaceful creature being framed by a psychopath. What if the Sheriff pursued the fake woodbooger and apprehended or, worse, killed the real woodbooger by mistake? How tragic that would be! Luckily, Dud held firm.

"Unless you have a warrant, Sheriff, you may not set foot upon our property."

"Then consider this my resignation from the Concatenated Order!" Sheriff Bagby did an about-face and marched toward his Ford Explorer. "And I'll be back with a warrant!"

As soon as he left, the members of the Order started buzzing. Dud and Daddy got to work assigning guard duty to all the Squires and Pages. They would spend the night on the mountain to keep out trespassers.

Momma and the Ladies Auxiliary produced food from I don't know where to sustain the men. Tents and sleeping bags appeared. Before you could say woodbooger, the men of the Concatenated Order were headed up Woody's Mountain.

"This is dangerous!" insisted Mike to anyone who would listen. "Someone is going to get shot. Wouldn't it be easier to just let the bigfoot hunters have a look around? What are they going to find? A sapling arch. That's it! They're not going to find the woodbooger because there's no such thing!" I knew Mike was worked up because he said the W-word.

"Take a breath, son," said Daddy as he laid a soothing hand on Mike's shoulder. "There's no need to worry. These men know this mountain. The outsiders don't."

"But there could be violence."

"There won't be. The men of the Order aren't armed. Remember, this is a wildlife sanctuary. No hunting. We just want to protect the critters living on that mountain."

Mike took a deep breath and raked his hand through his hair, a gesture he always made when he was calming down and pulling himself together.

"Do you need my help?"

"Or mine?" I added.

"I think we have it under control. The first shift is headed up the mountain, and they'll be relieved at dusk by the second shift. The Loyal Knights of the Order will have an emergency meeting tonight. Mike, I would appreciate it if you would attend."

"My pleasure."

"What about me—" I started to say when Momma cut me off.

"We've got the word out now, Cal. There will be more food arriving for the second shift just before sundown." Then Momma gave me *the look*, the look that said "Shut your mouth or there will be dire consequences." You can't mistake *the look*.

Then a movement caught my eye. Past the gate, I could see someone coming down the trail.

"Look!"

It was Jeannie Shoecraft. She was wearing khakis, a twin set, pearls, and sneakers, and she carried a basket that, from the way she swung it haphazardly, appeared to be empty.

"What's all the fuss?" she asked.

Everyone spoke at once, demanding what she'd seen on the trail.

"Why, I didn't see anything. I went up the mountain to pick ramps, but I didn't find any. I guess it's too late in the season."

Momma quickly filled her in on the latest woodbooger shenanigans, which shocked her to the point she started to swoon. I took the basket from her, and Mike helped her sit down.

"And to think that criminal might have run right past me when I wasn't looking."

While Momma patted her hand, I glanced in the basket. Sure enough, there were no ramps, but there were a few red grapes on a stem. I held them up.

"Mrs. Shoecraft, maybe you should finish your snack?"

She laughed a little hysterically and took the fruit from me.

After a few minutes and a few grapes, Jeannie felt better and headed to her car. As I watched her drive off, I wondered why she, too, was lying. Just a few days before, I had seen oodles of ramps, that garlicky wild onion so beloved by Appalachian cooks, all along the trail. Why had she been on the mountain that day, and what was the basket really for?

CHAPTER 16

The drive home was quiet. I was both pondering the lies of Jeannie Shoecraft and the look my mother had given me. What everyone else was thinking, I could only guess. As we pulled into the driveway, Momma finally spoke up.

"I had a word with Gladdy Tidwell. Tyler Skaggs was first attacked around six in the morning."

"Now how does Gladdy know that?" asked Daddy.

"The sheriff's wife was in the tearoom with her closest friends, and she spilled the tea, so to speak."

"Well, that's useful," said Mike.

We climbed out of the truck and went into the house. I immediately headed to the war room to add Jack Skaggs to the suspect list, and maybe Jeannie Shoecraft, although I really couldn't see it. What I found in the attic turned my blood to ice.

The chalkboard had been turned around to display my brother's name. Next to it, Jeremy had scrawled some language I won't repeat, clearly directed at me. I sank into one of the folding chairs with a groan. Just when I thought I couldn't make my relationship with my brother any worse, how had he known to look behind the chalkboard? Was I that predictable? Worse, had my thoughtlessness spurred Jeremy to a desperate action?

My thoughts were interrupted by a bellow from my father. I ran down the stairs to find everyone heading back outside.

"Tyler's waking up!" Momma said.

We were on the move again.

Sheriff Bagby was in Tyler's room when we got there. He growled as we entered, but Betsy threw herself into my mother's arms, so he couldn't very well order us to leave.

Tyler's eyes were open, but he still looked fuzzy around the edges, as if his consciousness were both here and wherever the coma had taken him.

"Now, son, you just take your time, and tell me what you can remember," instructed the Sheriff gently.

I reached for Mike's hand. The suspense was killing me. Was Tyler about to unmask his attacker?

Um…no.

"I'm sorry, Sheriff. I don't remember a thing. You said I was attacked on Woody's mountain? I don't even remember going there." Tyler started to tear up in frustration.

"There, there," said the doctor while frowning at the Sheriff. "It's quite all right, Tyler. In cases such as these, it's quite normal to have memory loss. Your memories should return with time," he looked meaningfully at the Sheriff, "and rest."

"Don't you worry, son," said Jack. "You're going to be just fine." Then he broke down. "I'm so sorry we fought."

That seemed to be our cue to leave and let the healing begin between father and son, so everyone except the Skaggs family slipped into the hallway. That's when Hi Graham, mayor of Luthersburg, came running down the hall.

"Sheriff! I need to confess!"

What the heck?

"I did not see this coming," I whispered to Mike.

"Me, neither."

Hi came to a stop and bent over at the waist, panting. He raised one finger as if to say "Give me a minute?" A minute later, he repeated the gesture, but Sheriff Bagby had no time for it.

"What is this all about, Hiram? I haven't got all day."

Hi took a huge breath and attempted to say his piece.

"I was there (*pant*) on Woody's mountain (*pant*) with Tyler (*pant*) the morning he (*pant*) was attacked."

"And you're just now telling me?" the Sheriff roared. Somewhere, a nurse shushed him.

"I didn't attack him (*pant*) I just wanted to talk (*pant*) to convince him not (*pant*) to defect. I asked him to meet me there." Hi's breathing was settling. "But he was determined to go through with it."

"So, you picked up a rock and beamed him when he turned his back!" The sheriff smiled bitterly.

"I didn't! I swear." Hi looked around at all of us, his eyes pleading for understanding. "I swear I never touched him!"

"So why come clean now?"

"Because I wanted you to hear it from me, not Tyler."

"Hiram Graham, you are under arrest for the attempted murder of Tyler Skaggs." Sheriff Bagby brandished the cuffs.

"But I didn't do it! Ask Tyler! I left!"

Daddy patted Hi's arm. "Tyler doesn't remember anything…yet."

"Doesn't that just beat all? I should've kept my mouth shut! Shitake mushrooms!"

"Sheriff, can't you wait until Tyler remembers before you make any arrests?" pleaded Daddy. "After all, Hi is the mayor of Luthersburg."

"And give him a chance to get the heck out of Dodge? No, sirree! Seems to me the members of the Concatenated Order are good at slipping away and staying hidden." He was referring to when a large portion of the town helped my father fake his death. He had stayed hidden for years. Hi had been a loyal friend, and now it was coming back to bite him in the butt.

"As I recall, you were a great help," replied Daddy evenly.

Sheriff Bagby glared at him for a moment before he spoke. "More's the pity. You have the right to remain silent…"

Momma drove home from the hospital because Daddy was so mad he couldn't see straight. Every so often, phrases sprang from his mouth like "doesn't have the sense God gave a mule" and "traitors at every turn." In the back seat, Mike and I kept up a running conversation with our eyes and facial expressions. It went something like this:

"Is your dad going to be okay?"

"Momma will set him straight."

"Do you think Hi did it?"

"No way. He's a lamb."

"But if he thought his mayoral career was over?"

"Even if, I still can't believe it."

My mother made a pit stop at Cahill's barbecue to pick up something for dinner. She made Daddy go inside with her. When they returned with bags oozing the delicious scent of fried chicken, Daddy seemed a bit more with it.

"Don't forget," he said to Mike as he buckled his seatbelt, "we have the Concatenated Order tonight. We'll head out after supper."

Before I could even take a breath to protest that I wanted to go too, I felt Momma's eyes in the rear-view mirror. I held my tongue. Momma generally had a reason for the things she did. I hoped she had a good one for allowing blatant sexism and usurpation of a daughter's place in her father's heart!

Chill, Jill. He's bonding with Mike. That's a good thing.

Oh, whatever.

Momma's controlling gaze stayed on me all through

dinner, which was more than a little unnerving. I forced my attention on fried chicken, mashed potatoes and gravy, coleslaw, and yeast rolls, which wasn't a hardship. The Cookseys are stress eaters, so no one was picking at their food.

When Daddy rose from the table and started collecting plates, Momma stopped him.

"Jill and I will take care of the dishes. You go on and get ready for your meeting."

"I have time to help—"

"You go on now. Mike, you go too. Cal, don't you need to find him a fez?"

"That's right! Come with me, son."

Mike gave me a helpless look and followed my father out of the kitchen. I turned to my mother and planted my hands on my hips.

"What gives?"

"There's no time for explanations. Grab some plates! We've got to get these dishes done. As soon as they've cleared the driveway, we're out of here." She started scraping and stacking, so I followed suit.

A few minutes later, Daddy appeared in the kitchen wearing his red fez.

"Come in here son and show off to the ladies!"

Mike came shuffling into the kitchen sporting a fez of his own and looking so, so uncomfortable.

"You've never looked hotter," I deadpanned.

Mike gave me a look that spelled out in no uncertain terms that he was doing this for love and that I owed him.

"We're off!" cried Daddy. "I don't know how late we'll be."

"I'm taking Jilly to the Ladies Auxiliary, so you might beat us home if the canasta gets too heated."

They were about to exit when Jeremy came through the door.

"What's this?" He looked from Daddy to Mike and back again. "Do I get a fez too?"

"We're on official lodge business," said Daddy. "Hi Graham has been arrested."

"So I heard. Are you hatching a plot to break him out of the hoosegow?" Did I detect a note of hurt under Jeremy's sarcasm?

"Of course not!"

"Just as well," yawned Jeremy. "I have a date with Lacey Shoecraft."

"Well, we're off then." Daddy hustled out the door with a captive Mike.

"Have you eaten?" asked Momma. "There's chicken from Cahill's."

"I'm taking Lacey to dinner." He snagged a leftover roll and sauntered out of the kitchen, but his walk was too nonchalant to be natural.

"His feelings are hurt," I said to Momma, once I heard Jeremy on the stairs.

"Yes, they are." She didn't meet my gaze, just continued drying the last of the dishes.

"Maybe Daddy should have included him."

"Your father has his reasons. Now scoot!" She snapped a dish towel at me, and I jumped. "Grab your purse!"

With said purse in hand, I stepped out the back door, and darkness descended on me.

CHAPTER 17

I was in a car, my mother's car, to be exact, with a hood over my head. My own mother and a couple of her friends had kidnapped me. I was highly annoyed.

"I just want you to know that I know exactly where we are," I complained. "Really? Is all this necessary?'

No response.

"Gladdy Tidwell, I know you're sitting next to me. I can smell the Shalimar on you. Everyone knows that's your signature scent. And Helen Graham, your charm bracelet has been jingling on your wrist since you slammed the hood on my head. I heard that charm bracelet in church every Sunday for eighteen years. It's like an old friend. Honestly, this is a farce!"

My mother sighed in exasperation, a sound I knew all too well. It made me smile. I was getting to her, so I prattled on.

"Gladdy, you should update your fragrance. Give Fall Fantasy a try. It's a bit more youthful. Now let me see if I can name all the charms on your bracelet, Helen…"

A short time later, the car came to a stop.

"Just as I expected. We're at the Scott house."

"Oh, for the love of Peter, Andrew, James, and John, will you SHUT UP?"

I giggled.

Jingling Helen took my arm rather fiercely and pulled me from the car. I attributed her violence to the fact her husband had been arrested, but it could have been my snarkiness. Then she and Gladdy marched me around the house to the backyard.

"Let me guess. We're headed for Shirley's she-shed. How exciting!"

"I'm going to strangle her," muttered Gladdy.

"Get. In. Line." Momma was mad as a yellowjacket run over by a lawn mower. I could feel her vibrating several feet away.

We stopped, and I heard a door open. I was ushered unceremoniously through, marched about six more feet, and deposited in a velvet-covered chair, again with more force than was necessary. When they finally took the hood off my head, I was going to crow with laughter.

"Jillian Elizabeth Cooksey," intoned Shirley Scott in stentorian tones, and the laughter stuck in my throat. This was a different Shirley. "You have been selected. Do you accept?"

"Do what?"

"You have been selected. Do you accept?"

This had to be about the Ladies Auxiliary of the COW unless Momma had joined a coven, which I highly doubted.

"Uh, sure."

"You must take the blood oath. Repeat after me. I, Jillian Elizabeth Cooksey, do solemnly swear that I will never divulge what I see and hear within these four walls."

I repeated the oath. Then someone took my hand and pricked my finger.

"Ow!" My finger was rubbed against something, possibly paper.

"Hey, if I've just given my soul to the devil, I'm gonna be pi—"

"Jillian!"

"Angry! I'm gonna be angry!"

"Remember your oath," cautioned Shirley, and then the hood was yanked away.

It took a moment for my eyes to adjust to the light, and when they did, my jaw dropped.

Seated in semicircular rows before me were all my mother's closest friends, the wives of the Loyal Knights of the Concatenated Order, but like I'd never seen them before. Each lady was robed in deep red and wore a red hat as well. Every woman's hat was unique, and all styles, from fascinators to fedoras, were represented except for one—the fez. I smiled inwardly, appreciating the joke, but the women before me weren't in a joking mood.

"Welcome to the Red Chamber," pronounced my mother formally.

The Red Chamber?

I looked around the interior of Shirley Scott's she-shed, a domain that had always been off-limits to kids and husbands. Now I knew why. From floor to ceiling, the entire space was red. The ladies sat on parson's chairs slipcovered in red velvet. The walls were draped with red brocade, completely obscuring the windows. Even the ceiling was upholstered in red brocade. As my eyes adjusted to the overabundance of crimson, gold accents began to emerge from the background in the form of fringe on the drapes and chairs and a series of Egyptian statues arranged down the sides of the room, most featuring a lioness wearing a pharaonic headdress. Sekhmet! (My trips to the Metropolitan Museum were paying off.) What I had always assumed to be a sewing room or potting shed was actually some sort of temple...or bordello. Both Cleopatra and Belle Watling would have felt quite at home in Shirley's she-shed.

Having taken in my surroundings, my eyes returned to the flower of Luthersburg womanhood before me.

"Are those the old choir robes from First Baptist?"

The women groaned.

"Daughter, you know how to ruin a moment."

"We are trusting you to keep the secrets of the Red Chamber and to treat this honor with the respect it deserves," intoned Shirley.

I decided to put my smart aleck away. "I will treat the order with the respect it deserves," I replied sincerely, and Shirley nodded solemnly.

"Wives of the Loyal Knights of the Order have been inducted into the Red Chamber for decades. Your significant other is being knighted this very evening, and even though you aren't married to him, you are the daughter of the Right Honorable Yeti, and you should be privy to the same secrets. Plus, your Momma thinks a wedding is imminent."

I gulped.

"It's nearly time," interrupted Gladdy Tidwell.

"Time for what?" No one paid me any attention. I heard a mechanical sound and turned to see a curtain opening at one end of the shed to reveal a large television.

"Jill, move your chair," urged Momma. I got up and moved my chair next to hers. Now I was facing the screen too. The lights dimmed as a picture came up on the screen, revealing a room very similar to the one I was sitting in, except it was draped in blue velvet. The shot was from up high, probably a fish eye lens in a corner of the room because I could see almost the whole thing.

"What am I looking at?" I whispered to Momma, but all I got in return was a "*Shh.*"

Then a curtain parted, revealing a doorway, and a line of men led by Dud Scott processed into the room. They were robed in blue velvet and sported their crimson fezzes. Dud carried a ceremonial sword, and my father carried a large bowl of fruit.

A bowl of fruit?

"Is that the Concatenated Order?" My demand was met with a collective "*Shh!*"

So much shushing. Jeez.

The procession came to an end with Mike bringing up the rear. He, too, was sporting the blue robe but no fez.

"Step forward, brother Michael, and kneel," commanded Dud. Mike complied and knelt before the Supreme Squatch. "Insomuch as you have taken the blood oath and sworn never to reveal the secrets of the Concatenated Order of the Woodbooger, even though you are a reporter, I hereby knight thee, Sir Skunk Ape, and grant you all the rights and honors accorded to a Loyal Knight." Dud tapped Mike on both shoulders with the sword, and Lester Tidwell stepped forward to set Mike's fez upon his head. "Arise, Sir Skunk Ape, and take your place among the brotherhood."

Sir Skunk Ape! Mike was going to hear about this later. I was surprised he wasn't blushing with embarrassment.

A thought occurred to me.

"Momma," I whispered. "Do they know we're watching?"

My mother looked me in the eye and slowly shook her head. Then she smiled a wicked little smile that had me wondering if all Jeremy's mischievous ways truly came from my father's side.

"You mean you bugged the Concatenated Order?" I must have nearly shouted it because the shushing was long and loud. "Does Daddy know?" I hissed in Momma's ear.

"Of course not!" she hissed back. "And you're not going to tell him. You took the oath!"

Oh, my stars! My family was turning out to be much more complicated than I had ever expected. I almost longed for the days when I thought my father had died of a heart attack and my brother was just a scoundrel. Now there were more secrets and lies than you could shake a stick at.

I turned my focus back to the feed. Mike was being congratulated by all the other Loyal Knights.

"We have a few minutes," announced Gladdy Tidwell. "Time for cake!"

"A few minutes until what?" I asked.

"Just hush and eat some cake," replied Momma.

A Texas sheet cake was produced from somewhere, and soon a plate was thrust at me with a huge slice. I noticed everyone else's slices were smaller. They were probably trying to keep me quiet. Soon the ladies of the Red Chamber were tucking in. I had soooooo many questions, but I had a feeling I would get no answers until the drama played out and I could corner Momma at home.

On the screen, the men were toasting their new inductee with what appeared to be moonshine, since it came out of a mason jar. I was glad to be eating cake instead.

I finished my slice, and another one came out of nowhere. The ladies really wanted to keep me quiet.

The joke's on them. More cake for me!

Halfway through my second piece, the men on the screen finished their moonshine and began forming up into rows. I watched as Daddy guided Mike to a spot in the second row of three.

"It's starting! It's starting!" cried one of the ladies, and everyone got very still.

On the screen, another curtain parted to reveal a door. My father opened it with a flourish and then took his place in the front row. Dud Scott stepped forward and produced something that looked like a large kazoo. He stood in the doorway, raised the item to his lips, and blew. A bellowing sound filled the air, strange and yet somehow familiar. He finished, waited a moment, and then repeated the performance. Then he stepped back into place in the front row, and everyone, Loyal Knights and their good ladies alike, waited with bated breath. I had no idea what I was waiting for, but the anticipation still had me perched on the edge of my seat.

Five minutes passed, ten, fifteen. The men on the screen began to squirm. and the ladies around me began to shift.

At twenty minutes, the men began to look questioningly at each other, and Jeannie Shoecraft began collecting plates and forks from the Red Chamber. A few minutes later, Dud turned to face his knights.

"Well, I guess he isn't coming tonight." The tight formation of knights began to dissolve, the men murmuring in what sounded like concern to me.

"Who isn't coming?" I asked the ladies around me, no longer attempting to whisper. "Who?"

Momma placed a hand on each of my shoulders as if to brace me.

"The woodbooger," she said.

A well of joy and laughter sprang up from somewhere in my gut, and a grin erupted on my face.

"I knew it! I just knew it!"

I had so many questions, and I wasn't leaving Shirley Scott's she-shed without some answers.

The meeting of the Loyal Knights broke up quickly after the Woodbooger was a no-show. The men quietly filed out, and the lights were extinguished. Shirley Scott turned off the feed at that point, and some of the ladies seemed like they too were going to bolt.

I was just about to order everyone to stay until I had my answers when Momma touched my arm.

"Be patient."

Soon the only members of the Red Chamber left in the she-shed were Momma, Shirley, Gladdy, and Helen. Oh, and me. I was now a member, whether I wanted to be or not. I looked at my mother and her closest friends and realized I was looking at her very own Posse.

The apple doesn't fall far, does it?

"Sit down, Jill," ordered my mother, and Gladdy thrust a third piece of cake at me.

"Now, wait just a second. I can be quiet without having cake shoved in my mouth!"

"Sorry," said Gladdy, and she moved to take the plate from me. I clutched it tightly.

"My cake!"

With eye rolls all around (was I that exasperating?), the ladies sat down to face me.

"Loretta," said Shirley, "it's your story to tell."

"Thank you, Shirley," said Momma, and she began.

The story of the Concatenated Order of the Woodbooger

"Back in the 1930s, Luthersburg was in the grip of the depression. One of the best ways to make money in these mountains that didn't involve criminal activity was to gather ginseng for shipment to Asia. Many folks hunted ginseng and delivered it to buyers in Richmond or Baltimore. It was on one of these ginseng hunts that your great-grandfather, Josephus Braswell Zaricor, ran into a spot of trouble. He was up on what you know as Woody's mountain but at that time was called Zaricor's Ridge, and it was a windy day. Now most folks know to stay out of the woods when there's a big wind, but Sephus had a deadline to meet. He had a ginseng buyer lined up and was scheduled to meet him in three days, so he had to be on the mountain.

"Then tragedy struck. He was digging ginseng when the wind forced a dead branch from a big tulip poplar, and it fell on him, breaking his leg. He had a compound fracture and was in agony. He just had to hope that his people would come looking for him before he bled to death or got gangrene. He also knew he was going to miss the buyer, but that was the least of his troubles.

"At some point, he passed out, and when he came to, it was dark. Even though it was summertime, he was bitterly cold. He felt his end was near.

"Then the woodbooger appeared. At first, Granddaddy thought he was hallucinating. He'd heard tales of the woodbooger all his life and never took them seriously. But when the woodbooger gently lifted him from the ground and began to descend the mountain, he knew it was real.

"The woodbooger, Woody as Granddaddy came to call him, carried him to the family cabin and gently laid him on the porch. Then he made a great bellowing sound to get the family's attention and ran off into the woods. When my grandmother peeked out the door, shotgun at the ready, she found her husband on the porch. The doctor was called, and the leg was set and saved.

"Josephus Zaricor never forgot what the woodbooger had done for him. He was the sole provider for his family, and if he had died on the mountain, heaven knows what would have become of them. Granddaddy wanted to thank his rescuer, so he got the idea of fashioning a duck call that would mimic the bellowing sound of the woodbooger. It took him a while, but he finally perfected it, and when he called, the woodbooger came.

"Eventually, Granddaddy shared his secret with his nearest and dearest, those he could trust with the secret. He and his closest friends started the Concatenated Order of The Woodbooger, and he eventually donated Zaricor's Ridge to the order to keep it as a nature preserve. That's how he repaid the woodbooger for saving his life—by protecting him and his offspring for as long as he could."

"But you and Daddy denied the woodbooger existed!"

"For his protection! And your Daddy doesn't know that I

know, although he should have figured it out by now since Josephus Zaricor was my grandfather."

"And that ceremony tonight? It was meant to call the woodbooger, right?"

"It was, but he didn't come. For the first time in living memory, he didn't come."

"So, you've seen it happen." I was breathless with excitement.

Momma smiled. "Many times."

"Oh, my stars!"

"They always call the woodbooger when they induct a new Knight. They reveal the secret, and the only way to get most people to believe it is to show them a real woodbooger."

"What would have happened if he had shown?"

"They would have welcomed him in and shared fruit with him. The woodbooger is a vegetarian, kind of like a gorilla, except even gentler."

My head was spinning, and I had about a thousand more questions.

"Why didn't he come tonight?"

Momma looked to her friends for answers, but they all shrugged their shoulders.

"I don't know."

"Is it because he's afraid? Because he knows people are hunting him?"

"Could be."

So many thoughts crowded my mind, making it difficult for me to focus, but beneath all of them was a feeling of utter joy in my heart. I was happy to be right in believing in the woodbooger, but I was even happier that the world still held surprises.

When we got home, we found Daddy and Mike subdued. Even though I had seen the secret ceremony, I hadn't seen any interactions between my father and my boyfriend, but I could smell the tension.

They were both seated in the living room. Daddy was doing a Sudoku, his go-to in times of stress, while Mike was on his laptop with his earbuds in. I touched Mike's shoulder, and he looked up at me without smiling, but he did take out his earbuds.

"Did you have a good meeting?" I hoped I sounded normal and not like I'd been spying on them. *Gahhh!* How did my mother do this every time the COW had a meeting?

"It was very interesting," said Mike neutrally, too neutrally, because my father broke his pencil lead on his sudoku book. Before I could probe further or work to resolve the tension (I hadn't decided on a course of action yet), Momma's phone rang.

"What? Where?" Her tone had both men jumping to their feet. "We'll be right there." She hung up. "The woodbooger's been spotted on Main Street again. He just robbed the gas station!"

When we got to the Philips 66 on Main, the only store open at that hour, we found the Sheriff taking a statement from the station attendant while his deputy leaned against a squad car.

"I promise, Sheriff, that's all he took. An armful of orange creamsicles out of the freezer case."

My heart plummeted. I knew someone who loved orange creamsicles.

Just then, more sirens began wailing in the distance but getting closer every second. A moment later, several vans and trucks screeched to a halt in the gas station parking lot. The bigfoot hunters and the press had arrived. They descended on the sheriff, peppering him with questions.

"Quiet!" he roared. Then he stepped up on the island, right between the gas pumps, to give himself a little bit of height. "I said quiet! Tonight, the infamous woodbooger attempted to rob this gas station, but the attempt was foiled thanks to the quick thinking of the station attendant and the presence of a guard dog. The attendant, Mr. Craig Kennedy, ordered his German shepherd to attack the woodbooger after he attempted to make off with a dozen ice cream bars."

"Is that a joke?" asked a voice from the crowd.

"No, it is not," said the Sheriff with a clenched jaw. "It is now my pleasure to reveal to you the woodbooger you have all been searching for."

The crowd of onlookers held their breath.

"Deputy!" The sheriff nodded to the younger man who opened the car door and hauled out a man in a gorilla suit.

Sugar honey iced tea!

"Ladies and gentlemen," said the deputy with unexpected panache, "I give you the woodbooger." He yanked the head off the gorilla to reveal my brother, Jeremy Cooksey, who smirked at the crowd.

"What can I say? I love a good creamsicle."

The crowd went wild.

"Dude, you're a legend!" shouted Kenny Beveridge from atop the police cruiser. (How'd he get up there?) Then he shook a can of beer and popped the tab, letting it rain down on everyone like champagne.

That's when all hell broke loose.

IT WAS the wee hours of the morning when we finally arrived home. Jeremy had only avoided arrest because the cashier finally noticed the money he'd left on the counter when he took the creamsicles. (I suppose that when confronted with the bigfoot making a late-night ice cream run, you tend to overlook small details like that.) Jeremy's tacky gorilla suit and lack of motive for attacking Tyler also helped. Still, my brother wasn't completely in the clear.

"I'll be watching you, boy," declared Sheriff Bagby. Jeremy was now a person of interest in the case, and not just to me.

Law enforcement and, worse, our parents, now had deep suspicions. If things were tense in the family before Jeremy's escapade, they were now bordering on a meltdown.

"In the dining room. Now!" ordered my father. I dutifully headed in that direction, but Jeremy refused.

"I'll skip the recriminations if it's all the same to you," he drawled laconically. "I'm a bit tired."

"You will join this family meeting," demanded my father.

"I won't."

"Then you will leave this house."

My hands and feet suddenly felt like ice. I'd never heard my father sound so angry, so cold, and I'd never heard my brother sound so insolent.

"I'll pack my things," he said and headed up the stairs.

What was happening? I knew Jeremy was angry I had put him on the suspect board, and I knew he was hurt when Daddy took Mike to the COW meeting. Was this his way of striking back?

Without warning, the day caught up with me and threatened to overwhelm me. My family was falling apart, and I was now subject to a blood oath that prevented me from discussing the one thing I needed to talk about to clear the air. I couldn't even inquire about Mike's thoughts and feelings because I wasn't allowed to reveal that I knew about his experiences. I was well and truly trapped in a web of my mother's making.

My mother.

"Pardon us," I said to the room as I grabbed her arm and pulled her into the kitchen.

"We have to tell Daddy and Mike that we know."

"Already? You're caving already?" Momma laughed disgustedly.

"This secrecy is about to break our family apart."

"Don't be melodramatic."

I didn't bother to contradict her.

"Fine," I said. "How do you see this situation playing out?"

"Your brother will stay with a friend until he cools off. Your father will rant and rave until he falls asleep. You and Mike will go to your rooms, and everything will look better in the morning."

"Will it? I'm not so sure. Tomorrow, Jeremy is still going to be under suspicion for attacking Tyler Skaggs. Mike is still going to be wondering if his potential future father-in-law and friends are trying to deceive him, and I still won't be able to do anything to save my relationship because of a blood oath. Tomorrow is looking pretty awful from where I'm sitting."

"It's unfortunate the woodbooger didn't appear," admitted my mother. "It certainly threw a wrench in things; however, we've been keeping the secret of the woodbooger for almost a hundred years. We're not giving up now."

"You could at least talk to Daddy. You could admit your knowledge to him and still keep the secret. Tell him it was passed down in your family. You don't have to reveal the Red Chamber."

Momma's eyes shifted from side to side, a sure sign she was conflicted. I pressed on.

"You can tell him you passed the story to me, which isn't a lie. If you reveal your knowledge of the woodbooger, Mike may not feel like he's being tricked, and we can all talk about what this means for the case...and for Jeremy."

Momma didn't answer.

"Just think about it, okay?"

I went to the dining room but found it empty. Mike and Daddy were nowhere to be found. Upstairs, the master bedroom door and Mike's door were both closed, but I could see light at the bottom of both. I knocked lightly on Mike's door. He opened it part way, which I took as ominous.

"Hey, how are you?" I searched his face for clues about his feelings, but his guard was up.

"I'm fine."

"Do you want to talk?"

"No. I...I just need to be alone for a while."

Crap.

"Okay." I tried to smile at him, but I think I grimaced instead. "I'll see you in the morning."

The door was shut before I'd even turned away.

Is it any wonder I called my Posse?

"SECRETS CAUSING TROUBLE? THAT NEVER HAPPENS." Surya laughed bitterly. "I just wish you could tell us what the secret is."

I was on a video call with my Posse, and it felt so good to be with my friends, even virtually.

"But we totally understand that you can't break a confidence," said Kate authoritatively. "Don't we ladies?"

"Yeah, yeah," moaned Surya, while Anupa and Liz nodded in agreement.

"Ten years ago, I wouldn't have said we were a family of secrets and intrigue. Now, I'm beginning to think we're the Borgias. My whole perspective has shifted. I feel off balance."

"Hardly the Borgias," said Liz. "No one has been poisoned."

"But the list does include gambling, faking a death, and keeping a secret that, as you put it, would blow the collective mind of the entire world," countered Anupa. "Pretty heavy stuff."

"I think it's time to grow up," said Kate. "When we come to understand that our parents are people just like us, complicated and messy, then we've truly matured."

"I don't want to grow up!" I whined. "I want family game night!"

Everyone laughed, but I wasn't entirely joking.

"I think you need to prioritize your relationship," said Liz. "If Mike is your future spouse, then he needs to come first."

"After what he witnessed, he may be rethinking our future."

"Jeez Louise, I wish you would spill the details!" cried Surya, the least patient of my friends. "It all sounds so dire. You're killing me, Smalls."

"I'm sorry! I wish I could."

"What if we guessed it?" Surya began bouncing up and down on her couch. "If we guessed it, could you tell us then?"

"Not even then. Blood oath."

"She wouldn't have to tell us," laughed Anupa. "Her face gives her away every time."

Curse my truthful face!

"Ooh, let me try!" cried Surya. "Let's see. Your father's lodge is hiding the Holy Grail."

"I'm going to turn off my camera if you don't stop."

"Nah, that's not it," said Anupa. "How about Elvis is alive and living in Luthersburg with Marilyn Monroe?"

Kate snorted with laughter. "Those are so cliché! I've got a better one."

"Camera is about to be turned off. I'm warning you." Kate didn't listen.

"There's a stone circle near Luthersburg, and your entire family are time travelers who came through the stones."

"Talk about cliché!" cried Surya. "You said yours was better!"

"Turning off the camera now." I clicked the camera icon just as Liz began to speak.

"How about bigfoot is real and your whole family is part of a conspiracy to hide the truth from the world?"

Gulp.

"Hey, that's not half bad," said Surya. "What with the wood-booger stories in the news, that could be it!"

"Jill, turn on your camera so we can check if it's true," demanded Kate.

"Haha! Jill's face, the lie detector test. I told you I was turning my camera off, and I meant it." I hoped my bratty tone of voice hid the terror that gripped me that I was about to reveal the secret.

"She hasn't denied it," put in Anupa.

"I categorically deny it," I said, all the while praying the Lord would forgive me for lying. *It's for the greater good, Lord.*

"Okay, okay." Kate attempted to calm the waters. "Enough with the secret guessing. We need to respect Jill's privacy."

I switched my camera back on.

"Thank you, Kate, for being a grownup." That earned me a raspberry from Surya. "Now, how am I going to mend things with Mike?"

The girls were quiet, thinking. Had I stumped them? If they couldn't help me, I didn't know where else to turn.

Finally, Liz spoke.

"Jill, I think you might have to break your oath."

"It was a blood oath!"

"Jill," began Kate cautiously, "did you sell your soul to the devil?"

"Of course not!"

"Then I think this is an oath you can break."

Could I?

CHAPTER 19

When I came down to breakfast the next morning, the winds had shifted yet again. Daddy, Momma, and Mike were sitting at the table, and the tension was palpable. Everyone was staring at their plates while their breakfasts cooled. When Daddy saw me, he jumped up from the table.

"Jilly-bean! Good, good. Sit down, sweetheart."

Daddy pulled my chair out for me, and I sat.

"Your mother has been relating to us how she shared the story of the woodbooger with you, and how she knew it herself. I should have expected, with Josephus Zaricor being her grandpappy, that she would know." He turned to Momma. "Honestly, Loretta, I don't know why you didn't tell me forty years ago."

"Calvin, I was just trying to preserve the secrets of the Concatenated Order, same as you," she sniffed.

He laid his hand on hers. "Of course you were. You're an honorable woman."

So honorable she was spying on Daddy and his lodge brothers. At least she had the good grace to blush at the compliment.

Daddy turned to Mike.

"Son, I know it's a tough pill to swallow, but you've heard it from both of us. Won't you believe us?"

Mike looked stricken, and my heart went out to him. My beloved was a journalist who dealt in facts, not hearsay. Seeing was believing for Mike McCall. It was an occupational hazard.

"I just...It's not...Excuse me."

Mike rose from the table and walked out the back door. Naturally, I followed. I found him pacing around the firepit, muttering to himself. When he saw me, he threw up his hands in exasperation.

"It's an impossible situation!"

"It is."

"It's too much pressure!"

"I agree."

He planted his hands on his hips and narrowed his beautiful blue eyes.

"Are you trying to placate me?"

"Nope."

I sat on one of the log stools and gestured for him to do likewise.

"I really do agree with you. You're in an impossible situation. Faced with no proof whatsoever, just the word of two people you know to be honest...mostly...you're being asked to believe in something many consider a hoax. For a journalist who needs evidence, this must be so very hard."

Mike exhaled and practically collapsed on the stool next to mine. Then he dragged me into his arms and held me tight.

"Thank you for understanding," he murmured into my hair.

"Of course," I murmured into his shoulder

"Your parents must hate me."

I pulled away so I could look him in the face.

"No way. They may be frustrated that you don't believe them, but they couldn't hate you."

"I want to believe your parents. I do. They're honest people, except for the whole faking your father's death thing, but there were exigent circumstances. But bigfoot? I'm a journalist, Jill. I need proof."

I stroked his face soothingly then kissed him gently. I didn't share what I was thinking. *If it's proof you want, it's proof you're going to get.*

When we rejoined my parents, they were deep in conversation that ended when they saw us.

"Young Michael," said Daddy, "sit, sit. We feel terrible about pressuring you. Loretta has been explaining to me about…what did you call it?"

"The Code of Journalistic Ethics."

"Yes, yes. Evidently, you're the only journalist following it these days, and for this we must be grateful."

"Your code of ethics requires proof before reporting," clarified Momma. "And since you have conflated reporting with personal belief, we must respect your need for more proof before you believe us."

It sounded like an apology and acceptance but with the teensiest edge to it. Pure Momma.

Mike thanked them for their understanding, and Daddy slapped him on the back. Momma passed him the biscuits, and I breathed a sigh of relief. It wasn't peace, and it wasn't global thermonuclear war. It was détente, and it was acceptable to me. Everyone was in improved spirits as we ate our sausage and biscuits, not only because of the fragile truce but also because Momma received news from Gladdy Tidwell that some of the bigfoot hunters had left town. When Jeremy was apprehended in the gorilla suit, some of the groups took it as a sign that Luthersburg was experiencing a hoax and took off. The Bigfoot Brigade, sadly, was not among them. Jeremy had an alibi for the attack on Tyler in the hospital, so the Bigfoot Brigade lived in the hope that a real woodbooger was on the loose. Still, they didn't know where to begin looking, and the Squires and Pages of the Concatenated Order were able to end their vigil on Woody's mountain and return home...for now.

The most pressing problem, in my book anyway, was Jeremy. We needed to get him back in the fold and fast. On his best day, my brother could cause himself and others no end of trouble. This wasn't his best day. Jeremy was a wounded animal, lashing out at anything and everything. We needed to save him from himself.

"I'm going to find Jeremy," I announced and set my coffee cup down resolutely. "Who's with me?"

Daddy crossed his arms, which I took as a bad sign. "After the stunt he pulled? He needs to think about his actions!"

"I agree," said Momma.

"Look," I began, "he promised not to impersonate the wood-booger again. He only did it because his feelings were hurt. It was a cry for help."

"What do you mean *again*?" asked Mike.

Oh, snap.

Three sets of eyes bored into me like laser beams. It came to me, all of a sudden, that my parents weren't the only people keeping secrets. *Borgias—every last one of us!*

"Um, well, it was Jeremy impersonating the woodbooger at the Brunswick Ball."

The table erupted in exclamations, head shaking, and recriminations. I let them run their course. This was just like dealing with angry clients. You had to let them vent their spleen before they would see reason. I waited them out, and when all that was left were angry looks, I spoke again.

"I found his gorilla suit and confronted him. He admitted to it, but he asked me not to snitch. He may have brought up a history of snitching on my part, and that may have played a role in my decision not to tell, but, in return, he promised me he wouldn't impersonate the woodbooger again. I felt it was a fair deal."

"And you trusted him to keep his promise?" asked my mother. "Bless your heart."

"Momma! How could you bless my heart? I can't believe you just did that!"

"I can't believe you trusted your brother!"

"He acted out last night because I didn't trust him. You didn't either. Jeremy discovered I'd added him to my list of suspects, and he was mad. And when you took Mike to the Concatenated Order but didn't invite Jeremy, I saw immediately how it hurt him. None of us trusted him, so why keep his word?"

"Did you expect me to trust Jeremy with the secret of the woodbooger?" demanded Daddy. "Imagine what he could do with that knowledge!"

"He'd find a way to monetize it," said Momma. "No doubt."

"I'm not saying we tell him about the woodbooger! We just need to bring him back into the family for his own good. I just want to protect him from himself."

"If you find him," began Mike, "how will you convince him to come home?"

Honestly, I had no idea.

"I'll come up with a plan while we're searching."

It took all morning to find Jeremy, and I still didn't have a plan when we finally caught up with him. It was a complete accident. Mike and I decided to take a break for lunch at Cahill's barbecue and stumbled upon Jeremy having lunch with the entire Shoecraft family. *What the what?* Jeremy usually avoided a girl's parents like a Wuhan live animal market.

We approached the table slowly and cautiously.

"Jill," whispered my beloved. "We're not on safari. He's not going to run."

"But he might charge."

We arrived at the table to hear Jeannie laugh joyously. It sounded like tinkling crystal, as I would expect from the elegant Mrs. Shoecraft. Then she caught sight of us.

"Jill. Mr. McCall. What a pleasure to see you!"

Both Tater Shoecraft and my brother rose from their chairs. I don't know how Jeannie did it, but everyone's manners improved in her presence.

"We don't want to interrupt your lunch," Mike said with a smile. "We just wanted to say hello."

"And to tell Jeremy we hope to see him at family dinner later," I improvised. Completely winging it! "Momma's going to make all your favorites tonight."

"Oh, how wonderful," enthused Jeremy with a smarmy Cheshire Cat grin. "Tell Momma I wouldn't miss it for the world. But let's not keep all that good home cooking to ourselves."

He turned to Jeannie and Tater. "Mr. and Mrs. Shoecraft, won't you join us tonight? And, of course, you Lacey. That goes without saying." He raised her hand to his lips and kissed it. Lacey and her mother sighed in unison.

"We couldn't possibly invite ourselves," protested Tater.

"You're not," replied Jeremy. "I'm inviting you. Momma will be thrilled, won't she, Jill?"

Momma was going to skin me alive, but I smiled my best PR smile.

"Of course she will. I'll let her know. It's going to be such fun!"

"We're so glad Lacey and Jeremy are dating," enthused Jeannie. "I don't know why these two didn't get together years ago."

Lacey shot me a look of pure hatred with a chaser of triumph.

"Isn't life funny?" Mike chuckled.

We said our goodbyes and put in our order at the counter—to go.

Once we were safely in the truck, I exploded.

"Jerkemy is doing anything he can to spite his family! Momma is going to kill me when she finds out she'll be spending the rest of the afternoon in the kitchen making dinner for eight. I want a spray of yellow roses on my casket and a Dixieland band at the cemetery. You have my permission to love again."

"How generous of you."

I sighed heavily, thinking of the coming retribution. "That boy is crazy!"

"Like a fox."

"Come again?"

"My gut tells me there's something else going on here. Something besides revenge on his family."

"You don't know Jeremy. His plans for world domination are nothing if not elaborate."

"That just proves my point. He's putting a lot of effort into the Shoecrafts, and we both think he has no honorable intentions toward Lacey. It's a lot of effort, but what does he have to gain?"

"Making his family cuckoo."

"There are easier ways to drive you all mad. I mean, it's not a far trip."

"Mr. McCall! You take that back." But he just laughed at his own joke.

"Okay, okay, I take it back," he finally agreed when I threatened him with a bath in barbecue sauce. "Don't you need to call your mother?"

"Don't remind me."

I picked up my phone and eyed it warily. At least I wasn't telling her in person. She'd have time to cool off before we got home. Maybe.

$\mathcal{M}$omma did NOT cool off before we got home, even though I made Mike take me into Shenandoah National Park for a picnic to kill time.

When we got to the house, she thrust a shopping list at Mike and ordered him to the Piggly Wiggly. Me she shoved bodily into the kitchen, tied an apron around my waist very snugly (it hurt), and set me to cutting up a chicken to fry, my least favorite activity on the planet, as she knew well. This was Momma's revenge.

"When you're finished with that, you have ironing to do. I want the best linens, the ones from Ireland. Tablecloth, place-mats, and napkins. When that's done, you need to polish the silver. All of it. Enlist Mike."

"Momma, you're going overboard!"

"You invited the cotillion teacher to dinner! Normally, I need a week to prepare for a visit from Jeannie Shoecraft. You gave me five hours! Now be quiet and get to work. I have to make a cherry pie with a lattice top because you promised your brother all his favorite foods!"

I shut up and got to work. When I finished cutting up the

chicken and disinfected the kitchen and my hands, I headed for the dining room to collect the linens. I found my father rubbing beeswax into the already glossy dining room table as if his life depended on it.

He glanced up at me.

"Daughter."

He resumed polishing.

Jeez! Ice, ice, Daddy!

By the end of the afternoon, Mike and I were sweaty messes. Momma and Daddy, however, as the injured parties, had taken the last half hour before the arrival of the Shoecrafts to make themselves presentable. When our guests arrived, I had a gravy stain on my blouse, and Mike had dried cream corn on his sleeve.

Good times.

Jeremy's favorite meal had always been homemade fried chicken, mashed potatoes and gravy, creamed corn, and lattice-topped cherry pie with homemade vanilla ice cream. (Boy had Mike enjoyed cranking that ice cream maker.) To the menu of childhood favorites, Momma added homemade rolls and her famous slaw.

I didn't want to eat any of it, but I made myself fill my plate as the dishes were passed and everyone else made polite conversation. I added some extra sugar to my already sweet tea, hoping it would perk me up. I was plum tuckered out.

I was jolted out of my sleepies when Lacey Shoecraft unexpectedly brought up Jeremy's hijinks from the night before.

"I wish I could have been there to see everyone's faces when the Sheriff unmasked the woodbooger," she laughed.

"It was straight out of Scooby-Doo," crowed Jeremy. "And then they wanted to arrest me because no one had seen the pile of cash I'd left on the counter to pay for all the popsicles!" Jeremy and all the Shoecrafts laughed.

"Such fun!" exclaimed Jeannie.

"Why did you do it?" asked Mike. He was smiling, attempting to join in the fun while trying to extract information. A Mike McCall specialty.

"Because those bigfoot hunters had it coming! After descending on the town and causing mischief and mayhem, they needed to be taken down a peg."

The incredulous looks on my parents' faces almost made me laugh.

Jeannie and Lacey beamed at my brother, but I just sat there wondering who was going to take *him* down a peg or two. The ladies were eating out of his hand, and neither had an inkling that Jeremy Cooksey was the OG mischief maker.

When the laughter died down, Jeannie asked Jeremy about his work in Atlanta. This I wanted to hear.

"I've been working for Malevia Group, mergers and acquisitions, that sort of thing, but I'm considering a move."

"You don't mean to leave Atlanta?" Jeannie seemed horrified by the thought.

"Not necessarily. I enjoy the city."

"It's such a vibrant place," gushed Jeannie. "What an art scene! The High Museum, the Fox Theater, the symphony orchestra. Plus, the largest airport in the world! You can go anywhere from Atlanta." Jeannie sighed wistfully.

"Well, you can go anywhere from D.C., too, and that's only a two-hour drive," put in Lacey. It seemed as if they'd had this conversation often.

"And with the Atlanta traffic," chuckled Jeremy, "it can take you two hours to get to the airport even if you live downtown."

Jeannie frowned, caught herself, and forced a laugh. I looked at Tater. He kept his eyes on his plate and seemed to be ignoring the conversation. I decided to draw him out.

"Isn't it wonderful that Tyler woke up, Mr. Shoecraft? You must feel good about that since you were one of the people who rescued him."

At first, Tater seemed surprised that someone had spoken to him, but then he took in my words and smiled.

"It does feel good to save a life. I'm glad that young man is going to be okay."

To my surprise, Lacey reached over and patted her father's hand.

"We're very proud of the work Daddy does, aren't we Momma? He makes a difference."

"Thank you, peanut." Tater leaned over to his daughter and kissed her on the cheek.

"We are indeed," said Jeannie. "Now, Loretta, this linen, it has to be Irish."

This family dynamic had some strange undercurrents. I didn't think it was an exaggeration to say that Jeannie and her husband inhabited different realities, and Lacey seemed to bounce back and forth between them. Did all children do that? Did I vacillate between my mother's world and my father's? If I did, I didn't notice because their worlds were, for the most part, the same. But there was a disconnect between Jeannie and Tater, I was almost certain. I say almost because my conclusions were based on the observations of one dinner. Maybe if Lacey and I hadn't fallen out and I had spent more time with the Shoecrafts I would know for sure.

Dinner continued with polite conversation, mostly concerning my brother's life in Atlanta. I was glad because I learned some things about Jeremy. He had season tickets to the Braves, he took jiu-jitsu, and his favorite place to get away from it all was Bermuda. Wow! Jeremy had a life beyond plotting world domination. Who knew?

Soon we were at the dessert course, and I was aching to move the conversation away from Jeremy and back toward the Shoecrafts, or even better, toward Tyler Skaggs. That meant a potential social gaffe on my part, and my mother might never forgive me, not with the cotillion teacher at her table.

Oh, well. Needs must.

"So Lacey," I asked. "How long ago did you and Tyler break off the engagement?"

Mike was lucky enough not to have food or drink in his mouth, but Jeremy about gagged on his homemade vanilla, and Momma had to wail on Daddy's back to keep him from choking on a cherry.

"I don't know what you mean." Lacey narrowed her eyes at me. "We weren't engaged. We were never that serious." She looked meaningfully at my brother. "He wasn't the right man for me."

Jeremy doubled down on his coughing fit.

"That's so funny." I laughed lightly. "Weren't you planning a wedding, Mrs. Shoecraft?"

Jeannie's face rapidly turned the shade of the cherry pie filling.

"Momma?" Lacey's eyes were full of questions and, if I wasn't mistaken, censure. Tater was frowning at his wife too.

Jeannie forced a laugh.

"Oh, you know how a mother dreams! I was never planning anything in earnest, my dear. Just window shopping. After all, I wouldn't want a wedding to sneak up on me and not be prepared."

Nice save, I thought, even if her embarrassed blush gave her away.

"That must be why Loretta is always picking up *Bride's Magazine*," said Daddy soothingly. "She's probably hoping young Michael will pop the question."

Everyone laughed except Mike and me. Hoisted by my own petard!

Meanwhile, Jeannie's coloring was returning to normal.

"Guilty!" cried Momma. "I just love to look at the dresses, don't you Jeannie?"

They launched into a discussion of wedding dress designers

while Lacey, Jeremy, Mike, and I paid very close attention to our desserts and coffee.

When dinner was over, I thought my brother might try to make a run for it with the Shoecrafts, so I slid my arm through his and held on tight. This seemed to amuse him.

"Oh, look, everyone. My little sis is holding on to me for dear life. Have you been missing your big brother?"

I tried to work up some fake tears, and I think I succeeded in making my eyes glisten just a little.

"It's just that soon I'll be going back to New York, and you'll be going back to Atlanta. We might not see each other for a long time. I just want to spend some time with you."

"Isn't that sweet," cooed Jeannie. "Now Jeremy, I insist you give Jilly some attention. We'll see you tomorrow. Come on Lacey, Virgil."

Lacey looked expectantly at Jeremy, and I knew she was hoping for a kiss. I dug my fingers in tighter until her mother pulled her out the door and it was shut and bolted.

Mike was the first to speak.

"Does anyone else feel like they're living in a Jane Austen novel? All these dinners, teas, lunches, and picnics with subtext. Is that all people in the South do? Eat?"

I looked at Momma, who looked at Daddy, who looked at Jeremy, who looked at me.

"Yep!" we replied in unison.

"Well, okay then," said Mike resignedly. "Can we have a family meeting now?'

We tromped up the stairs to the attic, and I immediately erased the chalkboard, both sides. I wanted a clean slate so Jeremy would feel part of the team, even if we couldn't share every secret with him. You know, due to blood oaths.

Instead of taking a seat in my makeshift classroom like everyone else, Jeremy leaned against an old trunk and crossed his arms. His body language was resistant, but at least he was there with us. I started to speak when Mike interrupted.

"Jill, do you mind if someone else leads this meeting?"

Did I? Surprised by the request, it took me a moment to gauge my feelings.

"Not at all." I handed Mike the chalk and took a seat. He, in turn, held the chalk out to Jeremy.

"You have the floor."

Jeremy smirked, but he heaved himself off the trunk and sauntered toward Mike. I mean, it wouldn't do to look too eager, would it? My father looked confused at this turn of events, my mother less so. She always insisted that Jeremy's sneakiness came from the Cooksey side, but I was convinced that was a smokescreen.

"It all comes down to motive," said Jeremy as he began to scribble a list of names on the board. "Hiram Graham, Dud Scott, Beulah Kenilworth, Lacey Shoecraft, Tater Shoecraft, and Jeannie Shoecraft. Our prime suspects."

Daddy sputtered.

"How can you put Dud Scott on there? He's your godfather!"

"You mean THE Godfather. Dud Scott, as Supreme Squatch, wields a lot of power in this town. The COW lost a lot of members the night before Tyler was attacked, enough to make Dud more than a little nervous."

Daddy started to protest again, but Momma laid a soothing hand on his arm.

"Hiram Graham is on the list for the very same reason," continued Jeremy. "As mayor, he has been elected repeatedly by the Concatenated Order voting bloc. Those elections have always been close. With the COW bleeding members, Hiram Graham would likely lose the next election.

"That brings me to Beulah. She'd love nothing more than for Hi to be dethroned and to take what she sees as her rightful place as leader of all of Luthersburg. Ambition is her middle name. Now, on to the Shoecraft family.

"Lacey Shoecraft is utterly smitten with me," he smiled bitterly. "More fool her, but that doesn't mean she wasn't hurt when Tyler dumped her, and he did DUMP her. Even if she didn't see a real future with him, it still stung. Enough to kill? I'm not sure. She doesn't seem to be suffering from a guilty conscience.

"That brings me to Tater Shoecraft. Lacey is the apple of his eye, and she loves her Daddy. Jeannie may have tolerated her husband for the last thirty years, but Lacey has adored him. If he perceived an injury to his darling girl, well, that might push him over the edge. The one factor arguing against this scenario is his history and abhorrence of killing. That would be tough to overcome.

"And that leaves Jeannie Shoecraft, our illustrious cotillion teacher, the arbiter of good taste in Luthersburg. When Tyler came back to town, he was full of big talk. He was just here to regroup; then he would be off to bigger and better things in Raleigh or Nashville or even Los Angeles. When he and Lacey started dating, Jeannie was over the moon. Her daughter was going to succeed where she had failed. Lacey was going to get out of Luthersburg. One problem. No, two. No, three! First, Lacey has no desire to leave her hometown, her business, or her father, unless, of course, it's with me. Poor little fool. Second, Tyler decided not to leave Luthersburg. Overhead for his business, at least at the beginning, would be much lower if he operated out of his parents' basement. And third, Tyler didn't love Lacey. He didn't even give her a chance. He was, and presumably is, focused on getting his business off the ground."

"How do you know all of this about Tyler?" asked Daddy.

"Because we're friends."

Baffled, Momma, Daddy, and I just looked at each other dumbly.

"I have friends," muttered Jeremy through gritted teeth. "And not just Kenny Beveridge."

"You came to Luthersburg when you heard Tyler had been attacked, didn't you?" Mike asked.

"Yes." Jeremy inclined his head in gratitude toward the one person who wasn't treating him like a space alien, and I immediately felt ashamed of my behavior and grateful to Mike, who was successfully bringing Jeremy back into the fold. I could just kiss him, and I would, later.

"Why did you bring the gorilla suit? Why impersonate the woodbooger?" I asked. This part didn't make sense.

"To mess with whoever had attacked Tyler. I knew it had to be someone in town."

"Because the woodbooger isn't real," I finished the thought.

"No." Jeremy looked at me like I was an idiot. "Because the woodbooger would never attack anyone!"

You could have heard a pin drop.

"I know the woodbooger is real. In fact, I know everything."

Jeremy skewered each of us with his eyes, lingering longest on Momma and Daddy. "I knew you faked Daddy's death. I know all the rights of the Loyal Knights, and I know all about the Ladies Auxiliary, otherwise known as the R—"

"That's quite enough!" Momma jumped out of her chair. "How do you know all of this?"

"Because he was the sneakiest boy in town," I answered for my brother. "He never got caught for anything he did. Not for the mailboxes or the cheating or the stealing. No one had a clue. He was a master of deception."

"Thank you, sister."

"Everyone trusted the golden boy, which meant no one ever registered alarm at his presence," I continued. "He operated with carte blanche—"

"We get it." Momma cut me off.

Mike whistled low. "I bet you know all the secrets in this town."

Again, Jeremy inclined his head.

I looked at my parents. Daddy appeared positively flummoxed, working his jaw as if he wanted to say something but didn't know quite what. Momma, on the other hand, coolly appraised her boy-child.

"It seems I underestimated you, Jeremy. I thought I had your number, but I was wrong." I could hear the admiration in her voice. Who was my mother? Emperor Palpatine?

Shaking off that image, I asked, "So where does that leave the investigation?"

Jeremy gestured to the board. "One of these people attacked Tyler. I'd bet my BMW on it. We just have to figure out which one."

Now the debating began in earnest. Daddy and Momma were adamant that Dud and Hi were completely innocent. Mike doubted the Shoecrafts' motives for murder were strong enough. We all agreed that Beulah was capable of absolutely anything.

"So, we focus on Beulah." Jeremy circled her name on the chalkboard and stepped back to regard it.

Something didn't feel right to me. I cleared my throat.

"Do you think it's right to put all our eggs in one basket?"

"Dud and Hi are innocent," proclaimed Daddy. "I don't want to hear another word against them." He was still worked up from the discussion.

"If it makes you feel better, Jilly," said Momma as she laid a soothing hand on Daddy's arm, "Hi is being investigated by the police."

"And I'm still dating Lacey Shoecraft," offered Jeremy. "I can keep an eye on that family."

I looked at Mike, and we had a conversation with our eyes:

"Is that enough?"

"Probably not, but it will have to do."

"Beulah's probably the assailant, right?"

"Probably."

"Okay," I relented out loud. "Let's investigate Beulah."

There ensued another debate on how to do that.

"Surveillance! It's the private investigator's number one tool according to my professor." Momma was still taking classes at the community college. Was she getting a PI's license? Nah!

"Surveillance takes a long time," put in Mike. "With Tyler still in danger, we need faster results."

"We could toss her place," said Jeremy. "I'm sure we'd find something incriminating."

"Or we could beat a confession out of her," suggested Daddy with too much gusto for comfort.

"Let's try to stay on the right side of the law," suggested Mike patiently. I saw three pairs of eyes roll, all related to me.

"I have a better idea." I rubbed my hands together diabolically as the plan came together in my mind. "Let's set a honeytrap."

CHAPTER 21

"I can't believe I let you talk me into this," hissed Mike as I unfastened one more button on his shirt and rumpled his hair sexily.

My boyfriend was the honey in our honeytrap. He was going to Beulah's favorite watering hole to lure her into conversation and pump her for information.

"You are the only option! Jeremy can't jeopardize his relationship with Lacey (I couldn't believe I was saying those words), and Daddy is not a candidate for obvious reasons, the most relevant being that he and Beulah Kenilworth are mortal enemies. It has to be you."

"But I'm YOUR boyfriend! Why would she expect me to give her the time of day?"

"She may not expect it," put in my mother as she scrutinized Mike, "but when you do give her the time of day, she'll be receptive. Her ego will make sure of that. Maybe some more cologne, Jilly."

Mike coughed as I added another spritz of his body spray. I couldn't get enough of the piney scent myself.

"And when you express doubt about our relationship, now

that you've met my family and seen my hometown, she'll be completely convinced. Beulah is perfectly willing to think the worst of us, right Momma?"

"Indeed. Hateful woman!"

Fed up with our primping, Mike swatted our hands away and picked up his phone.

"Full charge. I shouldn't have any trouble, but I'll use my recorder as a backup."

Mike was going to go live on social media on his phone using a brand-new account that only the Cooksey family members had subscribed to. That way we could hear the encounter as it happened. Video wasn't important, so Mike planned to keep his phone face down the entire time.

"Wish me luck."

"Better you than me," said Jeremy. I elbowed him in the ribs. "Ow! And good luck."

I was about to wrap my arms around Mike's neck and smooch him for luck when my father beat me to it. Rather, he enfolded Mike in an enormous bear hug.

"My boy, you are making the ultimate sacrifice for this family and this town. It shall not be forgotten."

"Daddy, he's not laying his life down. Don't be so dramatic."

"Young Michael is going into the belly of the beast, and her name is Beulah. Farewell, brave soldier!"

I did finally manage a quiet word with Mike, away from everyone else, as he headed to the truck.

"Does the fact that Jeremy has seen the woodbooger alter your position in any way?"

Mike sighed.

"No, Jill. All the Loyal Knights of the Concatenated Order claim to have seen the woo—bigfoot. One more person isn't going to change my mind."

"Okay. I was just wondering." I leaned up on my toes and kissed him softly. "Farewell, brave soldier."

Thirty minutes later, Mike was seated at the bar in the biker hangout we had visited once before. I now knew that it had a name: Route 666 Tavern.

"The mark of the Beast! How fitting!" spat Daddy.

Jeremy assured us this was Beulah's favorite hangout, but when I asked him how he knew, he got cagey.

When Mike arrived, Beulah wasn't there, so he settled at the bar to wait for her, his phone face down. We heard him order a beer and chat with the bartender.

And that's all we heard.

Mike was into his third beer, and Jeremy was whipping the rest of us at Spades when things finally got interesting.

"Well, well, well, look what the cat dragged in."

It was Beulah. Mike didn't respond. *Why didn't he respond?*

"That's okay. You don't have to say a word. I understand completely."

"What do you understand?" *Finally!*

Beulah ordered a drink, and I heard her settle herself at the bar.

"Second thoughts."

"About what?"

"Now, Mike—Can I call you Mike?—don't be coy. At this point, you've seen the Cooksey family, including your girl-friend, in their natural habitat. You now know they're all nuttier than a squirrel turd."

"Always the lady," murmured Momma smugly.

"I expect you're having second thoughts about taking them on 'til death do you part."

There was a long pause while Mike ordered another beer.

"Put it on my tab," said Beulah.

"Wow," I whispered. Beulah was making this too easy.

There was another pause. I thought I heard a bottle set on the bar, lifted, and set down again.

"Let's say, hypothetically," began Mike, "that you're right." I could imagine Beulah smiling like a coyote at my boyfriend. "What would you do if you were me?"

Beulah barked a coyote laugh. "Run as fast as you can as far as you can."

Mike laughed, which didn't sit well with me.

He's just pretending. It's just pretend.

"I've been trying to decide which direction." They both laughed companionably. I heard the bottle scrape the bar again. "The thing is, I don't want to hurt Jill, but I want a clean break."

"Makes sense." There was a pause. "But I think the cleanest breaks come when you give the other person something to be mad about. Let Jill feel like the injured party. She'll hate you, but you'll be in the clear."

"Now that makes sense." I heard glasses clink. Had Mike just toasted Beulah's advice? "So how would you go about making Jill hate me?"

"The simplest way. Get caught cheating." There was a long pause, and I could imagine Beulah touching Mike's hand, letting him know that she volunteered as tribute. When we finally exposed her as Tyler's attacker, I hoped I'd get a chance to punch her in the face.

"Another drink?" asked Mike, the scoundrel. Beulah must have signaled her approval because Mike said, "Another for the lady."

All Cookseys present *harumphed*, except Jeremy, who watched us with open amusement.

"Tell me," continued Mike in low, sultry tones, the black-guard. "Why do you hate the Cookseys so much, I mean, besides the fact they're crazy and annoying."

What was that sound? Oh yeah. Just my teeth grinding.

"Isn't that enough?" laughed the she-coyote.

"To want to avoid them, absolutely," chuckled my ex-boyfriend. "But to hate them with the fire of a thousand suns?"

Coyote laugh again. Like fingernails on a chalkboard.

"They're part of the Old Boy network, and I just hate it. Calvin is at the center. I mean, almost the entire town helped him fake his death. Shouldn't he be in prison or something? Those old Woodboogers run this town. And the wives? They just enable it. Their husbands are part of a club the women are not allowed to join, but do they protest? No! They don't say a word. They just make their little Ladies Auxiliary, which is a fancy way of saying they serve the men. It's backward, but don't worry, their days are numbered."

We leaned closer to the phone. Was Beulah about to incriminate herself?

"I sense you're a woman with a plan." Did Mike have to say the word woman so sensuously? Nauseating.

"Not a plan, per se. I'm what you would call an opportunist. I make good use of the opportunities that come my way. I just need to give the Woodboogers enough rope. They'll do the hanging themselves." Then the she-coyote laughed and Mike joined in.

"Take Tyler," she continued, and we held our collective breath. "The Woodboogers of the World was utterly his idea, but when he came to me asking for help in getting it started, who was I to say no?"

"Boy, that opportunity was served up on a silver platter."

I heard a loud smack as if Beulah had slapped the bar in triumph.

"That's just what I mean. The Concatenated Order drove him to it! They're self-destructive. It's only a matter of time."

I looked at my father, and his expression was troubled. Beulah was the Medusa of the mountains, but she was offering up some very uncomfortable home truths.

"What do you think about all this bigfoot hoo-doo?" asked Mike in his most mellifluous tones. Perfect timing! The man was a pro! And yes, my feelings were all over the place. We can talk about that later.

I could imagine him leaning closer to Beulah and the hag moving closer in return. Their faces were close. Perhaps their lips were just a whisper apart. His handsome face and her horsey mug tète-a-tète. Would he kiss her? Would I then be expected to kiss lips that had touched hers? A shudder of revulsion coursed through my body.

"Seal the deal," whispered Jeremy, and I nearly clubbed him with Momma's favorite Hummel figurine.

"I know things," whispered Beulah. "The woodbooger...is real."

"Of course he's real!" boomed a third voice. "Good luck convincing this guy!" It was Larry from the Bigfoot Brigade.

"Son of a biscuit!" yelled Daddy. "He was so close!"

I sat back on the sofa and breathed a sigh of both frustration and relief. I had major cognitive dissonance.

"Those bozos need taking down a peg," muttered Jeremy. Uh oh. Jeremy was just the man to do it.

The conversation in the bar continued.

"You should come out in the woods with us sometime," offered Larry. "I could really open your eyes."

"I'll take you to the woods," protested Beulah. "I can show you a thing or two." She was trying for sexy, but the mood had been destroyed by the Bigfoot Brigade.

"Let me buy you a drink," offered Larry. "Barkeep, a round for my team and our new friends."

"Thanks all the same," said Mike. "I think I've had enough. Beulah, thank you for a lovely evening." There was a pause, and I couldn't help but imagine that Mike raised her hand to his lips. Was there any Listerine in the house? "Until next time." Over my rotting corpse.

When Mike got home, Momma and Daddy met him at the door. Jeremy didn't like to show enthusiasm, and I...I was in a war with my thoughts and feelings.

Daddy kept slapping Mike on the back as he ushered him

into the living room, while Momma kept asking if he wanted something to eat. Mike declined food. Maybe he was as nauseated as I was.

"Well done," said Jeremy, as Mike sat heavily on the sofa next to me. "She was eating out of your hand."

Mike made a little bow in acknowledgment.

"Yes, you were very convincing," I said crisply. Was that a look passing between Mike and my brother? Better not be!

"Beulah Kenilworth," said Mike as he turned to me, "is even more revolting when she's on the prowl than she is during the day. You couldn't see, but she was all tricked out and looking to score. The phrase 'mutton dressed as lamb' comes to mind."

"Really?" I couldn't imagine polo shirt and blue jeans Beulah dolled up to meet men at a biker bar.

"Really. She was odious."

"I guess you're a good actor then," I reluctantly admitted.

"He did fool you on the cruise ship," said Daddy. "A masterful disguise!"

"Would you have kissed her?" The question just flew out of my mouth, and I blushed hotly. My face was on fire.

"Probably. I've never locked lips with an over-the-hill wannabe biker babe, but it's on my bucket list."

Jeremy howled with laughter, and I stood up to flounce out of the room only to have Mike grab my hand and pull me into his lap.

"I most certainly wouldn't have kissed her." He wrapped his arms around me and nuzzled my neck. "I haven't had all my shots."

"Well, the most important thing we learned," said Momma as she put down a tray of chips and dips on the coffee table, "other than that Jilly has a jealous streak, is that Beulah knows the woodbooger exists. How did she find out?"

"Could it be knowledge passed down in her family, like it is in ours?" I asked.

"Not likely," replied Momma.

"The Kenilworths are relative newcomers to Luthersburg," explained Daddy. "Her people only arrived here after the war."

"Which one?" I asked.

"World War II."

"So that's what defines a newcomer," chuckled Jeremy. "She may have had a point about the Old Boy network."

Everyone avoided that landmine. A conversation for another time.

"Has someone at the Concatenated Order spilled the beans?" I asked.

"Impossible!" blustered Daddy. "The Loyal Knights won't even tell their spouses. I don't know if I can make you understand. It's a form of chivalry. We are devoted to the cause of protecting the Lord's most kind and innocent creature. We take that cause as seriously as we take our faith or our marriages. The Loyal Knights are just that—loyal."

I looked at Momma. "What if a spouse found out another way?" Momma was shooting daggers out of her eye sockets at me, but I was Wonder Woman, deflecting with my metal bracelets.

"The women of the Ladies Auxiliary are no less honorable!" insisted Momma. "If one of them found out the truth about the woodbooger and the Order, the secret would go with her to her grave. Take me, for instance. I know and have known my whole life. I haven't told a soul who didn't already know the truth and who wasn't already sworn to secrecy. No ma'am! It wasn't a member of the Re—Ladies Auxiliary."

Jeremy's face contorted as he tried not to laugh at Momma's near slip. I had a thought.

"Jeremy, how exactly did you find out about the woodbooger? Did someone tell you?"

He scoffed. "If someone had told me, I wouldn't have believed it. I saw for my own eyes. I snuck into the Concatenated Order's inner sanctum and saw the calling of the woodbooger."

"That's enough!" said Daddy. "No need to reveal our sacred rites. It's enough that your mother and sister know the woodbooger exists."

Momma and I sucked our teeth at the same moment. It pained me to admit it, but Beulah had a few things right.

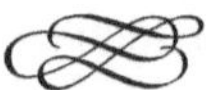

The next morning, we decided to visit Tyler in the hospital to see if he had remembered anything else and to see if he could shed more light on Beulah's motives and machinations. I was glad to see a Sheriff's deputy stationed outside his room. Hiram Graham had been released without charges filed because there wasn't enough evidence, and Sheriff Bagby wasn't taking any chances. I wasn't worried about Hi. I had Beulah on the brain.

Tyler was eating Jell-o and watching reality TV when we arrived. He and Jeremy bumped fists, and I set a vase of flowers on a table. Momma always says never to go to the hospital empty-handed.

"I haven't had a chance to thank you," said Tyler, coloring slightly in embarrassment, "for saving me. If you hadn't gone hiking…" He trailed off, and his color deepened as he no doubt thought about how close he had come to death.

"We're just glad you're okay," I said. "Have you remembered anything else?"

"Nothing." He sighed. "I don't even know why I was on the mountain. I don't remember going there."

"Tyler," Mike took over, "I know the police have already asked, but do you have any enemies?"

Tyler looked at my brother as if for help then shrugged. "Enemies who would want me dead? I just can't see it, unless the Concatenated Order wanted me dead for starting the Woodboogers of the World."

"What about Lacey?" I asked. "You broke up with her."

"Yeah, but who tries to kill someone just for breaking up with them?"

"Read a lot?"

"No."

"Go to the movies much?"

"Not really."

"Okey dokey." This guy.

"What about Beulah Kenilworth?" tried my brother.

"What about her?"

"She helped you start the Woodboogers of the World."

"Well, she gave me some advice."

"And she let you use her printer," pressed Jeremy.

"Sure, but I did all the work."

"Did you make her any promises?"

"Like what?"

"Did you promise her the Woodboogers of the World would vote for her in the next election?"

"No!"

"Did you promise to sleep with her?"

"Okay, Jeremy, now you're just being gross. I never...we never..."

"We get it. You never. So, Beulah was just a friendly Ruritan helping you out."

"Exactly. Wait, did she say something different?"

Jeremy reassured him that wasn't the case, and Tyler calmed down. We didn't want to get kicked out for riling up a patient with a traumatic brain injury.

"Well, you ticked someone off," said Mike prosaically. "It would help if you could remember how you did that."

"I'm trying."

We said our goodbyes, and Tyler promised to let us know if he remembered anything else.

Our next stop was security, where we asked to see the footage of the woodbooger from the night of Tyler's second attack.

Chuck Tinsley, whom I knew from high school, refused. "We already shared it with the police."

"C'mon Chuck. For old times' sake?"

"What old times? We didn't hang out." He turned to me. "And you turned me down when I asked you to the Halloween Dance."

"You never asked me to a dance."

"See! You don't even remember. There's no way I'm showing you that video."

"How about you show us the video and I won't tell your boss here at the hospital that you were the main supplier of all things pharmacological back in high school?" said Jeremy with a smirk.

"Come again?"

"You were a drug dealer! Tell me, do you have keys to the hospital pharmacy?"

Chuck's eyes got very wide.

"You wouldn't," he whispered. Jeremy just cocked an eyebrow in response. "Okay, you would."

The footage was terrible. Chuck explained that due to privacy laws, security cameras were limited and couldn't be high resolution, so the image we saw wasn't even as clear as when Steve Austin fought bigfoot on *The Six Million Dollar Man*. All we had was the woodbooger coming down the hall and passing the camera, and it looked pretty real to me. Unlike Jeremy's gorilla costume, this Bigfoot suit looked like something other than a great ape. It was more like a human but covered in dark brown fur—sort of a cross between a caveman and a grizzly bear.

"I can't tell if it's a man or a woman inside the suit," muttered Mike.

"Look at the exaggerated walk," I said as I started the clip again. "The perpetrator was giving it her all, really trying to look convincing."

"You say 'her' as if it were a foregone conclusion," Jeremy pointed out helpfully. "It might not be Beulah."

"Beulah Kenilworth?" Chuck was suddenly interested. "She was here that night."

"What?"

"She delivers care packages for patients every Wednesday. The candy stripers hand them out. I saw her when she came in and later after the woodbooger poop hit the fan. You don't think that's Beulah in the woodbooger costume, do you?"

"Why not?" asked Mike.

"Like I said, she was delivering care packages for the patients. She does good things. She's the head of the Ruritans after all!"

I didn't even try to explain that Beulah was a diabolical, power-hungry megalomaniac. I couldn't fight care packages.

I couldn't fight the Sheriff either. Our next stop was his office where we tried to convince him to take a harder look at Beulah.

"Look, Sheriff," said my brother. "She was at the hospital the night of the second attack. She's tall. She could easily have impersonated the woodbooger. All I'm saying is she's worth looking into."

"And what about motive?" countered Sheriff Bagby. "Why on earth would she want to hurt Tyler Skaggs? By breaking up the Concatenated Order, he was probably doing her a favor! She has no motive. Zero! Nada!"

"Chaos is her motive!" It just flew out of my mouth. "She's creating chaos to destroy Luthersburg as we know it, and out of the ashes will rise a Ruritan Reich!"

He laughed at me. Looking back, I'm not surprised.

"Spoken like the loyal daughter of the Right Honorable Yeti." He verbally patted me on the head, but I knew it would be counterproductive to assault a police officer. "Now, if you'll excuse me, I have work to do."

"What now?" asked Jeremy as we emerged on the sidewalk.

I looked at Mike and smiled my best "Get out of Jail Free" smile. My wonderful boyfriend sighed.

"Now it's time for another honeytrap."

CHAPTER 23

"Since the Ruritan headquarters at the corner of Main and Poplar is right near the spot where the wood-booger was sighted before he headed for the nature preserve, it only follows that Beulah was impersonating the woodbooger, and she's keeping her costume in the Ruritan offices." I was pumped for Honeytrap Part Two. I had a good feeling that we were going to get some answers.

"There are so many holes in that argument, I don't know where to start, so I won't." Mike was less enthused.

We were sitting in the café about to execute phase one of the plan: The Fight. Mike and I were supposed to argue, and I was supposed to flounce out of the café in high dudgeon.

Phase two was called The Slink. Mike would slink down to Beulah's office for an understanding shoulder to cry on. This would distract Beulah while Jeremy and I executed phase three: The Search. We were going to find Beulah's woodbooger suit.

The beautiful thing about the honeytrap was that we could build on it indefinitely. I have to say, I was quite the little mastermind, and I was being very professional about it. I had compartmentalized my emotions, and I told Mike he could even kiss Beulah if he had to. He choked on the breath mint I had given him just before my brave declaration, and I had to do the Heimlich, but I knew he was impressed with my sang-froid.

Jeremy was waiting for me around the corner from the Ruritan offices. The sooner I started this fight with Mike, the sooner we could catch Beulah and put her behind bars.

"Are you ready?" I asked Mike.

"To be pimped out to a cougar? As ready as I'll ever be. Just so you know, Jill, you owe me big time. BIG time." He was serious. Was I asking too much? I couldn't think about that question right at that moment because we had an attempted murderer to catch. I'd think about that tomorrow.

"I love you," I whispered, and then I let loose. "I'm just sick of you judging me and my whole family! To think I even considered spending the rest of my life with you! You're nothing but a lowdown Yankee!"

"His people are from Kentucky," inserted a man from the next booth.

"I don't care! From where I'm sitting he's a conceited Yankee who thinks he's better than the rest of us!" I stood up and grabbed my purse. "Don't follow me!" I stormed out of the café and down the street in sight of a good portion of Luthersburg's citizenry. *That ought to do it.* News of the argument would reach Beulah any minute. By the time Mike made it to the Ruritan offices, Beulah would be ready for her beau.

I didn't stop until I reached Poplar and hung a left. I met Jeremy a few doors down, by the alley. He had his phone out, already following Mike's live social media broadcast. Again, we weren't going to be able to see anything. I just hoped the audio would give us enough clues to know when the coast was clear. He gave me an earbud and kept one for himself.

After a couple of minutes, I heard a door open and a bell ring. He was in the Ruritan headquarters.

"Hello, again." Beulah.

"Are you alone? That is, is anyone else in the office?" Mike sounded stressed.

"Just little ol' me." I could hear the smile in Beulah's voice, and my nose wrinkled in response.

"Can we talk? It's just...things have gotten worse."

"Of course." To her credit, the she-devil was playing it cool. I had her pegged for a desperate woman who would come on too strong given the least provocation, but she was proving more subtle.

Whatever.

"Can we talk somewhere more private?" Mike was doing a great job putting trepidation into his voice. "This isn't a conversation we want anyone walking in on."

"We can use the storage room...It has a lock on the door."

And there it was, the Hussy Express, right on time.

We heard thumps as they walked down the hall and the sound of a door shutting. Jeremy hurried around the corner to the Ruritan office. With the speed of a slug on a lettuce leaf, he opened the door, attempting not to jingle the bell. It worked, mostly. One teensy jangle had us holding our breath, but no one emerged from the storage room. The conversation inside carried on without a pause.

"Since we've been back in Luthersburg, Jill has been a different person. In New York, she's...approachable, open-minded. Here, she's just plain bossy."

I tried to ignore the substance of the conversation as Jeremy and I began searching the building. The storage room was on the right side of the building, so we started on the left. Jeremy tossed a small, unused office, while I searched a kitchenette.

"That's because in this town, she's practically royalty. Big fish in a small pond. Aren't you glad you're seeing the real Jill before it's too late?"

"But is this the real Jill? Or is the real Jill the girl I know in New York?"

The cabinets were clear, as was the fridge. I even checked the microwave. No sign of woodbooger fur.

I met Jeremy in the hall. He'd had no luck in the small office either. Together we headed for Beulah's office, next door to the storage room. We would have to be very careful and quiet.

"I thought you were ready to move on," said Beulah with a little edge to her voice. Was she growing impatient with the glacial progress of our break-up?

"I thought I was. I think I am. I'm just not sure. We've been through a lot together."

We had, hadn't we? I thought about all the turbulent seas we had weathered together and apart as I carefully opened the drawers of the Ruritan filing cabinet. Nothing in the top or the middle drawer.

"Maybe I can help you make up your mind." Beulah's voice was filled with determination. And then, all I could hear was movement, like people bumping up against furniture or the wall.

"Should we?" I heard Mike say. "I don't know."

"Hush, darling. Let Beulah make it better."

"I'm not so sure..."

Great day in the morning! Mike and Beulah were making out!

In my shock, I closed the bottom drawer a bit too loudly. In truth, I might have slammed it. As soon as it happened, I knew I had screwed up. Jeremy was pantomiming frustration and a desire to strangle me, nothing new there. Me, I was feeling a whole cocktail of emotions. Disappointment that I had screwed up, shame for letting down the team, and above all, rage that Beulah Kenilworth was having her wicked way with my man.

"What was that?" Beulah cried. At least her lips were no longer touching Mike's.

"What was what?"

"That noise. I think someone's in the office!"

I knew what I had to do. We had discussed the possibility, but now it had to happen. I wasn't too upset. I was about to have words with that harlot!

Leaving Jeremy to make sure the office was as Beulah left it, I stormed down the hallway and burst through the door. Or, I would have if it hadn't been locked. I started pounding.

"I know you're in there, Mike McCall. Gladdy Tidwell said she saw you make a bee-line for Beulah's office. You come out here this instant and face the music."

The door opened, and there was Mike with shirt buttons open and fuchsia lipstick on his chin and cheek. Wait! Was that his belt buckle undone?

I launched myself at Beulah like a rabid bobcat. Jeremy grabbed me around the waist, forcing all the air out of my lungs, while Mike attempted to get hold of my claws, I mean hands.

"Let me explain, Jill."

I tried to yell some more, but I had no breath.

"Beulah, I'll call you."

'Stay, lover," she pleaded. "You don't have to go!"

Mike feigned confusion. (For his sake, I hope he *was* feigning.) "I...I don't know what to do. I need time to think."

They dragged me out of there, and Jeremy didn't put me down until we reached the parking lot of the Concatenated Order.

"Steady girl. Steady."

"I'm not a horse!" I swatted at Jeremy and then turned my swatting on Mike.

"Why are you hitting me? The mission's over!"

"I don't know! *Arghh!*" I stalked a few feet away to get control of myself. Why was I overreacting? The mission had gone to plan, even the failsafe. Why was I so worked up?

"I think I'm just having trouble getting out of character."

That seemed a likely excuse. I looked at the men, and their wary expressions told me they had doubts. "I'm fine now. I guess I'm a method actor."

"You're the Meryl Streep of Luthersburg," quipped Jeremy. "Now can we figure out what's next? We didn't find a woodbooger costume in the Ruritan office."

"It was the perfect place for her to keep the costume. The woodbooger appeared right at the corner of Main and Poplar, right by Ruritan headquarters!" I stomped my foot in frustration.

"Maybe it's too perfect." Mike scratched his chin thoughtfully. "Maybe someone wants us to think it's Beulah."

"Holy Moses!" Jeremy and I said at the same time.

Maybe Beulah wasn't the woodbooger after all.

CHAPTER 24

We drove home in silence, each of us pondering who might be trying to frame Beulah Kenilworth. Beulah was a tidy solution to the problem, one I liked very much for obvious reasons, but we weren't the only people in town who disliked her.

When we got home, we marched directly to the attic stairs.

"Council of war!" I called out to my parents.

"What happened?" cried Daddy, as they scurried after us.

I went to the chalkboard and picked up the eraser. Then I put it down and picked up the chalk. Then I put it down too.

"We're flummoxed," I finally admitted.

"No costume?" asked Momma.

"No costume," said Mike.

"That doesn't mean she didn't do it!" cried Daddy.

Mike explained our thinking, that Beulah might be too convenient and that someone might be trying to frame her.

"What do you think, Jeremy?" Momma asked.

"It's possible," he admitted. "It was a mistake to put all our eggs in Beulah's basket."

Duh!

"So, who else is good for it?" asked Daddy, his face going florid with frustration.

He wasn't going to like the answer.

"Hiram Graham."

Daddy didn't like the answer, and he let us know in no uncertain terms. But while Daddy blustered, Momma remained calm, which was odd. Up to now, she had defended Hi vociferously.

"We saw Hiram the day the woodbooger appeared on Main Street! He told us what had happened. How could he be the woodbooger? Answer me that!" Daddy paused to take a breath, and I jumped in.

"He could have doubled back. Hi could have appeared on the corner of Main and Poplar, run up Poplar toward the lodge, then doubled back, leaving the costume in an alley."

"I mean," began Jeremy, "how convenient was it that Hiram was there to tell everyone the woodbooger had gone toward the nature preserve?"

"He might have staged the sighting right near the Ruritan offices just to throw suspicion on Beulah," added Mike.

"What's his motive?" Daddy threw up his hands in frustration.

Momma sighed. "Cal, even I can see Hiram has motive for days. Tyler threatened to erode the Woodbooger voting bloc, and Beulah is his toughest competition for mayor."

"Fine! Hi has motive. You know what he doesn't have? A killer's instincts! He just couldn't do it!"

"We never know what we can do until we're pushed too far," said Jeremy thoughtfully. Was he speaking from experience?

Momma and Daddy agreed to invite Hiram and Helen over for dinner that evening. We needed to spend some time with one of our chief suspects whom we had ignored because of ties of friendship and brotherhood. Helen Graham was happy to accept the dinner invitation on their behalf, admitting to Momma that since Hi had been arrested on suspicion of attempted murder, they hadn't had many invitations. That knowledge hurt my heart. Hi and Helen were like family, part of my life ever since I could remember.

Yes, he could be a killer. I had to keep reminding myself of that fact. I had seen enough of murder in the last couple of years that, rationally, I knew most people had a breaking point. I couldn't let myself be sentimental simply because I was visiting my hometown.

Jeremy went off to do some work, and I went to help Momma in the kitchen. She didn't need my help, so I went to find Mike. A conversation between the two of us was long overdue. I found him in my thinking spot on the porch swing.

He smiled when he saw me, but his smile faltered when he saw the concerned look on my face.

"What's happened?"

"Nothing yet. Can we talk?"

"Of course."

Even though I had come out on the porch to have a heart-to-heart with Mike, I didn't quite know where to start.

"Give me a moment to gather my thoughts."

"That sounds ominous. What's going on, Jill?"

"It's just…I know it was pretend, the conversations between you and Beulah. I know it was pretend. I mean, you couldn't possibly be interested, could you?"

Something akin to a giggle welled up from deep inside Mike, and soon he was guffawing with tears streaming down his cheeks. It was infectious, and I started to laugh, realizing that the thought of Mike being at all interested in Beulah Kenilworth was ridiculous.

As his laughter abated, Mike pulled me close.

"I needed a good laugh. Thank you. But just so that we are one hundred percent clear and there is no doubt in your mind,

I am not, never have been, nor will I ever be attracted to Beulah. Never, ever, ever." That started us laughing again.

"Okay, okay. It was very insecure of me to even wonder," I admitted. Then I pulled away from him just a little bit to give me some space to look into his eyes.

"Oh no. I feel a *but* coming on."

"Just a little *but*," I said. "The things you said about my family..."

"First of all," countered Mike, "Beulah is the one who said things about your family. I just let her think that I agreed with her. Secondly, I was spitballing, trying to come up with something that would convince that woman that I could turn my back on the most beautiful, wonderful woman I've ever known in favor of a woman whose last name says it all. Kennel worth. Bow wow!"

"So, you don't think I'm a different, bossier person here than I am in New York?"

Mike cocked his head to the side in thought.

"You're a little different here than you are in New York because you're in a different environment. I'm different here too. We're not in the city rat race trying to survive. We're in a small town with family and friends. We're going to act differently. It's not a bad difference, and you're certainly not bossy. How could you be? Your mother bought all the bossiness at the Piggly Wiggly and she's not giving it up to anybody else."

I chuckled because he was right.

"What about the family?" I asked. "Are the Cookseys crackers?"

"Of course they are," he said, "but so are the McCalls. And as I told you before, I love your brand of crazy. I have from the very beginning."

His lips stifled any more paranoid questions from me, and soon I felt nothing but warmth and contentment. Yes indeed, I felt perfectly content in Michael McCall's arms.

DINNER WITH HI and Helen was awkward, to say the least. They were on their very best behavior, acting more formally than I'd ever seen them. Normally, they would make themselves at home in my parents' house. Helen would help Momma in the kitchen, and Hiram would tell stories with my dad and laugh. Everyone would be relaxed and happy.

Not so that evening. From the moment they entered the house, they were on edge. Unfortunately, this nervousness was contagious, and I saw my parents engaging in stilted conversation and fussing over their friends the way they would over strangers. Mike, Jeremy, and I shot each other looks all through dinner. None of us was keen to jump in and defuse the situation, probably because we didn't quite know how. Luckily, Daddy suggested we take dessert out by the fire pit.

In the dusk of evening, with lines softened and faces somewhat obscured, I felt Hiram and Helen relax for the first time. Momma had made blackberry cobbler, and Daddy suggested we add a little chocolate in the form of s'mores. Genius! The last time Hiram sat around our firepit was when Mike and I were trying to smear marshmallows across each other's faces, before Tyler had been attacked and the world had turned upside down. Firepit plus s'mores did the trick, and soon people started telling stories. I wondered if I should jump in and ask Hiram to tell us more about what happened with Tyler on Woody's Mountain, but I didn't have to.

"I was an idiot," he began. "The night of the Brunswick stew festival, when I saw so many of our members at the interest meeting for Woodboogers of the World, I was filled with panic. You remember that night, don't you Cal?"

"I do. You and Lester and Dud paid us a visit."

"I couldn't sleep that night, so I called Tyler and asked him to meet me at the lodge the next morning. I told him I wanted to discuss the situation. We hiked up the trail a piece, with me making my case for keeping the Concatenated Order whole. I'm ashamed to say what happened next."

I held my breath. Was Hi about to tell us that he had whacked Tyler in the head with a rock?

"Tyler would not be swayed by my arguments, which, looking back, were pretty desperate and thin. So, I decided to appeal to his altruism. I did a bad thing." He looked at Helen, Momma, and me. "Ladies, and Jeremy, could you excuse us, please? I need to talk to my lodge brothers alone."

Well, if that didn't beat all! Hiram was about to reveal crucial information to our investigation, and I was being sent packing because I was a woman. Scratch that! Because I wasn't a member of the Order, which I couldn't be because I was a woman.

Momma and Helen stood up. I looked at Jeremy. His face was inscrutable. Then I stood up and picked up my cobbler. Momma smiled at me in gratitude that I hadn't spilled the beans. I looked meaningfully at my brother. He rolled his eyes and got to his feet, and the four of us went to the porch where we had our own interesting conversation.

"The charade is becoming tiresome," said Momma unexpectedly, "especially since both of my children know about the woodbooger."

Helen gasped. "How does Jeremy know?"

"Jeremy knows everything!" Momma threw up her hands in exasperation. "He even knows about the Red Chamber."

"But how?"

"Suffice it to say that Jeremy knows more than is good for him!"

"I am a vault," said my brother solemnly.

"Do you think the Concatenated Order and the Red Chamber will ever come together?" I asked half-jokingly.

"You don't understand," said Helen. "It's for their own good.

The Order is full of good intentions, but so is the road to you-know-where."

Jeremy opened his mouth to reply but was interrupted by shouting from the firepit. Leaving vanilla ice cream melting into blackberry goop, we hustled back to the fire.

"You broke the sacred trust! I can't believe you told him!" Daddy was so mad that he hadn't noticed his blackberry cobbler had fallen to the ground, a first for Daddy.

"What happened?" I picked up the bowl, which had landed face-up. Score!

"Hiram told Tyler about the woodbooger!"

"Don't tell her!" shouted Hi. "What I did was bad enough!"

"She already knows," said Jeremy. "And so does your wife."

"What?"

"Never mind that," said Mike. "You told Tyler about the woodbooger's existence to try to elicit his sympathy and keep him from starting the Woodboogers of the World?"

"It was a Hail Mary pass!" cried Hiram. "A Hail Mary!"

"What you don't realize is that you've given yourself an even greater motive for his attempted murder," sputtered my boyfriend in frustration. "The case could be made that you tried to suffocate him in the hospital to keep him from telling the secret."

"But it didn't matter," cried Hi, "because he didn't believe me! Not one word. He laughed at me and called me a foolish old man. I was gonna take him up to see the woodbooger because we all know that people don't believe unless they see it for themselves, but he wouldn't come."

"So, he called you a foolish old man, and when he turned his back, you picked up a rock and beamed him," said Momma surprisingly.

"Loretta!" cried Daddy.

"I'm just thinking like a prosecutor," said Momma. "Criminal Justice 101."

"No!" cried Hiram. "I left Tyler on that trail before I could say or do something to make things worse." Helen put an arm around her husband in a show of love and solidarity.

"Have you told the police all of this?" asked Jeremy.

"Of course not! I can't tell anybody that the woodbooger exists!"

"Do you see the cognitive dissonance here?" I had to ask.

"How do you gals know about the woodbooger? Who told you?" Hiram demanded. Personally, I thought he had bigger fish to fry.

"My grandfather started the Concatenated Order," said Momma with a sniff, "and that knowledge has been passed down in my family. I passed it down to my children." Cool lie, Momma. She had passed it down to me, but Jeremy got that information all by himself. She was just trying to protect the Red Chamber.

"If you didn't tell her, how does Helen know?"

Helen looked to Momma, her eyes wide with panic, but Momma had no answer for her.

"I...I...I saw him for myself!" Good work, Helen!

"You did? Honey, why didn't you ever say anything?"

"I...I...I had my reasons," was all she would say. She hadn't lied. She had seen the woodbooger for herself on the video feed from the Concatenated Order, and she did have her reasons for not saying anything to Hiram about it, mainly because she didn't want to out the Red Chamber. Technically, Helen had told the truth.

"We will speak more on this," said her husband gravely.

"I'm sure we will," murmured Helen.

"What happens," asked Mike, "when Tyler remembers everything, including that you told him that the woodbooger is real?"

"Hopefully, he'll just think the same thing he thought on the mountain—that I'm a foolish old man."

"I don't think so," put in Jeremy. "He was attacked by the 'woodbooger' in the hospital." He made air quotes around woodbooger. "He could put two and two together and come up with you as the culprit."

Defeated, Hiram ran his hands over his face.

"Maybe he's right. Maybe I am a foolish old man and my time as mayor should end."

"You've been an outstanding mayor!" said Daddy. "The best Luthersburg has ever seen. Your leadership has kept the small-town economy thriving. People are happy to live here, and that's thanks in large part to you. Don't you ever call yourself a foolish old man again! That's an order from the Right Honorable Yeti!"

Hi looked up at Daddy with tears in his eyes.

"Thank you, Calvin. I appreciate it."

"Things aren't as bleak as they appear," continued Daddy, finding his groove. "When Tyler gets his memory back, he'll remember that you left him on that mountain in perfect health."

"Unless he's actually an attempted murderer," hissed Jeremy in my ear.

"Let's all fill our bellies with cobbler and s'mores, then go home and get a good night's sleep." Daddy didn't have to tell me twice. I was no closer to knowing whether Hiram or Beulah was a better suspect, and I needed chocolate.

"Things are gonna look so much better in the morning," said Daddy.

CHAPTER 25

*E*xcept they didn't look better in the morning. The landline ringing shrilly at seven o'clock had the whole house jumping out of bed.

"I knew you wouldn't answer your cell phones this early," said Dud Scott at the other end of the line so loudly we could all hear. "We've got a full-blown woodbooger emergency on Main Street!"

Soon we were throwing on clothes and racing for the car. Daddy drove like a bat out of hell until we reached Main Street, where we had to slow down because it appeared that a tornado had ripped through Luthersburg.

Trashcans were upended down the street with litter flitting about everywhere in the morning breeze. Signs that hung in front of businesses were now hanging askew or lying on the ground. Mrs. Thompson's flower cart, which normally sat in front of her shop, was now lying broken in the middle of the street, flower petals mixing with the trash that was being wafted around the town. Worst of all was Tidwell's Tearoom. The enormous plate glass window that fronted the establishment had been smashed. Inside, tables were overturned, and art was ripped from the walls. An enormous breakfront that held Gladdy Tidwell's collection of teacups no longer graced the back wall. Instead, it had been toppled and lay on the floor. I imagined all of the teacups underneath, smashed to smithereens. Up and down Main Street, the people of Luthersburg wandered in a daze.

As soon as we alighted from the truck, Dud and Shirley came running.

"The candle shop has one of those fancy doorbells with a camera, and it caught the woodbooger tearing down their sign," wheezed Dud. "The woodbooger did this!"

"Is that the only security camera on Main?" asked Mike incredulously.

"Never needed them before," replied Dud defensively.

"There's one other," said Jeremy quietly. He played with his phone for a moment and then held up the screen for us to see. It was a wide shot of Main Street, and it seemed to be taken from the belfry of the First Baptist Church.

"You've got a Luthersburg Cam?"

"Can't a fellow get homesick from time to time?"

I believed in the woodbooger more than I believed that Jeremy ever got homesick. One day, he and I were going to have a nice long talk. It might involve him being tied up, a bare light bulb, and a length of rubber hose. I was going to know his secrets!

"We'll talk about this later," said Momma ominously. She might help me tie my brother up for the interrogation. "Right now, we need to see the footage from last night."

Jeremy fiddled with the phone some more and found the footage of the vandalism. The woodbooger had emerged from around the corner at Main and Poplar, just like the other time, and had systematically worked its way down Main wreaking havoc as it went.

"What's the time stamp?" asked Mike.

"3:37 a.m.," replied Jeremy. "While the good citizens of Luthersburg were fast asleep."

We continued to watch the video, and something soon became apparent. This wasn't the bigfoot from *The Six Million Dollar Man*. This cryptid was full of rage, but it didn't translate into infinite strength. The woodbooger was working hard at creating devastation.

"Look how it topples that trashcan," I pointed out. "It's not easy. The woodbooger is straining. Shouldn't that be easier for something so muscular and imposing?"

"Meaning those muscles are probably fake," said Mike, "created by a padded costume."

"This is no woodbooger," said Daddy. "This is a human impostor!"

A screech of tires had us all looking up as The Bigfoot Brigade came roaring down the street. The truck hadn't completely stopped before Larry descended.

"This is never-before-seen devastation! Bigfoot has made his presence known in Luthersburg in a way he hasn't anywhere else. This can mean only one thing. There's a rabid Sasquatch on the loose!" Upon hearing this declaration, people up and down the street stopped what they were doing. Parents clutched their children, men clutched their concealed firearms, and little old ladies clutched their pearls. "Citizens of Luthersburg, heed my warning. Lock your doors and stay inside! Let the professionals handle it."

"That's right," said Sheriff Bagby as he appeared from inside Tidwell's torn-up tearoom. "Let the professional handle it. That would be me! Get back in your truck, leave town, and let me handle the investigation."

"We will not be dismissed," said Larry. "This is a public street. We have the right to be here."

"Not if you're inciting a riot! You can't yell fire in a theater when there's no fire, and you can't yell 'rabid woodbooger' in this town when there isn't one. You're scaring folks to death!"

"For their own good!"

"If you don't clear out, I will arrest you for disturbing the peace. Have I made myself clear?"

Without another word, Larry marched to the truck and climbed back in. Daryl made a violent U-turn, and they sped out the way they'd come in.

"Sheriff," I cried, "we have video. The woodbooger is a person in a costume."

"Of course it is!" The police officer muttered something to himself along the lines of "three years to retirement," but he took the phone and watched the video anyway.

"Can you send me this video?" he asked Jeremy, who nodded in the affirmative. "Good, and at some point, we're gonna talk about why this camera exists. You feel me?" Jeremy grimaced but nodded again.

It was Sunday morning, but instead of attending church, we spent the next few hours helping our friends and neighbors clean up, all the while reassuring folks that they had nothing to fear and that there was no rabid woodbooger. Our soothing words fell on deaf ears. The town was worked up. Even Gladdy Tidwell was enraged.

Clutching shards of broken teacups to her bosom, she shouted to anyone within a half-mile radius, "Whatever or whoever did this had better give his heart to Jesus because his butt is mine!"

We showed everyone Jeremy's video and explained how the perpetrator had to be a person in a costume, but the image of a great hairy beast smashing the tearoom carried more weight than our explanations.

When the street was mostly cleaned up, we headed back to the house for yet another council of war.

"So, who do you think was in the woodbooger suit? Beulah or Hi?" I asked once my Avengers were assembled in the attic. The responses were surprising. Momma and Mike shouted Beulah, but Dad and Jeremy voted for Hi. Momma was stunned.

"Cal, how could you?"

"You saw how hard the perpetrator had to work to tear up the town. Hiram Graham is no Dwayne Johnson!"

"Neither is Beulah," said Mike. "She's tall like Hiram, but she most likely isn't any stronger."

"There's another thing," said Daddy. We waited for him to finish, but he chewed his lip and looked at the floor.

"Out with it, Calvin," ordered Momma.

"I should have thought of it before," said Daddy, "but it was only when we were looking at the video that I remembered."

"What," I said softly and encouragingly, while my inner monologue was shouting "Spit it out!"

"We, the Order I mean, used to have a woodbooger costume. One of the members would wear it when we marched in parades or visited kids in the hospital."

"I vaguely remember that," said Jeremy. "What happened to it?"

"We had to retire it," said Daddy, "after a child saw the person in the costume take the head off. The kid lost his mind."

I thought back to my time in children's television and shuddered. I learned the hard way that kids freak out when the human in the suit is revealed.

"The thing is," continued Daddy, "the suit in the video could have been the one we used to have."

"What happened to it?" asked Mike.

"I dunno. It probably got put in storage at the lodge, or maybe a lodge member took it home. It was over twenty years ago. But what if Hiram remembered it?"

"And what if Beulah remembered it?" countered Momma.

"I think we need to find that suit," I said. "Daddy, Momma, it's time to call an emergency meeting."

While my parents and Mike, now a member of the Order, headed downstairs to activate their phone trees, I held Jeremy back. We needed to talk.

CHAPTER 26

The noise in the Red Chamber, a.k.a. Shirley's she-shed, was deafening. The main source of the noise had to be Gladdy Tidwell, who was spitting mad about the destruction of her tearoom and wanted to make sure everyone knew it. Not to be outdone, Mrs. Thompson worked herself into a fit of tears over the loss of her flower cart. Other shop owners bemoaned the destruction of their signage, and everyone in general tried to tell everyone else that they had been first on the scene to witness the devastation on Main Street. I sat quietly in the corner with my hands over my ears. The only other people keeping quiet were Shirley and Momma, who were trying to set an example, and Helen Graham, whose husband was living under a cloud of suspicion. I felt for her, but mostly I felt for my ears.

Momma had a quiet word with Shirley, and the two hustled to the kitchenette, brought out Mississippi Mud Cake, and started dishing it up. The overall tone of the room shifted to something less strident, and soon it was much quieter as the ladies' mouths were glued shut by marshmallow and chocolate.

"Now that we have your attention," said Shirley, "we'll bring this meeting to order.

"This morning's violence against our town wasn't perpetrated by the woodbooger," proclaimed Momma in no uncertain terms. "It was a human dressed up to look like the woodbooger."

"Ahmntshoobutnat!" Gladdy struggled with a bite of cake and tried again. "I'm not so sure about that!"

"We have examined the video footage," continued Momma. "The woodbooger is stronger than the person in that video. What we have is an impostor in a suit, and now we have to find that suit!" She explained how the COW used to have a woodbooger costume for parades that they stopped using decades ago.

"The question is, where is it now?" asked Shirley. "If anyone has any knowledge of the suit's whereabouts, please share with the group."

The ladies looked at each other, shaking their heads. Eventually, murmurs of "I don't have it," "I don't even remember it," and the like could be heard from the group.

"If you have any knowledge of the suit, if any memories surface, cause let's face it, we're not getting any younger, please get in touch as soon as possible," commanded Momma. The ladies nodded and murmured their assent. I was disappointed because I thought someone would have some recollection of the costume. I glanced at my watch and started.

"Momma," I hissed. "It's almost time!"

Quickly, the curtain was opened to reveal the television, and soon we were watching the COW meeting being brought to order. At first, it was like a mirror image of the Red Chamber. Dud and Daddy explained about the costume and asked if anyone knew where it might be. The men looked at each other and hemmed and hawed. Many of the members looked openly at Hiram Graham.

"Don't look at me! I don't have it."

"Well, we've looked all over the lodge and can't find hide nor hair of it, literally," said Dud. "If anyone remembers anything about it, please let us know ASAP. That's the only business we had tonight, and I'm disappointed we couldn't run that woodbooger costume to ground. It might have answered some questions."

"Hold up! Don't adjourn the meeting just yet." My brother entered the frame.

"Jeremy! What are you doing here?" hissed Daddy.

"The sacred rights of the Concatenated Order of the Woodbooger have been violated!" Dud proclaimed.

"I'm just getting started." Jeremy marched over to one wall and pulled a curtain that revealed a large television, and I wondered how many of their "emergency" meetings were simply about watching football. Jeremy fiddled with the remote and his phone, and a few moments later, an image appeared on the screen—an image of the Red Chamber watching the Concatenated Order.

A collective gasp shook Shirley's she-shed, a gasp we could also hear through the television on a slight delay. The Order also had audio.

"It's time you knew," announced Jeremy, "that your wives have been spying on your meetings for years. Gentlemen, I give you the Red Chamber!"

The two rooms, separated by miles, exploded simultaneously.

"Turn it off! Turn it off!"

"Women in our sacred space! Betrayed! Just like Eve in the Garden!"

"How are they seeing us?"

"Dolores, how could you?!"

"There must be a camera!"

"Women ruin everything!"

"Let's find it!"

"What kind of monster did I marry?"

"The cat's already out of the bag. What's the point? It's over!"

But the women were still crawling over each other to find the camera.

"Ladies!" I screamed. "Before you destroy that camera, stop!" Out of the corner of my eye, I saw myself appealing to the women on a tiny screen. It was a little trippy. "We have an opportunity here to make something greater! Please, hear me out." I turned to where I knew Jeremy had hidden the camera.

"Shame on you, Jeremy!" I cried. "I know you have good intentions, but you went too far." In the room on the other side of town, my brother hung his head in shame. It was a nice touch. "Still, perhaps my ill-advised but well-meaning brother has done us all a favor. Yes, gentlemen, these are your wives, the Red Chamber. For decades, they've worked tirelessly to support your work. Would any Woodbooger event be possible without their help? Therefore, don't they deserve to be part of the organization? Are your wives simply slave labor? Think about it!

"Separately, you've accomplished great things. You've funded the children's wing of the hospital, making sure the kids of this town don't have to travel far afield for excellent care. You've preserved Luthersburg's traditions, like the Brunswick Stew Festival, the Christmas parade, the Harvest Festival, and the Easter egg hunt. This town is practically Stars Hollow thanks to you."

"What is she talking about?"

"I have no idea."

I tried to keep my audience in mind.

"Your dedication to tradition has made this a wonderful place to live. And let's not forget your greatest achievement— the preservation of a species. You've kept the secret and protected the woodbooger's habitat for almost one hundred years! Now someone is impersonating the woodbooger and trying to frame him for many crimes. Twice attempted murder and vandalism. In this dark and desperate time, let's all come together to find this impostor, this threat to our community, and put him or her behind bars! Most important of all, let's protect the woodbooger! Imagine what you could accomplish if you worked together, one body and one mind."

I heard my voice echo from the speakers of the television. Then there was silence. I had done it. I had convinced the Woodboogers and the Red Chamber to join forces!

"*Yeah, that's a hard pass for me.*"

"They don't serve cake. If we want cake, we'll have to make even more."

"*I can't get a word in edgewise at home. Here my voice is heard.*"

"*But you don't say nothing.*"

"*That's not the point!*"

"We had a finely tuned system," hissed Momma, "and you've destroyed it."

"My misguided son and daughter do have a point," said Daddy above the din, which settled as he spoke. "We've relied on you heavily for so long, but we didn't fully include you. You found a way to include yourselves, and it serves us right."

"*I don't know about that.*"

"Hush, Willard!" said his wife.

"*It begins.*"

My cell phone vibrated in my pocket. It was Mike.

"I hate to interrupt this pivotal moment in Concatenated Order history, but no one here knows anything about the woodbooger suit."

"I know. We were watching."

"Yeah." There was a pause. "Anyway, does anyone in the Red Chamber know where it is?"

"Not an inkling."

"Then I'm coming to get you. We have some breaking and entering to do."

"I thought you wanted to avoid anything illegal."

"I don't see that we have much choice."

"Well, if you hurry, you can catch up to Jeremy."

"What?" I watched the screen as he looked around the room to no avail.

"He lit out about five minutes ago. That's his MO. Wreak havoc and slip away to avoid the aftermath."

"I have a feeling this was a joint operation."

"I have no idea what you're talking about."

Daddy was still talking as I quietly left Shirley's she-shed, and I had hope for a new Woodbooger tomorrow.

CHAPTER 27

$\mathcal{A}$t Mike's insistence, we headed to Hiram and Helen Graham's house for the aforementioned B and E. He wanted to search the mayor's house for the woodbooger costume in the hope that Honeytrap Part Three could be prevented. I knew it was pointless, but I humored him. After all, I wasn't the one who had to seduce a monster.

Hi and Helen lived in Luthersburg proper on Sycamore Street, two blocks off Main. We were riding in Jeremy's BMW, which cornered so beautifully that I felt like I was riding a roller coaster. I was slightly breathless when we pulled up to the Graham house, and Mike helped me alight from the back-seat of the two-door coupe. The house was a classic craftsman bungalow with a wide front porch and dormer windows. Concrete planters spilling geraniums flanked the front steps. Mike and I surveyed the property, considering the best points of ingress, but Jeremy walked confidently up the porch steps, went straight to the planter on the left, dug into the soil, and produced a rock. The rock opened on a hinge, and Jeremy produced a house key.

"Ta-da!"

"Jeremy, whose house haven't you burgled in this town?"

My incorrigible brother smirked. "I prefer to avoid breaking when I enter."

The Graham house was just as beautiful as I remembered. Hi and Helen had no children, and they had put their energy into restoring the Craftsman home to its original condition and filling it with antiques. We bypassed the communal spaces in the house, certain the Woodbooger costume would be hidden someplace private. Jeremy took the first floor, while Mike and I headed upstairs.

The second floor of the home consisted of three bedrooms served by a large family bathroom. One room was a guest bedroom. Another was Helen's sewing room. She was a skillful seamstress who made custom dresses, did alterations, and made heavenly quilts which sold in shops all over the region. Mike took the guest room while I inspected the sewing room.

Helen's domain was well-organized and efficient. I immediately went to the closet, which revealed antique wooden cabinets with dozens of little drawers filled with notions. None of the drawers was large enough to contain a huge, furry costume, so I moved on. Several sewing machines were set up on tables around the perimeter of the room. Bolts of fabric standing on end filled the corners. A table for cutting and piecing stood in the center of the space, and it looked like Helen was in the process of cutting out pieces for a wedding dress. The white satin was a dead giveaway.

I looked under sewing tables, behind bolts of fabric, and everywhere else big enough for a costume but found nothing. I headed for the master bedroom and found Mike already there looking through a dresser.

"The guest room is clean."

"So is the sewing room."

While Mike finished with the dresser, I headed for the closet. It was small, like most closets of the era; therefore, it was crammed full. I started at the top and worked my way down. Many boxes were stacked on the shelf at the top of the closet, most of them large enough to hold a costume. I took a photo with my phone so I could replace the boxes exactly as I'd found them. Then I began taking down the boxes and arranging them on the bed. Most were hat boxes that revealed a glorious collection of millinery. I recognized a few from Easters past, but some were antiques I had never seen before, probably family heirlooms. One box contained loose family photos from the last one hundred years or so. I quickly put the top back on that one so I wouldn't get distracted. Other boxes contained paperwork and various odds and ends. No costume.

Following the photo, I rearranged the boxes at the top of the closet and moved my eyes downward. A quick perusal of the clothes on the rack failed to reveal a furry costume, so I moved to the floor of the closet. The couple's shoes were hanging on a rack on the inside of the closet door, and the floor of the closet was taken up primarily by an antique trunk.

"Now we're talking!" The trunk had brass fittings, and I flashed back to Nancy Drew number seventeen, *The Mystery of the Brass Bound Trunk*, a particular favorite. Wouldn't it be smashing to find the incriminating clue in a trunk just like Nancy did?

I flipped the latches and pushed...and nothing happened. The trunk was locked.

"Allow me."

I looked over my shoulder to find Jeremy with a hairpin. I scooched over, and he went to work on the lock. Before he could finish saying "The downstairs is clean," I heard a click. I pushed my brother out of the way (because this trunk was MINE) and lifted the lid.

"Oh!" The sight took my breath away. Sky blue satin, dark blue velvet, pink ribbon lacings, and oodles of lace bespoke a gown that Marie Antoinette would have been happy to wear. I carefully extracted it from the trunk and laid it across the bed. Next was a woolen officer's coat and breeches in the style of the Continental Army. Under that, a fringe-covered flapper dress and a pinstripe suit worthy of Al Capone.

"Halloween costumes?" I asked Jeremy.

"That or the Grahams have an imaginative romantic life," chuckled my brother. I'd have to ask Momma if she had seen Hi and Helen in any of these costumes. If not…

As I reached underneath the pinstripe suit to lift it out, I felt fur. Shitake mushrooms! I flung the suit over my shoulder. It may have landed on the bed, or it may not. I didn't care because I was staring into the face of the Woodbooger.

"It's the wrong color," said Mike matter-of-factly over my shoulder. "It's too light."

Indeed, the Woodbooger in the hospital video and the Main Street surveillance footage was the color of dark chocolate. This costume, according to the Crayola box, was closer to burnt sienna.

I lifted the head out of the trunk and handed it to Jeremy. Then I lifted out two furry gloves and handed them to Mike. Finally, I lifted out the body of the suit. It came out as a block, the wrinkles fixed and holding fast. This costume hadn't been out of the trunk in donkey's years. When I tried to shake out the wrinkles, bits of fur filled the air like a blown dandelion. I coughed.

"I think it's safe to say this isn't the Woodbooger we're looking for."

"Why didn't Hi and Helen tell anyone about this costume?" asked Mike. "It doesn't match the video. It could have cleared him."

"Unless he has a second suit," said Jeremy. "Think about it. This one is in no condition to fool anyone. If Hiram is the Woodbooger impostor, then he must have acquired a different suit. If he and Helen confessed to having this one, the Sheriff might have gotten a warrant to search the home.'

"Or," I added, "maybe they just forgot. It hasn't been out of this trunk in decades."

"But Helen most likely made the costume," countered Mike. "I doubt *she* forgot it. She was probably protecting her husband."

"Whatever the reason, we need to make sure there isn't a second costume in the house."

I finished the bedroom while Mike and Jeremy perused the attic. Then we all tromped out to the garage, which didn't reveal a second Woodbooger costume either. While Hiram wasn't necessarily innocent, this avenue of inquiry was a dead end. That left one option.

I rubbed my hands together gleefully.

"It looks like Honeytrap Part Three is a go!"

CHAPTER 28

*B*eulah Kenilworth lived outside of Luthersburg, right next door to Aunt Minty. Next door didn't mean the houses were close to each other. Aunt Minty lived on twenty acres. Her house wasn't close to anybody, but the two properties abutted. That Aunt Minty was nearby comforted me as we approached Beulah's lair. I had imagined some ramshackle Southern Gothic monstrosity full of rotting corpses and insane relations, so I was both disappointed and relieved to find that Beulah lived in a tidy mid-century brick rancher. The fake wishing well in the front yard was sufficiently offensive to fuel my sense of superiority (I hate a fake well!), so I was mollified.

We arrived in the rental pick-up because Beulah would expect Mike to be driving it. Jeremy and I were crouched down in the back seat of the crew cab. Mike parked the car parallel to the front of the house so we could slip out the passenger side door without anyone in the house seeing us. Once Mike had her distracted, we would enter the house and begin our search. After two successful attempts, we had this honeytrap thing down to a science. Mike was again going live on his social media account. This time Jeremy and I were listening on our respective phones so we could be further apart during our search. Mike was going to try to get Beulah to take a walk in the moonlight, thus getting her out of the house and out of our way. He was also hoping a moonlit stroll would be romantic enough to forestall any kisses or cuddles. *Blech!*

The door opened before Mike could even knock.

"Hello, lover. Have you finally decided you need a woman instead of a girl?"

"I have."

"Then what are you waiting for? Come in."

Said the spider to the fly.

"Wait…I want to do this right. I want to court you."

I almost lost my lunch. Was Beulah going to buy this? A long pause followed during which my heart rate accelerated like a Chevy at Bristol Motor Speedway.

"That would be lovely," Beulah finally replied breathlessly. Huh? Was it simply Mike's charms, or did Beulah entertain fantasies of hearts and flowers? I thought of her more as a "wham, bam, thank you ma'am" sort of gal, but perhaps that was just for show. Underneath, Beulah was a woman just like any other, who wanted to be cherished, and Mike McCall was good at cherishing.

Sugar. Honey. Iced. Tea.

"There's a beautiful moon out tonight," said Mike.

It's the same moon that's out every night. Jeez!

"Care to take a stroll in the moonlight?" Mike offered his arm.

"I do." Beulah invested those two words with such import that I was certain she was imagining herself walking down the aisle with my man! Delusional! But it worked. Beulah put her arm through Mike's and they strolled down the porch steps and around the corner of the house.

Jeremy and I wasted no time alighting from the truck and creeping toward the front door. I let Jeremy handle the opening and closing of doors because he was the sneakiest Cooksey sibling with more practice. I made a mental note to check my apartment for hidden cameras.

The front door opened into the living room. A door to the right revealed a staircase to the attic.

"I got this," said Jeremy before he sprinted silently up the stairs. How did he do that?

I perused the living room, looking for obvious hiding places. This was a formal room, sort of a front parlor, with a sofa, end tables, occasion chairs, and a coffee table, all very modern, sitting on laminate flooring so new I could smell it. Someone had recently redecorated. I looked between the sofa and the wall, but that was the extent of hiding places in this room.

An archway led from the living room to the dining room. Beulah was using it as a home office, and it was full of Ruritan paraphernalia. Several large tanks of helium reclined in the corners of the room next to boxes of balloons and string. I made short work of the boxes, the desk drawers, and the filing cabinets.

Nothing.

I bypassed the small up-to-date kitchen and headed to the den. The heart of the house still had shag carpeting and wood paneling. A recliner loveseat had pride of place in this room, facing a huge TV. Bookshelves lined the walls, full of DVDs and Blue Rays. I perused the titles.

Red, White, and You.

Vote for Love.

Meet Cute on Main Street.

Mayor of Lovetown.

Oh, my stars!

I picked up *Mayor of Lovetown* and read the blurb.

"When Cassie Truehart runs for mayor of Valentine, Tennessee, she expects to win by a landslide. After all, she's the local girl everyone loves. Cassie doesn't expect competition in the form of a big shot from the big city. Jake Romeo wants to start a political career in small-town America. Becoming the mayor of Valentine is the first step, but a feisty redhead with the face of an angel is determined to get in his way. Can Cassie win the election even if her heart votes for love?"

I looked at some more blurbs, but they were all basically the same movie. Small-town politician meets big-city hunk.

Beulah meets my boyfriend!

We had accidentally played right into Beulah's greatest fantasy. Mike McCall was her dream man come to life, and we had served him up on a platter for her consumption. I was the worst girlfriend ever.

I thought back to the night the Woodbooger tore up Main Street. It occurred not long after I interrupted Beulah and Mike in the Ruritan supply room. Mike had chosen to follow me instead of staying with her. (Like he had a choice.) Could she have been so angry that she tried to destroy the town? I replayed the scene in my mind and blanched.

"Gladdy Tidwell said she saw you making a bee-line for Beulah's office."

Tidwell's tearoom was the only business with smashed windows, the only one sacked by the Woodbooger. Had Beulah taken revenge on Gladdy? I felt terrible that my lie might have brought such destruction to a Luthersburg institution.

Was this more evidence against Beulah or mere speculation? My emotions were making it difficult to see things clearly. Jealousy and frustration might have been a clear motive for tearing up the town, but what might have been Beulah's motive for attacking Tyler? We hadn't identified a satisfactory motive, even though we all hoped Beulah had done it.

I suddenly noticed how quiet it was. My heart started pounding along with an alarm bell in my brain. Beulah and Mike were no longer talking. In fact, there was no audio whatsoever. For whatever reason, we had lost the feed.

Jeremy bounded into the room, scaring me half to death.

"Find anything?"

"Not yet," I replied. "Look at this." I showed him the movies, but he just shrugged.

"So, she has terrible taste in movies. Big deal! We need to hustle. They could be back at any moment."

That's when we heard the front door open.

"Are you sure I can't tempt you to sit on the porch?" I heard Mike say. "It's such a lovely night."

"I'm getting eaten up by skeeters! Besides it's cooler in here."

Jeremy grabbed my arm and pulled me toward the kitchen. We leaped for the back door, but it wouldn't budge. It was deadbolted with a key from the inside, and the key was nowhere to be seen.

"Why don't you make yourself comfortable on the settee, and I'll get us some cold drinks? Beer? Coke?"

"Beer would be great!" said Mike overloudly. Jeremy and I looked around the room in desperation. Next to the stove on the inside wall was a door that I prayed wasn't a pantry. Miracle of miracles, it revealed a crude set of stairs leading down to the basement. It must have taken mere seconds for us to slip through the door and close it behind us, but I felt the whole time like I was running through quicksand. We heard Beulah moving about in the kitchen, and Jeremy gestured to me to come further down the stairs. At the bottom, he whispered in my ear. "We might as well check out the basement while we're here." Minimal moonlight made it through the tiny windows at ceiling height, so we turned on the flashlights on our phones.

Basement was a generous term for the space. Root cellar was more accurate. The space had been hewn out of rock. Not a cinderblock to be seen. The walls were uneven, with plenty of nooks and crannies for creepy crawlies to hide in. I shuddered and flashed my light above my head to see if there were any spiders above me. Big mistake. I was standing under a messy black widow nest. The red hourglass on the plump abdomen glowed like a neon sign. Jeremy slapped his hand over my mouth before I could scream. Then he moved me several feet over and shined his light to show me that I was out of danger. Even so, a slight tremble set in.

"Just keep your head down and start looking around. Keep yourself busy." Jeremy's advice was sound. Activity would help keep my fear at bay. I bent at the waist and started scanning the perimeter of the room. Every so often, I looked up to make sure no arachnids were mounting a surprise attack from above.

Scan the ground. Scan the ceiling. Scan the ground. Scan the ceiling.

Mostly, I encountered empty mason jars. I also found an old high chair. Had that been baby Beulah's? Next to it was a large oval frame containing a severely foxed photo from the late 1800s or early 1900s. It showed a man and a woman who had to be Beulah's ancestors. The woman had the same fierce jawline and eyes set too close together. A piece of fabric draped over the frame obscured some details, but when I reached out to move it, I learned it wasn't fabric. It was a snakeskin. Before I could scream, a whispered exclamation from Jeremy snagged my attention and prevented me from betraying our presence with a solid bout of hysterics.

"I found it!"

I rushed to his side. His light shone on an open cardboard box containing a dark brown bigfoot costume. We silently high-fived, something we hadn't done in over a decade. It felt good to be on the same side with my brother.

"Mike, honey," we heard Beulah call out from the kitchen. "Would you be a dear and fetch another six-pack from the basement? It's right at the bottom of the stairs."

"Sure thing, babe," said Mike, and my stomach curdled.

I flashed my light to the bottom of the stairs as Mike came through the door.

Huh? No beer there.

As he came galumphing down the stairs, the door slammed behind him, and a deadbolt turned with a resounding click. Mike ran back up the stairs.

"Beulah?" He tried the door and pounded softly. "Honey, what's going on? Are we playing a game?"

The only answer was a crash that sounded like the entire contents of Beulah's silverware drawer had been thrown at the door, then a series of thumps as various kitchen implements followed in rapid succession.

"Beulah's miffed," whispered Jeremy. "What did you do, Mike?"

"Nothing! She must have caught sight of one of you in the window. She suddenly complained about mosquitoes and wanted to come back."

"We didn't hear anything. The feed stopped."

Mike checked his phone.

"Crap! It froze up, probably due to spotty service out here."

We all looked at our phones. The words "No Service" were plain to see.

"How do we call for help?" A feeling of panic was starting to rise from my stomach and threatened to take over the rest of me.

"Try WIFI," suggested Jeremy, but there was nothing.

"There's no internet service unless you have dial-up or satellite," I said. "Aunt Minty told me. She has satellite."

"That explains all the DVDs," said Jeremy.

"Well, then we need to escape."

We tried the windows first, but they were tiny. Only a child under two could have fit through them. Then we scanned every nook and cranny for a doorway, even though we didn't expect to find anything. Sadly, we were right. Solid rock all the way around.

"That just leaves the door," said Mike. "Jeremy, any chance you can pick the lock?"

"If I had a bump key, but I didn't bring mine."

Mike climbed the stairs and listened. Silence. Beulah must have stormed off in a huff.

"The hinges are on the kitchen side, so we can't pry the pins." Mike inspected the lock. Then he descended the steps, took them again at a run, and slammed his shoulder into the door. It didn't budge, and Mike bounced off and tumbled down half the steps before he caught himself on the banister.

"Nice try," said Beulah from the other side. "It's a steel-reinforced security door. Good luck!"

"Beulah, why have you locked me down here?" Mike tried the ruse one more time.

"Cut the crap! I know you're down there with those Cooksey brats. I saw blonde hair through the kitchen window. I'm no fool, but you are. You're a fool for messing with the wrong woman!"

"We found the costume, Beulah," I shouted. "We know you've been impersonating the woodbooger."

"You don't know nothing!"

"I know you were so angry at Gladdy Tidwell for telling me Mike had gone to visit you that you trashed her tearoom and the rest of Luthersburg with it! Jokes on you, she never said that. I lied."

"Jokes on you. I figured that out about half an hour ago. I'm not stupid! You made that up because you were snooping around my office."

Fair enough.

"Well, I also know that you attacked Tyler Skaggs because you expected something in exchange for your support of the Woodboogers of the World. You wanted votes, but he didn't deliver. Did he decide to run for mayor too? That would have put quite a crimp in your plans." I was just guessing, hoping to provoke a response, and I got one. Beulah laughed long and loud. Not what I was expecting. Was Beulah losing her marbles, or was I completely off base? I looked at the two men, but they just shrugged, equally perplexed.

Beulah's laughter finally trailed off to hiccups.

"I already told you Tyler didn't promise me anything. I'm an opportunist. Ask your boyfriend." I remembered her conversation with Mike at the bar.

"What does that mean?"

"It means I didn't attack Tyler. Not the first time anyway. Someone else did me the favor."

"Who did it, Beulah?" demanded Mike.

"I only saw one other person on the mountain that morning, and that was Hiram. Maybe it was him."

"You were there?"

"When Hiram passed the Ruritan office on the way to his beloved lodge, I didn't pay it much mind, even though it was the crack of dawn. But when Tyler passed by not long after, I got worried he was gonna cave, so I followed."

"You heard Hiram tell Tyler about the woodbooger!" I cried. "That's how you knew it was real!"

"Tyler called Hiram a crazy old man, but I believed him. It explained everything about the Order and why they're so dad-blasted protective of that nature preserve. If the woodbooger is real, it all makes sense."

"Did Hiram attack Tyler?" Mike demanded again.

"I don't know! I didn't stick around to get caught by Hiram, Tyler, or a woodbooger."

"But when Tyler's attacker tried to frame the woodbooger,

you ran with it." I was beginning to see it all clearly. "You attacked him again. You appeared as the woodbooger on Main Street, and you tore up the town. Someone else started the fiction, but you continued it. Why would you do that? Once you knew the woodbooger was real, why would you try to expose him?"

"Why wouldn't I?" barked Beulah. "The woodbooger means nothing to me. It's just another animal in the woods."

"And another opportunity," seethed Jeremy, "to bring down the Concatenated Order."

It was so simple now that I understood. "Poisoning people's minds against the woodbooger would also poison them against the Order, and the Order is the only thing standing in the way of Ruritan domination."

Beulah started slow clapping. "You finally got there. Not the brightest bulb, but you made it."

I started to grind my teeth and made a concerted effort not to. I would not let Beulah Kenilworth damage my dentition.

"If Beulah didn't attack Tyler the first time, then who did?" asked Jeremy. "It has to be Hiram."

"Tyler was hit on the back of the head, right?" asked Mike. We nodded. "That means he didn't see his attacker. Hiram might have thought he could confess to meeting Tyler without being convicted because Tyler never saw him do it. If there's no other physical evidence that proves Hiram wielded the rock, a jury would be hard-pressed to convict."

My heart plummeted. Our old friend was once again our prime suspect.

"I think a more important question," whispered Jeremy, "is why Beulah is confessing to us. She knows we'll tell the sheriff."

I took Mike's hand as a chill swept down my arms and legs.

"We need to get out of here."

Spiders and snakes were forgotten as a survival instinct took hold. Mike continued to pound the door with his shoulder while Jeremy and I assessed the windows. Unfortunately, they hadn't magically grown larger, and we were still stuck. They didn't open anyway, not that we wouldn't break them if it would help us escape.

"What if we remove the window and the frame? Do you think I could fit through it then?" I had been eating good Southern cooking for the last week and a half. The chances were slim because I was not.

"There isn't a grown woman alive who could fit through that window, even with the frame removed," said my brother. Despite impending death, I found that thought comforting. Vanity much? *Sort out your priorities, Jill!*

"The door isn't budging," said Mike a few minutes later. "I think our best chance is to take down Beulah when she comes to…comes for us."

When she comes to kill us was what Mike meant. He was trying not to panic me, the sweet man, but I was beyond panic. Adrenaline had taken hold, mercifully, and I was thinking clearly.

"How do you think she'll try to kill us?" The men blinked at my question. "Gentlemen, this isn't my first dance with death. We need a good plan, and that means thinking through all the scenarios."

We finally agreed that Beulah's best option was to shoot us. That way she wouldn't have to get too close and risk being overpowered.

Just then, the basement got darker as one of the windows went black, blocking out the moonlight. Then another. And another.

"It won't be long now," said Mike. "She's covering the windows to make sure no one sees. Maybe even to muffle sound."

"We're so far out in the country," said Jeremy, "why is she even bothering?"

"Aunt Minty's house isn't too far away. Maybe Beulah's afraid she'll call the police if she hears gunshots."

"Jill, this is rural Virginia. Gunshots are like birdsong—ever present."

My brother had a point.

"Our best bet," said Mike, "is to wait at the top of the stairs. When she starts to open the door, we push together. Hopefully, she'll be thrown backward. Then Jeremy and I can disarm her."

"That's a good plan," I said, "but I can help disarm her too."

The two men had a silent conversation that probably went like this.

"Is she for real?"

"Just humor her."

I resolved to be part of the takedown, whether they liked it or not.

"We should get in position," said Jeremy.

"Wait. I just need a moment with Mike."

"Make it quick."

As Jeremy climbed the stairs to listen out for Beulah, I pulled Mike to the other side of the cellar. It didn't afford us much privacy, but at that moment, I didn't care.

"Mike…I love you."

"I know." He pulled a smirk in the best Han Solo fashion.

I punched him in the arm.

"Be serious! I think the odds are good, but there's still a chance we might not survive this."

He pulled me to his chest, and I relaxed and sighed contentedly, despite the situation. Mike always made me feel that way. No matter where we were or what was going on around us, his arms always felt like home.

I knew what I had to say.

Pulling away slightly so I could look him in the eye, I smiled at my beloved.

"Mike, I brought you to Luthersburg to see if you and my

home were compatible. But the truth is, you are my home. Wherever we are, as long as we're together, I'm home. Mike, my love, will you—"

"Jill, what's wrong with your voice?" demanded Mike. He sounded stressed, his voice rising an octave higher than normal. Was my proposal unwanted? Was he trying to change the subject?

"Honey, I'm trying to—" I gasped. I sounded like a chipmunk.

"Are you two almost done?" demanded Alvin, I mean Jeremy. His eyes widened in shock at the sound of his voice. "What is happening?"

"Christmas, Christmas time is here," sang Mike. Then he giggled. It was surreal.

"I think Beulah's trying to poison us with helium," I chirped. I remembered all the tanks in her office.

"That's hilarious!" squeaked Jeremy. "It's inert. Wow! I never thought being held captive could be so funny." He laughed and sounded like a magpie chattering.

Mike chuckled too, and he sounded like a dolphin. Was I trapped in a nightmare?

I picked up a mason jar and ran to the window. I began beating the glass with the jar, hoping to break the window. Instead, the jar cracked, slicing my hand open. I dropped the shards and pressed my shirttail to the wound.

"Jill, honey, don't panic," cheeped Mike.

"I'm not panicking!" My voice was obnoxious. "We need to break these windows to vent the gas, or we'll asphyxiate."

They looked at me like I was crazy, so I had to waste time and oxygen explaining because that's what you want to do when the room is filling with toxic fumes. My friend Surya worked in product PR, and her firm had been hired by a balloon manufacturer to run a safety campaign and improve their image after two people had asphyxiated from inhaling helium. It didn't happen often, but it was possible. Beulah had multiple tanks, and if they were full, she could gas us to death. There wouldn't be a mark on our bodies, except for the cut on my hand, and she could arrange our bodies in the truck with an empty helium tank. People would just assume we were three bored idiots who deserved a Darwin award.

At least the helium hadn't yet impaired our judgment because Mike and Jeremy immediately began searching for something to break the windows. Mike found a rusty, cobweb-covered wrench in a dark recess (shiver). He shook off the dust and some of the cobwebs, dislodging a black widow which fell to the ground. Without thinking, I pounced on it with my foot, squishing it to smithereens with repeated stomps.

"I think it's dead," smirked Jeremy as I gave it one last pounding for good measure.

Mike wielded the wrench like a baseball bat for maximum power and began swinging at the first window. It cracked on the first blow and shattered on the second. He knocked the fractured glass out and moved on to the next. Jeremy and I put our faces to the opening, but the fresh air we were hoping for eluded us. Whatever Beulah had used to cover the windows was blocking the air.

Jeremy gave me a leg up, and I reached through the window to dislodge the covering. It felt like the rough backing of wall-to-wall carpeting. I pushed against it, but it wouldn't budge.

"You try," I told Jeremy. "I can't move it."

We looked around for something for him to stand on, but there was nothing. Mike was still busting out windows, so I got down on all fours.

"Stand on my back," I told my brother. "Like we used to do when we were kids and we were trying to get to something Momma had put out of reach." Usually candy.

"You used to stand on *my* back," Jeremy reminded me. "I don't want to hurt you."

"I'd rather be hurt than dead."

"Touché."

Jeremy put one foot on my lower back, a good choice because my pelvis could take some of his weight, and stood up. I let out an *oof* as a band of pain wrapped itself around my lower abdomen, but I didn't cry out. Jeremy needed to move the barricade. He didn't need distractions. The pain in my lower abdomen eased slightly when he rested his other foot on my upper back, using my shoulder blades for support. Now I had two bands of slightly lesser pain. Not an improvement. While Jeremy pushed, I prayed for strength and deliverance.

Suddenly, he jumped off my back. I collapsed on my side and curled into a ball. The pain began to recede.

"It moved a little," he said. "There's a bit of fresh air coming in." He helped me stand, and I lifted my face to the window. A touch of cooler air tickled my cheek.

"Let's try the others," said Mike, now done with smashing windows. He and Jeremy took turns giving a leg up while the other tried to push the carpet barricades away. When they were finished, each of us had a window to stand under and a small stream of air to hopefully combat the helium. Beulah's tanks would run out eventually. We just had to hold out until then.

As I leaned against the rock wall, no longer caring about creepy crawlies in favor of precious oxygen, I prayed continuously. We had done all we could. Prayer was the only thing left, so I leaned into it. As always, I was comforted even as I was reminded that so much about life was out of my control. Hadn't the last few years shown me that truth over and over? I laughed at myself even as I prayed. Work, relationships, family, and even other people's opinions were so beyond my control, and yet I tried over and over to control the uncontrollable. I was tilting at windmills, and I had to stop.

My epiphany was interrupted by noise overhead. A lot of

noise. It sounded like World War Three had started. I could make out voices raised in anger, footsteps pounding all over the house, and objects being knocked over. I tried to cry out "We're down here! We're down here!" but my voice was still cartoonish. I couldn't achieve any volume. Mike and Jeremy tried as well, but together we just sounded like a nest of chipmunk kits. Ridiculous.

When we heard the click of the deadbolt, we all three surged toward the stairs. The door opened, revealing Larry, Darryl, and Mario of The Bigfoot Brigade.

"Is Big down there with you?" asked Larry hopefully.

We ran up the stairs and into the fresh air, collapsing at the kitchen table and completely ignoring the three doofuses who disappeared into the cellar. A moment later, we heard a cry of anguish from the cellar, albeit a cartoonish one.

"Another hoax! When will it end? When will you reveal yourself, Sasquatch?"

"Sounds like they found the costume," said Jeremy in his normal voice.

"Perhaps we should turn off the gas," suggested Mike, no longer a chipmunk.

A moment later, a sad and defeated Bigfoot Brigade emerged from the cellar. Larry carried Beulah's woodbooger costume with the solemnity of an undertaker.

"I'll take that," said Sheriff Bagby as he strode into the kitchen. A deputy followed with Beulah in cuffs. Loathing radiated off the Ruritan leader, but she was silent, smart enough not to say anything without a lawyer. She didn't need to talk. Her snarl said it all.

Behind law enforcement was the entire Concatenated Order and the Red Chamber, crammed into Beulah's brick rancher.

"How? Why?" So many questions were swirling in my brain that I couldn't get a fully formed one to come out of my mouth.

"What my overcome sister is trying to say is how did you know we were here?"

The sheriff started to answer, but Momma beat him to it, earning her a glare.

"We didn't. Someone called in a woodbooger sighting to the sheriff, the Bigfoot Brigade, and the Concatenated Order. Said it was roaming around Beulah's house."

"Who called it in?" asked Mike.

"It was anonymous, from a burner phone," said Sheriff Bagby, finally getting in a word edgewise.

A suspicion tickled my brain, and I turned to Mike.

"You don't think…"

"Most definitely."

"When we arrived," continued the Sheriff, "we saw your truck outside, but Beulah denied any knowledge of your whereabouts. She said you must be trespassing on her land, but I wasn't buying it."

"None of us did," put in Daddy, earning him a glare too.

Someone had called in a woodbooger sighting knowing the cavalry would show up and rescue us. I had a very good idea who the bugler was, and she lived next door.

"Folks, this is a crime scene," announced the Sheriff. "I need y'all to clear out and let my people get to work."

"You heard the man," said Daddy. "Let's vamoose. We can reconvene at my Aunt Araminta's house next door. I already called her, and she knows we're coming."

The lodge members and their wives began filing out of Beulah's house, leaving the police, The Bigfoot Brigade, and us.

"What will you do now?" I asked the three doofuses.

"We're outta here," sighed Larry in his normal voice. "I don't think Big inhabits this area after all. It's been one disappointment after another."

"I think what we have here is a small town trying to cash in on bigfoot," added Darryl. "Well, we're not going to help you!"

"Yeah!" said Mario.

I bit my tongue to keep from laughing. Oblivious much?

"Well, happy hunting," said Mike.

With a tight nod from Larry, the three swept from the room and hopefully from our lives.

After giving our statements to the Sheriff, we followed everyone else to Aunt Minty's house. The living room, library, dining room, and kitchen were chockablock with people celebrating the end of the fake woodbooger's reign of terror. Hiram and Helen seemed particularly happy that the cloud of suspicion under which they'd been living had finally lifted. A pang of sadness gripped my heart because I was going to destroy their momentary happiness by once again accusing Hiram. Beulah had admitted to everything except the first attack on Tyler, and, as much as I hated the thought, Hiram was once again the prime suspect.

We entered the kitchen where Aunt Minty was busy making and putting out food for the impromptu party. The little dynamo was in her element bossing around Momma, Gladdy, Shirley, and Jeannie. My gaze paused on my old etiquette teacher, who was busy making an elegant fruit tray, complete with strawberry roses. That's when the penny dropped, and I suddenly saw things much more clearly. Maybe I wouldn't be destroying Hiram's happiness after all.

Calmly, I walked over to Mrs. Shoecraft, the tastemaker of Luthersburg. She looked up at me and smiled as she continued to arrange fruit.

"You know who attacked Tyler," I said quietly. All the women working in the kitchen paused.

"We all know," said Jeannie. "It was Beulah." She tried to pick up another strawberry, but her hands were shaking.

"I mean the first time. Beulah didn't pick up that rock and smack Tyler with it, but you know who did because you were there. You were picking ramps on Woody's Mountain. It's always best to harvest in the morning. You came across Tyler, and the opportunity must have seemed like a godsend."

"It wasn't his fault," whispered Jeannie. "You have to believe me. He thought I was in danger, otherwise he wouldn't have done it. He's not violent. Everyone knows that." Her face became blotchy as she struggled to hold back her tears.

"You were trying to talk some sense into Tyler, weren't you? You wanted him to marry Lacey and take her away from Luthersburg. You wanted Lacey to have the life you always wanted."

"A better life!" Jeannie's tears were falling freely now. "A life of opportunity."

"But Tyler wouldn't listen. He didn't love Lacey, and all your plans to save her were falling through. At some point, Tyler got angry."

"I know I got hysterical," choked out Jeannie, "but he didn't need to put his hands on me. If he had just kept his hands to himself…"

"He pushed you away, didn't he?"

Jeannie nodded. "He wouldn't have done it if Tyler hadn't pushed me to the ground. He was concerned for my safety!"

"And that's when your husband, a gentle man who abhorred violence, stepped in to protect you," said Mike.

"No!" cried Jeannie, face twisted in horror. "It wasn't Virgil…It was the woodbooger!"

Mike said a bad word, to which my mother responded, "Language!"

"I'm sorry, but this is just too ridiculous. She's trying to cover for her husband by blaming a mythical creature. It's like we're back at the beginning again. People are committing these crimes, not cryptids! And I don't know why you're covering for your husband. Tyler put his hands on you. Virgil's attorney can easily make the case that he was trying to protect you. Plus, Tyler isn't going to die. It's not like Virgil is facing a murder charge!"

"Michael!" Aunt Minty's exclamation effectively silenced my agitated boyfriend. "I need some Coca-Cola for my Coca-Cola cake. Be a dear and run down to the shelter and get me some."

Mike took a deep, steadying breath.

"Of course." Without further ado, he opened the shelter door and descended the stairs.

"It was the woodbooger," whispered Jeannie. "Not Virgil."

"Of course it was," said Momma. "Jill, how did you know?"

I explained that I remembered Jeannie on the mountain at odd times, carrying her basket with bits of fruit in it. She always claimed she was hunting for ramps, even when she came home empty-handed despite the abundance of wild onions on the mountain.

"You were saying thank you by taking fruit to the woodbooger. It was the least you could do. After all, as the etiquette teacher, you taught us to always write a thank you note."

Jeannie cracked the faintest smile. "Tyler wouldn't have hurt me badly, but the woodbooger couldn't have known that."

One thing didn't make sense. "Why didn't you get help for Tyler? Why did you leave him on the mountain?"

"I thought…" Jeannie's voice broke. "I thought he was dead. Beyond help. There was so much blood, and the woodbooger was crying…" Jeannie disintegrated into sobs, and the ladies of the Red Chamber moved in to comfort her.

"Jill!" came Mike's strangled cry from below. It sounded like he'd gotten into the helium again. "Can you come down here for a moment?"

I looked at Aunt Minty and found the twinkle in her eye twinkling its little twinkle off.

"You little stinker." I smiled as I headed for the shelter, and my favorite aunt winked at me.

As I walked slowly down the stairs, I tried to imagine the sight that would meet my eyes at the bottom, but nothing prepared me for reality.

Mike hadn't made it farther than two steps from the stairs before he'd frozen in place. I joined him and put my hand in his to help lessen the shock. Then I looked up.

Two adult woodboogers sat on a sofa with two juveniles, all watching Animal Planet—all except one, clearly the patriarch, who was looking at us. I smiled, and he smiled back. This then was the gentle giant who had tried to protect Jeannie and in doing so had started one of the most interesting chapters in Luthersburg's history.

I led Mike further into the shelter and saw more adults and more kids sitting on furniture and the floor playing and snacking on fruit, nuts, and popcorn.

"How much you want to bet Minty brought them here to protect them from discovery by the bigfoot hunters?"

Mike didn't respond. At that moment, I don't think he could. I wasn't bothered. Before too long, we would have a lot to talk about.

So, what did the bigfoot/Sasquatch/Yeti/Skunk Ape/wood-booger look like?

Let's just say that no costume devised by man could ever do him justice.

AND I SERIOUSLY ENVIED HIS hair.

CHAPTER 30

It was the last day of vacation, and I was determined to show Mike my favorite spot, Bridal Veil Falls. We set off from the trailhead by the Woodbooger lodge just as we had on the fateful day we discovered Tyler on the trail, only this time Daddy hadn't accompanied us. He was too busy with the Concatenated Order to go hiking, and I was glad of it. I wanted this hike to be romantic because I had something I wanted to say.

When we passed the spot where Tyler had lain all those days ago, I breathed a sigh of relief. Nothing was going to stop this hike. It was still early in the day, and the air was cool as we climbed through forests of tulip poplar and thickets of rhododendrons in bloom. I noticed that the ramps were now in flower, past the point of harvesting and eating. Jeannie Shoecraft wouldn't be climbing the mountain to harvest, but I suspected she would still make offerings of fruit to her protector.

Tyler still hadn't regained his memory. He and many of the residents of Luthersburg believed Beulah Kenilworth had conked him over the head, even though the Sheriff hadn't been able to tie her to that original crime. He had plenty of evidence that she had attacked him in the hospital, torn up the town, and tried to kill us, so he wasn't too concerned. She would do time no matter what.

I wondered what would happen if Tyler did regain his full memory. Was his brain a ticking time bomb? If he remembered meeting with Hiram and Jeannie on the mountain and then being struck, he would expect Jeannie to know who had done it. Of course, he might be too embarrassed about his behavior, pushing Jeannie to the ground like that, to admit he remembered.

Luthersburg was still a tangled web, but maybe a bit less so.

At least the Red Chamber had come clean. The Order and The Chamber were now coming to terms with each other and trying to reorganize to better preserve the secret of the wood-booger and all their other charitable endeavors. Speaking of charitable endeavors, the Ruritans had a new president who had no political ambitions. Hiram's position was most likely preserved for the time being. Still, he would be challenged in the future, and I hoped he would be able to concede graciously when the time came.

Our hike brought us to a scenic overlook, and Mike and I paused to view the town in the valley below us.

"It looks so peaceful from up here," chuckled Mike. "How deceptive."

"I promise you that I never knew just how much drama this town contained. Otherwise, we would have stayed in New York."

"Nonsense," said Mike. "This trip has been illuminating, to say the least, and I wouldn't have it any other way. I mean, now I know the woo—bigfoot is real. How many people can say that? I'm pretty sure all of them live in that town right down there."

"It *was* illuminating," I agreed. "But the biggest shocker

wasn't the woodbooger. It was finding out your people come from Kentucky!" I laughed as Mike picked me up and spun me around.

"Has it only been a little over a week?" he asked as he put me down. How bizarre that it only took a week to change our perspective entirely.

Out of the corner of my eye, I sensed movement, and as I turned my head to see fully, a juvenile woodbooger waved at me from behind a tree. I waved back, and Mike grinned as he made out the creature.

"That will never get old."

"Only slightly less surprising," I said as we moved on up the trail, "was learning that Jeremy may have switched teams from the Sith to the Jedi." In the last couple of days, several executives from The Malevia Group had been indicted thanks to an anonymous whistleblower who I suspected was my brother. Combined with the fact that Jeremy had come to Luthersburg to help a friend and the fact that he was still dating Lacey Shoecraft even after the woodbooger case was over, I began to hope that my brother was a good guy. I loved Jeremy, but now I was starting to like him. Ew! Gross!

I began to hear the far-off hiss of the falls, and I quickened my pace, pulling Mike along behind me.

"Hurry! We're almost there!"

Without warning, Mike picked me up and ran down the trail, me squealing and laughing the whole way. The hiss became a dull roar as we got closer, and without warning, the trail opened up to reveal a stream. To our left was Bridal Veil Falls tumbling down the mountain into a crystal-clear pool that fed a smaller stream that crossed the trail and tumbled further down the mountain to our right. We had reached my favorite spot.

I wiggled out of Mike's arms and sat on a nearby rock to take off my shoes and socks. Mike shook his head resignedly and followed suit. Feet bare, I grabbed him by the hand to pull him toward the pool, but he didn't budge.

"What's the matter?"

In answer, Mike grinned and got down on one knee. He pulled a velvet box from his pocket and opened it to reveal a little piece of the starry sky brought down to Earth.

My heart stopped, and my face split into a grin of my own.

"Jillian Elizabeth Cooksey, partner in crime and love of my life, will you be the Laura to my Almanzo, the Nancy Drew to my Ned Nickerson, the Anne Shirley to my Gilbert Blythe. Will you marry me?"

He'd been looking at the bookshelves in my bedroom. The Anne to his Gilbert? Of course, I would marry him. So would you!

"I will," I said.

And I did.

The End

ACKNOWLEDGMENTS

I always have so many people to thank when I finish a book because authors rely on the support of their families, friends, and communities so much. First, thanks to my husband, Matthew, for listening to me complain about all the things that get in the way of writing. You deserve a medal. Thanks also to my family members who went on research jaunts with me, encouraged me, and listened to me talk about this book for two years. A special thanks to my parents for loaning me their timeshare every time I needed to go on retreat, which was quite a few times. Without those retreats, this book wouldn't exist.

There's a special group of people that I think of as my writing angels. Without fail, when I needed it the most, one of them would say something encouraging to me about my writing or about how much they were looking forward to the next book. Mia, Sarah, Amanda D., Melissa, Jessi, Amanda C. (amandasuecreasy.com), Aunt Diane, Theresa, Lynn, Becky, and so many others (I know I'm forgetting names at this moment that will occur to me in the middle of the night), thank you for your kind words that meant more than you know. Writing a novel while being a teacher is really hard, and your encouragement kept me from giving up.

As always, my alpha reader, Melissa Hamill (melissahamill.-com) was a shoulder I could lean and cry on, and my beta readers, Mom, Sarah, and Cate, kept watch for errors I could no longer see. Their eagle eyes give me the courage to put the books out there.

I love cemeteries. As an amateur genealogist of seventeen years, I've spent a lot of time in them. Cemeteries inspired my two fictional fraternal organizations, the Concatenated Order of the Woodbooger and the Woodboogers of the World. In the past, members of fraternal orders sometimes had special headstones that indicated their membership during their lifetimes. The tombstones are how I learned about Woodmen of the World, the Freemasons, and other organizations. I don't know exactly how the idea of a fraternal order that protects the bigfoot came into my brain—like Athena, it pretty much sprang fully formed—but I know the cemetery visits, *In Search Of*, and *The X-Files* most likely played a part.

Now, about the woodbooger...

I've been fascinated by bigfoot (the woodbooger) since the Seventies, when Steve Austin battled a robot bigfoot on *The Six Million Dollar Man*. Mysteries like bigfoot, the Bermuda Triangle, and the Loch Ness monster continue to capture my imagination, and I know I'm not alone. Since I started writing this book, I've noticed a huge uptick in bigfoot interest. Maybe it was always there and I just became more aware of it. Maybe we all want to believe the world still holds some mystery despite technology. Whatever the reason, bigfoot, it seems, is everywhere, making the world more interesting. Well done, sir. Well done.

There *is* a woodbooger sanctuary in Virginia, in the town of Norton, to be exact, at the intersection of state routes 58 and 23 in Southwest Virginia. The town declared part of its trail system a woodbooger sanctuary after a television show about bigfoot was filmed there. So, there are people who care about the woodbooger, even if they can't actually produce one on demand. That's good because Luthersburg, Virginia is completely fictional, as are its residents and its woodboogers.

James 1:2-3

ABOUT THE AUTHOR

Lesley St. James began her career in film and television before moving to public relations and then to education. A devoted, lifelong reader of mysteries, she always knew the kind of books she would write. When she's not writing or teaching writing, Lesley enjoys traveling, movies, and genealogy. She resides in Virginia with her husband, Matthew.

For more books, newsletters, and information,
please visit www.lesleystjames.com.

lesleystjames.com/category/buy-the-books/

www.ingramcontent.com/pod-product-compliance
Lightning Source LLC
Chambersburg PA
CBHW030817210726
48290CB00002B/633